Hides
the
Dark Tower

Edited
by

Kelly A. Harmon and
Vonnie Winslow Crist

Pole to Pole Publishing
Baltimore

Hides the Dark Tower

ISBN-10: 1941559077
ISBN-13: 978-1-941559-07-9

Hides
the
Dark Tower

My first thought was, he lied in every word,
That hoary cripple, with malicious eye
Askance to watch the working of his lie
On mine, and mouth scarce able to afford
Suppression of the glee, that purs'd and scor'd
Its edge, at one more victim gain'd thereby.

What else should he be set for, with his staff?
What, save to waylay with his lies, ensnare
All travellers who might find him posted there,
And ask the road? I guess'd what skull-like laugh
Would break, what crutch 'gin write my epitaph
For pastime in the dusty thoroughfare,

If at his counsel I should turn aside
Into that ominous tract which, all agree,
Hides the Dark Tower.

~ From "Childe Roland to the Dark Tower Came"
    Robert Browning

Table of Contents

The Tower *by Laura Shovan* 9

Beneath the Bell Bay Light *by A.P. Sessler* 11

Squire Magic *by Larry C. Kay* 21

Who Abandon Themselves *by Jeremy M. Gottwig* 29

The Tower *by Richard Chizmar* 35

Ancient Spin *by Steven R. Southard* 49

The Siege of the Ravelin *by Ray Kolb* 51

Leaving the Tower *by Rie Sheridan Rose* 63

They Warp the Fabric of the Sky *by Kelda Crich* 67

The Tower of the Sea Witch *by Peter Schranz* 79

Kiss of Death *by Jeremy Zimmerman* 85

Soul for Sale *by M.J. Ritchie* 101

The Enchanted Tower *by Edward McDermott* 107

Freak Justice *by Brad Hafford* 117

The Sorcerer Climbed Her Tower *by Jeff Stehman* 131

The Long Road Home *by Andrew Gudgel* 135

Core Craving *by N.O.A. Rawle* 147

Annie the Escaper *by Meg Belviso* 149

Dark Ascent *by Daniel Beazley* 161

The Field Trip *by Alex Shvartsman* 167

Night in Nineveh *by Jonathan Shipley* 175

For the Feather Dusters *by Briana McGuckin* 187

The People's Avenger *by Robert E. Waters* 191

The People of the Town *by Kane Gordon* 207

Giving a Hand *by Kelly A. Harmon* 213

To the Flame *by Evan Dicken* 227

Deep Into That Darkness Peering *by Anatoly Belilovsky* 241

Smoke and Sprites *by Vonnie Winslow Crist* 249

The Blind Queen's Daughter *by G. Scott Huggins* 255

The Tower

Laura Shovan

The tower's tip
seems out of reach,
a stone lantern
glowing
in the woods.
I part thorns,
stand
in the tower's
long shadow.
If I climb the stairs,
scale the walls
slick with moss,
what will greet me
at the top?
A treasure room,
a long-haired girl,
all the tongues
of the ancient world,
or an empty window
where the dark eye
resides.
If lightning strikes
as I reach the top
and I fall,
forget who I am,
the stones
will tell me how
to build again
with my bare hands,
salvage
what I can.

Beneath the Bell Bay Light
A.P. Sessler

Kevin rose from the bay just beside his white sports boat, bobbing with the gentle waves while he inhaled stinging lungfuls of salt air. He pulled his goggles to the top of his wet, jet black crown and cleared his sinuses with a finger to each nostril.

Two seagulls strategically circled the boat from above, waiting to see if Kevin had risen victorious with another net full of knobbed porgy. With the near-empty net in hand, his left arm launched over the side like a grappling hook, giving him the necessary leverage to pull himself up.

His right arm emerged with a band-powered spear gun in hand. He dropped it inside the 20-foot boat and pulled himself out of the water, over the side, and onto the floor. The squawking seagulls circled above as he opened the cooler to store his latest catch.

Inside, sparkling fish scales reflected sunlight like Archimedes' metal shields about to set a far-off ship aflame. It was almost mesmerizing, even to Kevin.

He closed the cooler and scanned the horizon for more-productive fishing spots. Along the endless line of blue sky and green sea stood a lighthouse. It seemed a proper hang out for any well-educated school of fish. Standing at the side-mount steering console, he started the motor and set his sights for the distant tower.

As the coordinates on his GPS tracked his location, he saw the oceangoing landmark was listed as Bell Bay Light. As he got closer, his electronics picked up a smattering of moving objects and an increasingly shallower bottom.

When the depth finder read ten feet, he let off the throttle. Nine. Eight. Seven. He killed the motor and came to a stop. The finder read five feet. He dropped anchor to avoid running aground on the mound of rocks that formed the lighthouse's foundation.

The dilapidated tower blocked the midday sun, casting its cold shadow across the water and over Kevin's boat. The light's red brick had long ago been bleached to an ugly orange. The mound of rocks beneath the structure extended ten or so feet, ending in a mossy mess of green hair that stretched back and forth with the tide.

A ladder ran up the cylindrical light, its bottom half rusted from the unceasing salt spray. Its top ended at a railed walkaround encircling the glass-walled lantern room. At the base of the ladder, just behind it, sheets of rusted metal leaned against the lighthouse wall, and before the ladder stood a wood pylon stained green by the sea.

Kevin gazed at the walkaround of the extinguished beacon. The same sense of adventure that led him to dive thirty feet in search of dinner that morning now inspired him to scale the old ladder and declare himself king of the mountain.

He climbed out of the boat and dropped into the chest-high water. He waded through until he reached the slippery rocks, and with great trepidation, made his way to the few feet of dry surface that surrounded the base of the lighthouse.

He approached the ladder, and after rubbing his palms dry with clenched fingers, he began his ascent. The rusted rungs provided sufficient grip until about half-way up. It made sense that the higher he climbed, each rung would be smoother than the previous, but it was more than that—his hands were wet. If from sweat, he wasn't sure.

He stopped to examine a palm. It was smeared with what looked like chocolate syrup. Perhaps his sweaty hands had loosened a bit of ground-in dirt from the otherwise clean-looking rungs.

He continued his ascent. Now the bare soles of his feet felt that same, strange moisture. He turned his head and tried to examine a sole, but it proved a foolish move. When he returned the foot to the rung it slipped forward and crashed into the light's harsh brick exterior, busting his big toe.

Instinctively, a hand went to nurse the wound before Kevin second-guessed himself and returned the hand to the rung. His fingers gripped tight around the rung but nonetheless slipped right off, sending him reeling backwards, off the ladder, into the air, where gravity did its worst, bringing him crashing down onto the rocks below.

≈

It was black. His face tickled, though the sensation soon bordered on painful pricks. He opened his eyes. A series of segmented legs scurried over his right eye.

"Oh, God. No. Get off!" he shouted.

His neck tickled, too. He gazed down at his body, spread over the rocks at the base of the light, covered with half a dozen curious rock crabs conducting their examination.

One ran across his forehead and down his hair. Soon it wandered off.

"Get off me, get off, get off, get off!" he shouted and shook from side to side, or at best attempted to, but only his head turned either way—his body lay perfectly still

"Oh, man. Why can't I move? What happened?" he thought aloud, then remembered the slippery ladder.

The crabs continued to cross his body, from one bare end, cross his black and yellow swim trunks, to his other bare end. Some traded places, while others gathered at various points as if deciding what to do with their helpless Gulliver.

He screamed; though screaming proved painful.

One crab deserted the premises.

"Come on!" he shouted. "Get off already. Leave me alone!"

The crabs ignored him, clearly not intimidated. He spit at them until his mouth was dry. They merely tolerated his abuse.

He began to blow on them. One by one, as they came closer to the dark entrance and its noisy breeze, they fled to the rocks.

He groaned. "Thank God."

With the crabs having diverted his attention, he hadn't noticed the flock of seagulls circling overhead. One by one, they swooped down toward his body.

Kevin screamed. He willed his limbs to shield his head from the onslaught of birds but his hands remained flat on the ground. Wings flapped and claws spread only inches from his face. The most he could do was close his eyes.

With a squawk, a seagull took a nearby rock crab in its beak, and just as quickly as they had dropped in on their dinner guest, they took flight.

His eyes flashed right and left, then to his feet—not a crab remained. He gazed at the flying scavengers above, downing their meals in quick gulps before departing on the wind.

Kevin exhaled in relief and knew his heart had slowed its pounding. He soon felt the baking warmth of the sun, now west of the lighthouse. It dried him from head to toe, until he felt a bit like a jellyfish dragged onto the beach. He licked his parched lips and tried to swallow—another painful exercise. He glanced at his right hand.

You're my dominant hand, he thought. "Move," he said.

Not a finger twitched.

"Move, damn it!" he yelled, but his hand sat uncompliant.

He looked to his left hand and repeated the vain exercise with the same results. He thought about wiggling toes, but when he looked at them they sat perfectly still.

He stared at the sky above and watched the clouds roll by until his eyelids grew heavy.

~

Kevin heard the sound of waves lapping nearby. A salt mist covered his face. He opened his eyes. The ladder that lead to the top of the light disappeared into a cloud of fog just feet above him. He scanned his periphery, only to find the bank of fog surrounding the minuscule island.

Above the continual breaking of waves upon the rocks he heard a soft but steady sloshing rhythm. He peered into the fog from whence the sloshing came, but his vision could not pierce the thick wall of white.

"Hello?" he called out. "Is there somebody there?"

The sloshing continued, growing louder. He knew its origin: the distinct sound produced when one slices the surface of water with an oar—someone was rowing nearby.

"I need help!"

Then, as if on the other side of a curtain, he saw the soft silhouette approach. The arms were in motion, rowing, just as he suspected. His heart pounded. His rescue was near.

The shape broke through the fog, like a hand fanning cigarette smoke away. Small wisps of gray curled about the emerging object—a rowboat.

"Oh, thank God," said Kevin. But there was no acknowledgment.

The bow of the boat came closer to his head, so much that he could now see worn wood beneath its chipped green paint.

"Hey!" he shouted. "You're going to run—"

The boat struck bottom, its front only inches from the top of his skull.

"You scared me," he said, breathing heavy; still there was no response.

Covered to the wrist by a thick, dark sweater, an arm reached over the bow holding an unhitched rope. With a flick of the wrist the loose lasso flew over his head, and landed around the wooden pylon near his feet with a tap.

The sole of a black shoe appeared overhead, attached to a leg in blue jeans bent at the knee. The shoe came stomping down.

"Watch—" Kevin started to say as the shoe landed to the right of his head.

The other foot swung over the bow and planted itself by his outstretched left arm.

"Hello?" Kevin said to the man towering above him like a giant.

From beneath, Kevin could only make out the chin covered in gray stubble the color of fog, that and the large nostrils of his long nose. The man approached the pylon, each step barely missing Kevin's immobile body.

"Can you hear me?" he asked the man, who continued to ignore him.

Kevin watched as the man stooped over, took the loose rope in both hands and fidgeted with the rope to secure his boat. When the man was finished, the rope formed a taut line suspended a little over a foot high from the pylon to the boat.

The man stood straight and approached the ladder. He pulled at the pane of sheet metal behind it and slid it left. Kevin heard the sound of metal grinding on rock, and he watched as the man took a step to the right and slid the next sheet right, revealing yet another sheet half the size of the previous two.

This one he pulled toward himself and laid it flat on the rock. His eyes locked with Kevin's before he stood straight and retrieved a key from his pocket to unlock the door that had been hidden behind the rusted metal.

"You mean that was there all along?" Kevin asked. "Why did I bother with the ladder?"

The man glanced back at him before opening the door and entering the dark lighthouse. He pulled a hanging oil lamp from its mount and produced a lighter. With a few flicks, the narrow shaft was soon illuminated. His giant shadow spread across the spiral stair and onto the far wall, then disappeared as he pulled the door shut behind him.

"What about me?" Kevin asked in vain.

The lighthouse reverberated with mysterious sounds: a clanking here, a creaking there, a pounding or two; and then, after what seemed like hours to Kevin, the top of the light was set aflame. It burned phoenix bright, piercing through the fog like a blazing firebird captured in a small, glass cage.

It was then Kevin felt the rising tide soak his hair with its salty, freezing waves.

"Hey up there! Hurry down! I'm getting wet!" he shouted and began to tremble.

A black silhouette stood before the brilliant light, so intense, the figure appeared to burn and wither into nothing. Within seconds it emerged behind the creaking door at the base of the lighthouse. The man, now plainly keeper of the light, held several feet of rope coiled over one arm.

"Please," said Kevin with chattering teeth. "Get m-me up higher before I drown."

The keeper laid the length of rope on the rock by the narrow sheet of metal. With his back bent, he dragged the metal sheet until it was parallel with Kevin.

"That's b-brilliant," Kevin praised his rescuer. "And if you don't m-mind, please hurry. I'm freezing."

Starting with Kevin's feet, the keeper raised them and slid the bottom of the sheet metal beneath them. Continuing with the legs, he worked his way up to Kevin's head.

"Be careful. I think I b-broke my neck," he said.

The keeper gently raised Kevin's head with one hand and forced the top of the sheet to align with his body.

"Excellent job. You m-make a great nurse, and your b-bedside m-manner is perfect," said Kevin with a laugh.

The keeper smirked—the few teeth that showed through were the color of dingy pearls. His face was beige leather, tanned from too many years in the sun. He pinched the ends of the sheet between thumbs and fingers with a vice-like grip, and with his back hunched, he crab-walked in a semi-circle until Kevin's head was near the base of the light and his feet faced the ocean.

"Thank you so m-much," said Kevin. "I'm sorry I fell off your ladder. I just wanted to see the top."

The keeper shook his head. He reached over and took the rope he had laid down, and in true seaman fashion, began to weave a net of intricate hitches and knots over Kevin's body and beneath the sheet metal.

As he leaned over, Kevin couldn't help but admire the rugged man of the sea. Kevin didn't mind that he smelled like bad cologne and fish, or that the breath coming through his nostrils reeked of alcohol.

"How come you don't t-talk?" Kevin asked.

Without ceasing from his work, the keeper pulled at his dark turtle neck with one hand, revealing an open stoma, its edges surrounded by the same gray stubble that adorned his chin. Though he tried, Kevin couldn't hide his disgust. The keeper noticed and likewise, did his best to hide his offense.

"Is that why you work out here all alone? So you won't have to talk to anyone? That makes sense. If you don't have anyone to talk to, you won't miss talking."

The keeper flashed an angry expression.

"I'm sorry. I'm talking too much. I mean, why wouldn't you miss talking just because you don't have anyone to talk to? Who wouldn't miss it? That's like saying I won't miss diving anymore because I broke my stupid neck climbing your stupid lad—"

With that Kevin burst into tears. "Oh, God, I'm crippled now."

The keeper looked away with an awkward sigh as he continued tying knots.

"I'm sorry," said Kevin as he gained his composure. "I don't do this all the time, you know? I'm a tough guy. I haven't cried since I lost my grampa. He's the one who taught me how to dive."

Within seconds the tears resurfaced. A moment later, he calmed down. "I'm really sorry for screwing up your day. You didn't deserve to come home to this. I didn't mean to mess around and fall, I just thought this place was abandoned. I didn't see any boat, or –body. There was no light. Of course it was day, but I still didn't think anybody worked here."

The keeper secured his final knot. With a smile, he looked Kevin in the eye and gave him two pats on the cheek.

"Thank you so much. You really are a godsend. Are you going to call the Coast Guard now?"

Taking the leftover bit of rope in hand, the keeper stood and approached his boat.

"You're going to put me in the boat? Are you sure you can lift me? I mean, you're strong and all, but don't you think you might need help? I can wait on the Coast Guard to get here."

The keeper secured the end of the rope to a green, metal cleat on his starboard side.

"What are you doing? Is that so I don't fall out? Oh, wait. I just remembered. We can take my boat. It's got a motor. We'll get to the shore in no time. Plus it has my cell phone, wallet and ID, so you can tell them who I am. Or *show*, I mean. Sorry."

The keeper returned to the pylon by the ladder. He loosened the rope and tossed it in the boat.

"Wait. You're not going to drag me behind, are you?"

The keeper gave the boat a push and climbed in. He took up his oars and began to row. As the boat left the rocky mound, the rope went tight. With a scraping sound like nails on chalkboard, Kevin slid along the rocks, toward the rising tide.

"Are you sure this will float?"

His feet dipped into the frigid water.

"Man, that's cold. I think you're going to have to paddle faster so I won't sink. Can you do that?"

The keeper continued to row.

The sheet metal slid down the sloping rocks, into the water.

"Wait! I'm going under!" Kevin shouted as the water rose to his groin and hips.

The keeper kept rowing.

"You're gonna drown me!" Kevin shouted.

The water climbed up his chest.

"Stop it! Please! Oh, God, no!" he yelled as the water covered his face and he sank beneath the choppy surface.

He struggled against the ropes, fought to hold his breath, unable to feel his body from the numbingly-cold waters and helpless to use his limbs from the injury he sustained. He heard the muffled sloshing of oars and watched as they cut through the waves above him, stirring up a great bunch of bubbles.

He watched the dark bottom of the boat he thought was his salvation just ahead of him. Soon the oars left the water, and in their place came the loose end of the rope that condemned him, sinking down past him.

A change of current rushed through the bay, turning him to his side. As he fought to turn himself upright he heard a sharp snap. He fought to turn his head, but now even it was rendered immobile.

Kevin's little, cursed lifeboat overturned completely, and as he sank to the bottom of the bay he saw a dozen other fools such as he, bound by rope to sheets of metal or wood or bags of bricks, in various stages of decay.

When he beheld the aquatic graveyard of corpses he was soon to join—their exposed bones with things swimming carelessly through; their flesh covered in undulating plants and frozen expressions of terror—he did the only thing he *could* do: scream his last breath in a flurry of twisting, rising bubbles.

Squire Magic
Larry C. Kay

*B*etween the grey sea and the long black land rode a bloodied knight and his dirty squire. When his weary mount hit a rock on the dirt road, jarring his broken ribs, Sir Murten winced and groaned. Tied to his saddle in a burlap sack, his dented armor clanked like a bag of beach shells.

His squire, Reuel, winced when his master did. The blood on his clothes was that of Sir Murten and the creature. He had done his part, but had shed nothing but sweat. Reuel wished he could fix his master's armor, but it was one of the few mending spells he had not mastered.

Sir Murten checked the horizon and spotted the telltale smoke of Riev. He turned to his squire. "You showed me something back there, Reuel."

"I did?"

"You looked an ogre, mad with magic, in the eye and held firm."

"Your lessons, sir." Reuel was half-amazed himself. He had been thinking of his master's fate, not his own. Being brave for others was far easier, he had found, than standing for his own interests.

Murten grunted. "I taught you about steel and what small sorcery I know. The rest is guts."

"Yes, sir." Reuel sat taller in his saddle.

"I barely recognize the lad who came to me six seasons past. Despite your size, you were so meek I did not know the color of your eyes for four days." Murten chuckled.

Reuel grinned; he remembered. It had taken a full season to understand that Sir Murten taught with words not fists. He actually wanted his squire to ask questions. "Will you return the fee?"

"Why?"

"We didn't kill the ogre."

"We were tasked with killing an ogre turned wicked with sorcery. It can no longer practice magic. True it still draws breath, but only mountain goats need fear that. Besides, we need the coin. You eat enough roasted mutton to choke a dragon."

Reuel grinned. He felt his stomach was reason one that his parents had fairly thrown him at the visiting knight. His mending magic had been but an occasional thing then, good for shoes and pots, and failing more often than not. "Will you seek custom from the wizard in Riev?"

Murten spat. "Not that one. He may be the best spellwright along the coast, but he leaves his tower only to gloat or despise. We use our meager talents out in the world, as the gods intended, and so show the greater result."

Reuel knew his own talents were trifling, but not his master's. "But you have high magic, too. You can see through illusions."

"Aye. Which is why tower wizards hire me to go after their fellows. I'll take their coin, but not their company. We, who are Pledged to the Plain, build a tower of *reputation*. Small deeds every day, taunts and curses left unsaid, and the merciful stroke. Even your specialty can be a foundation for a mighty spire."

Reuel beamed at the compliment. Leather and cloth answered his call. Their horses were free of flies and hoof rot. Rust and mold and stains ran from him. Tin and lead bent to his will. Only iron eluded him.

"A tower wizard eats the work of his apprentices to foist his own ambition on the clouds." Murten's face grew grim, and Reuel knew his master chewed old wounds. He kept quiet, and imagined the beef stew waiting for them in Riev's best chow-house.

When the pair passed the city gates with a wave, they dismounted and led their weary horses through the bustle and stink. Riev traded on silver and slaves from the North, and steel and salt from the South. It had come into its wealth only in the last generation, and had only recently built a wizard's tower. Even so, filth still clogged the cobbles, and beggars still crowded any man dressed in silk.

A commotion in the plaza ahead of them caused both travelers to stop. Reuel frowned; he still did not trust towns and town folk. The fields were what he knew. Town folk might crowd about to see a hanging as much as a mummery show. Reuel preferred sleeping in a barn to any inn in town, but his master had a taste for sheets, and fettled ale, if they had the coin.

The duo approached cautiously, and found a strange scene. Reuel spotted a wizard in fancy blue robes, his cape billowing just right, intimidating a man they knew—a maker of saddles, a friend. Without warning, the wizard gestured and the saddler was held aloft in a chokehold of smoke. Reuel heard shouts to stop, but also cheers from the crowd.

What had the saddler done? Reuel cut his eyes to his master. Sir Murten's face hardened. Reuel knew his master would not ignore a slight, especially from a sorcerer.

Sir Murten dismounted. No words passed between knight and squire. Reuel knew his role: support his master. He was given leave to figure out what that support might be. Reuel noted that his master had left his long blades and his crossbow on the horse. This was not a killing ground. Still, he recognized the tension in his master's limbs as he accosted the mage.

"Lay off!"

The anxious crowd silenced at the knight's cry. The wizard turned, annoyed at such interruption of his sport. He found a solid, weary man with a wide stance and grim eyes.

Reuel noted a thin boy in an orange robe lurking behind the wizard. The apprentice did not seem a threat, so the squire focused on the enchanter. He recognized the haughty cast to the wizard's mien. He wished Sir Murten had strapped on his swords first.

The mage and fighter eyeballed each other. Finally, the wizard dropped the saddler, who lay on the ground coughing and groaning.

"Now, what is the mea—" began Sir Murten.

But the magic was not ended. It was diverted. Sorcerous chains of smoke assaulted Sir Murten, and grabbed him by his throat. Reuel groaned in sympathy as his master struggled against the foul air.

The wizard sneered. "I am Sortiarus. It is I who ask *why* and *wherefore*. Who are you to call me fair or foul? I am meat and drink to this town. Beloved by all. You shall be made to learn this."

The crowd reacted as before: some were content with a show, some hated such abuse; none were brave enough to tell Sortiarus to stop. Sir Murten twisted as the smoke raised him into the air. Reuel did not know what to do. His instinct was to rush the wizard, tackle him and thrash him. Even if it meant being hollowed by fell magery.

However, Sir Murten was not a saddle maker, nor just a sellsword. He grabbed the chains of smoke and rent them. Sortiarus scowled as the knight grabbed at a hunting knife, and advanced on him. This was beyond a lesson. This was serious ground made for blood.

The wizard incanted, his unheard words rippling the skin. Coruscating energy, purple and writhing, flowed from Sortiarus's staff and enveloped the knight. Sir Murten groaned, his wounds bled, but he moved closer. Growling, the wizard increased the pressure, and Sir Murten grunted, but he staggered forward, his blade sharp and intent.

Reuel had seen his master win against monsters and wizards both. He loved the grizzled warrior like a father, but he knew that once his master's blood was up he did not settle easily. Reuel's hope for Sir

Murten dwindled to a ghostly whisper as he saw both men narrow their gaze and focus their inner fire. For honor or reputation or sheer stubbornness, neither would yield.

Sortiarus flagged first, and Reuel cheered as his master, with a hard eye and a barbarian's cry, strove to plunge his knife to the hilt into the wizard's chest.

Sortiarus grabbed at an amulet about his throat, and lay a doom on his attacker that felled him like a sapling to a woodman's ax. Sir Murten made no cry, but fell to the dust and moved no more.

Reuel rushed to the fallen knight while Sortiarus, breathing raggedly, attempted to regain his composure. The mage's apprentice stood at his side.

He held Sir Murten's head, but the squire knew the truth. His master was dead. There was naught to be done but call for the priest, and the man with the shovel. Death was such a part of his life, but Reuel could not accept this finality. What did you do when the sun died? When rivers ran backward? You could only pray and weep.

The crowd hissed and booed. Sortiarus stood and assayed the town folk, his people supposedly. He frowned, then said, "You saw his mad eye. His blade hungered for my life. I had no choice." The crowd muttered. Some gripped their tools and thought of violence. The wizard raised his staff. "Look to your bounty, your green fields and full herds. I have done this for you."

Tearful, Reuel stood and listened to the wizard admonish the crowd. The wizard, with none now to gainsay him, spoke to their worries and their concerns. Reuel felt their righteous anger at a good man's death diminish. He did not need them.

"Wizard!"

Reuel stood as his master had, wide-legged, fists clenched, head down. Sortiarus turned and examined his new foe, and laughed. But Reuel had caught the fleeting fear in the wizard's eye. He was just a man who knew things most did not. He could still bleed.

Reuel squeezed his own will into a simple cleaning spell, and un-mending hex, and the fancy hat of the tower wizard disintegrated, its thread unraveling. Mending hexes, and their opposite, were low magic. They required no paraphernalia, no gestures, no incantations. Just willpower and intent.

Sortiarus ripped the remaining shreds of his fine hat from his head. "Do you think to test me with your squire magic? I have studied books written by the hoary dead. I will sunder your soul and raise your flesh from the grave to be my slave."

Reuel hesitated. He knew the wizard might speak truth, but it *felt* like tavern smoke, something to dazzle the locals. When Sir Murten had spoken, it was plain and powerful. This man shined and lied.

Sortiarus' apprentice stepped away from the wizard's shadow. "Let me, Master."

He nodded. A half-dozen paces separated solid squire from slim apprentice. The crowd hushed. This was something new. A tale to be retold in the quiet months of the coming winter.

The apprentice strode out as if the plaza was his stage. Gone was his earlier hesitation. His orange robes of silk flared as he assumed his position. Reuel thought this silk mule appeared very royal, but also something like a summer squash.

The apprentice spoke in cultured tones, full of learning and menace. "Hear me, you fat cabbage-eater. I am called Corlando. A third rank mage. Your mind is mush if you think saddle spells and broom hexes are going to mean a titmouse's tail against Ice Dagger and Stone Fist."

Corlando gestured grandly and began perilous incantations. Moonlight sparks flowed about his arms. The crowd backed up. Reuel grimaced at the fierce crackle of sorcerous doom. His bones thrummed from Corlando's whispered words of power. Reuel knew it must be a powerful, deadly spell because it took so long to perform.

With a half-dozen steps, Reuel crossed the space between them, and punched the weed-thin boy in the jaw. Corlando's well-prepared malevolence popped and faded. Before the gasp of the crowd finished, the apprentice's figure hit the ground, his fine robe askew, his pale legs akilter.

Reuel turned to Sortiarus. The wizard glowered and squeezed his staff, a fine oaken piece with iron bands on both ends. It glowed when Sortiarus began chanting.

Reuel noted the careful enunciation of words. He was a careful man himself. Everything in life required care to work properly. Ignored, horses could fall lame from a twisted shoe. Uncared for, swords dulled and broke. Even simple mud could clog a carriage's wheel.

Sortiarus raised his staff to lay a fulsome enchanting upon Reuel's brow, but the squire's jaw clenched. Instead of deadly sorcery, the metal bands rusted and cracked, the oak warped. In a heartbeat, the staff destroyed itself, and the unfocused power within knocked the wizard to the ground.

The crowd whooped and hollered. Reuel advanced on his prey.

Sortiarus grabbed for his amulet but it was lost, the chain broken. He fled to his fine stallion. He rummaged in his expensive saddlebags for a tome of ancient power. But even the mightiest books are held together with naught but glue. Reuel flexed his will, un-mended the volume, and the pages flew away in the wind.

Sortiarus spun about. The time for subtlety was past. A scroll saved time. A book recorded past power. A potion contained recipes of doom and puissance, but every wizard relied first and last on his own well of power. Sortiarus's eyes grew black, and his long, sable hair stood out with freakish energy. "I match thee, boy. Raw might against might. No tools."

Sortiarus stood only a few paces away from Reuel, sheathed in the selcouth energy that was his right through long years of study. Reuel seemed a lonely sow caught out in the wild when a wolf came down from the hills for supper.

Reuel whispered an unmending spell.

Sortiarus cut a fine figure, dressed in his magic and his rage… and not much else. Reuel watched with satisfaction as the wizard's face registered the effect of the unraveling cantrip on his fine silk robe. Magic required concentration, and the chill air on the sacred scrotum distracted Sortiarus, and his lethal magic died.

Naked but unbowed, Sortiarus began an invocation that would have summoned a demon, but it died in his throat as a cloud of dust choked him.

And then a swarm of horse-flies attacked the exposed flesh of the naked mage. The cow's milk of his breakfast curdled in his belly. The juicy pheasant rotted, too. Sortiarus puked.

The best spellwright of the coastal baronies squirmed on the ground in a pool of his own filth. Finally, he coughed out, "I yield, I yield."

Reuel could have cheered. Instead, he growled, ran, and grabbed Sir Murten's long blade, and stood over the retching wizard laid low by squire magic. He raised the sword high, his beloved master's death rattle searing his memory.

Then he remembered the knight raising the very same sword high over the defeated ogre, the beast squirming in pain as this man now did, and Reuel knew his master had shown mercy. But this man had shown none. What did he deserve but what he himself had sown?

Reuel shouted at the crowd, "My master lays dead at this one's hand, a blow fallen no grieving can mend." Reuel shut his eyes, but his inward eye turned on his heart. His master's oft-spoke words greeted him, "Think first, fight after."

The wizard hacked, and quivered, and turned to his slayer. "The treasure...of my tower...is yours. Spare me."

Reuel's muscles strained. He brought the sword down in a killing arc, and the wizard cringed. At the last, Reuel stopped his swing, and reversed the blade. He bashed the wizard's skull with the hilt, and his enemy crumpled.

"Keep your tower. I have my own."

Who Abandon Themselves
Jeremy M. Gottwig

*H**is joints ached as he climbed the three hundred icy steps* to the monastery. Shy Aubolis kept his pain to himself. "No need to complain to the Ether," he mumbled into the falling snow.

A blast of wind whipped the cowl from his brow and scattered icy flakes into his face. "Would the Ether listen, Shy Eel?" it seemed to ask.

Aubolis turned his back to the wind. He scrambled to secure his pocket but discovered it empty. Aubolis searched the steps and found the green envelope stuck to a nearby patch of wet ice. With his tail, he snatched the letter and moved it to an inside pocket.

"One thousand and twelve," he taunted as he tightened his sash. He had lost count of the years, but he had never lost count of her letters. "You have yet to steal a single one from me."

The wind laughed on its way down the mountain and across the frozen lake.

Aubolis repositioned his hood and studied the sky. Through a thin gash in the clouds, he spotted the familiar streaks of the planet Kain. Of Opal, the system's darker star, there was no sign.

The sanctuary spire disappeared into the clouds as it grasped for the star's purifying light.

"May the sky be cleared and True Mass be blessed," Aubolis whispered. He meant his words for the Ether, but a gust stole them away. "So be it," he added. Aubolis let the wind have its victory. He resumed his ascent and said nothing more.

The snow continued to fall. The wind faded, and by the time Aubolis reached the arched gates at the top of the stairs, it was nothing more than a breeze.

He passed into the sanctuary.

Pilgrims from across the Opalious System filled the pews. Photons webbed across the vault from the exposed spire crystal, but those who had traveled to Reev to bask in Opal's healing light remained in darkness.

"Another day without True Mass." Aubolis felt the letter through the fabric of his robe and wondered if he could accept the blame. "Without the burden of sin in my pocket, perhaps I might have reasoned with the wind," he considered. "Asked it to push the clouds away."

Aubolis removed his clawheals and slipped barefoot along the shadowy perimeter of the sanctuary. He passed through the mouth behind the altar and flipped back the cowl of his robe. From his pouch, he withdrew his luminescent shalh.

"How does the market fare, Shy Aubolis?" whispered a voice in the darkness. Aubolis lifted his shalh and caught the profile of Micha, who stood watch over the proceedings.

"Have you attended to the spire, Young Micha?"

Micha frowned. "That is Shy Pike's responsibility."

"As I understand it, Pike has taken ill. Did I hear wrong?"

"You did not."

"Then please: Attend to the spire. We must ensure that it is at full height."

"And what of the watch?"

Aubolis withdrew a skin of ceremonial spice from his belt and handed it to Micha. "Young Remus will need this. Bring it to him and ask that he take your place. I will stand watch until he arrives."

"But Remus is in the chapel preparing for Dark Mass, Shy Eel."

Aubolis frowned at the novice, who knew better than to address him by his familiar name. "Indeed he is," growled Aubolis. Micha winced and lowered his head. Aubolis continued, "And if he is not yet done, then he is taking too long. Hurry."

As Aubolis watched Micha disappear into the darkness, he regretted that he had not been available to manage the situation as it unfolded. He felt the envelope through his robe and whispered, "Sometimes you are too much the distraction."

In his heart, he enjoyed that so many young Shy called him Shy Eel behind his back. The name reminded him of his early years at the monastery, but his current position as one of the elders demanded formality.

"Shy Aubolis: Skinny as a Ruthus Eel," bellowed Young Par during a morning meal many years ago. It didn't take long for someone to reduce the proclamation to *Shy Eel*.

The elders at the time had tasked Aubolis with fetching items from the market city at the base of the monastery. Aubolis's legs and tail grew strong, but he never developed that layer of fat upon which the other Shy depended to stay warm.

Aubolis refused to abandon this role as he advanced in age and rank.

It was during one of those early trips to the market that he sent his first letter to Helon. He remembered how his hands shook as he handed the envelope to the system traveler. Weeks later he received his first reply. Their forbidden correspondence followed him deep into the years.

He once considered his nighttime chills part of his penance, but he had long since ceased to beg the Ethereal Murk for forgiveness.

It didn't take long for Young Remus to arrive. After a formal exchange, Aubolis departed into the inner cloisters and entered the plunging tower. He descended the spiral path toward his cell. The shalh, he held palm down to highlight his feet. He dragged his tail along the cold surface to offer quick aid in case he slipped.

A shout echoed from deep in the tower. Aubolis decided to ignore the disruption. He entered his small cell near the top of the spiral and dropped the shalh into its cradle on the wall. A second shalh embedded on the adjacent wall flickered to life. Aubolis withdrew the items he had retrieved from the market and placed each atop his reading desk. The envelope, he propped up on the stone shelf above his cot.

"This is a period of meditation, Shy Aubolis," he reminded himself as he studied the envelope. The green fabric had no place among the muted colors of his cell. He decided to push the letter beneath his cot with the others. He would read it later, he decided.

"You disrupt me," he told Helon.

Aubolis took the envelope and grunted to his knees. The letter never left his hands.

"It has been too long," he whispered. He knelt over his cot and peeled open the envelope. Flakes of red sealant scattered over his pillow. Once his fingers touched the paper, he knew that he had exceeded his ability to resist. His breath caught as he extracted and unfolded the letter.

Aubolis didn't recognize the handwriting...

Quiet One,

You must forgive the delay. It is not for lack of trying. No longer can my fingers wield the pen that has connected us these many years. I finally accepted the need to ask another for aid. She swears that she will keep our secret, but I do not trust her.

I am glad you are unable to hear my voice in its weakened state. These are my final hours. Is it wrong to be thankful that you will never view me through the lens of age? I like to believe that I am beyond caring, but that would be a lie. When you dream of me, be sure that I am young.

The truth is that I have become bitter, a fact that I have tried so hard to hide from you. I am bitter, because I am here, and I know that the power of Opal over Reev will keep you young long after I am gone, but I am also bitter because the knowledge of our transgression will live on with you. I am bitter, because we have never seen our child.

Could it be that Opal will keep you alive after even our child has died of old age?

I guess none of this matters. I wish that it did.

I have one final thought that I need to convey: I wish that I had never become your student. I wish your lessons had never enthralled me. I wish that you had been dull. And yet, sometimes when I find myself smiling, I realize that I am thinking of our tails twisted together in the depths of transgression.

Goodbye, Quiet One. It is now up to you to complete our penance, and I hope you will fare better than me. Perhaps my passing will give you the strength you need.

Helon

Aubolis dropped the paper onto his pillow and watched it fold. He closed his eyes and tried to picture her young face looking up at him. It had been too long. Within his own mind, the sin that bonded them together ceased to matter long ago. He realized that he had thought of neither her face nor her flesh in years.

He realized that Helon had become her letters.

"And in the end, we are still so far apart," Aubolis whispered into the gloom.

The sound of the chief acolyte singing the Call to Darkness echoed through the plunging tower. Aubolis didn't have time to mourn. He left the letter where it lay and struggled to his feet. He changed into his purified robe.

"Shy Aubolis," whispered a voice from outside his cell.

Aubolis paused, but he did not turn toward the voice. "I hear the call," he said.

"Shy Aubolis, I have come to beg forgiveness."

Aubolis stood like ice. He said nothing.

"Earlier, I was wrong to speak to you in such a familiar manner. It was a slip."

"Young Micha, is it?" Aubolis asked. "There is nothing to forgive."

"But surely, there is."

Aubolis lacked the will to argue. "You examined the spire as I asked?"

"I did."

"What did you find?"

"The third lock had come loose. I tightened it and extended the spire. The pilgrims experienced True Mass. It was brief, but the donation boxes are full."

Aubolis sighed and smiled. "May they be healed," he whispered. He turned to Micha and added, "You should have been more attentive." Once the words met his lips, Aubolis concluded that he had placed Micha into a role for which he was ill-suited.

"Yes, Shy Aubolis. May I go?"

Aubolis lost focus as his mind trailed toward Helon and her final letter. "Things have changed," Aubolis whispered. "We must accept change." In a stronger voice, he added, "There is something I would like you to do for me."

"Another task?" grumbled Micha.

"Yes. Another. Do you know why they call me Shy Eel?" he asked.

Young Micha hesitated. "Because you are skinny?" he asked.

"Skinny and strong. And I am so because of my travels to the market city. But I am tired, and this is a responsibility I should have relinquished long ago." It took all his will to proceed. "I will pass this task on to you," he struggled. The rest came easier. "You will retrieve small items at the request of the elder Shy. Nothing more."

"But...what of the temptations? I have heard stories."

Aubolis met the young Shy's eyes. He knew Micha's history. Like so many, Shy Micha was here because of a transgression. "While you are here in this monastery, you will apply yourself. You will strive to become greater than your flesh. And some day, you may find that your weaknesses do not have the hold over you that you thought they did. Someday, despite the feelings in your heart, you may realize that you have already moved on." Aubolis looked down at the letter. "You may lament this discovery."

"I understand, Shy Aubolis. But perhaps another would be a better choice."

"Perhaps. But I chose you."

The chief acolyte sounded the final call.

The Tower
Richard Chizmar

This campfire story,
for Jimmy Cavanaugh

1

They found the first body on a Thursday.
A couple of kids on their way home from fishing Hanson Creek stopped at the base of the old water tower to take a leak and almost ended up pissing on the missing girl's Nikes.

In the old days, one of the boys would have stood guard over the body while the other ran into town for help. In these sadly modern times, they did what most kids would've done: they took out their cell phones, snapped a few pictures to show their friends later, and only then, called 9-1-1 to report their finding.

The police showed up remarkably fast, not even ten minutes later. Three patrol cars almost colliding in a nearby gravel parking lot, before making the short hike to the old water tower. They forgot to bring a roll of police tape—seldom used in a town like Edgewood, Maryland—so one of the officers had to jog back to his car to retrieve it—which is where he met the girl's hysterical parents.

Some things never change, regardless of the times: news travels fast in a small town.

The officer radioed ahead to warn the others that the girl's parents had arrived and were understandably upset. His Sergeant ordered him to hold them there in the parking lot, but that didn't work out so well, as both Mom and Dad bum-rushed the officer and beat him back to the crime scene by a good forty yards.

Once there, the dad—a bearded construction foreman of nearly 250 pounds—took one look at his daughter's body sprawled in the bushes and fainted. The kids whipped out their cell phones, of course, and took more pictures, before they were shooed away by the police, with threats to tell their parents. The boys grabbed their fishing rods and stringer full of crappie and yellow perch and beat it. The entire time, the mom was down on her knees, eyes closed and praying.

An ambulance arrived a short time later, but by then the dad was conscious and back on his feet, too distraught to be embarrassed by his fainting. A pair of police officers stood with him by a patrol car, trying to counsel him. The mom was still off praying in the weeds.

It took several more hours for the police to finish their initial investigation and remove the body. In that time, a crowd of townspeople had gathered at the scene. There was incessant whispering and pointing and quite a bit more picture taking. There were also two television reporters and a local newspaperman.

But by dusk, the scene was eerily quiet and practically deserted. A lone officer remained, sitting guard on a folding chair—the kind you might see at a backyard barbecue—reading a magazine by the glow of his flashlight and swatting at mosquitoes.

Behind him, lost in the shadows, the old water tower watched over the town.

2

The dead girl's name was Bethany Hopkins. She was twelve, tall for her age, nearsighted, and blonde. A straight "A" student, she was also captain of her swim team and a talented artist. She liked to wear her long hair in braids and was crazy for country music.

Bethany had gone missing the night before. She had eaten pizza for dinner at a friend's house and set out to walk the two blocks home just before eight—but she never made it.

By eight-thirty, her worried parents were combing the neighborhood; her dad on foot, her mom behind the wheel of their brand new SUV. By nine-thirty, worry had turned into panic, and they had called in the police. The police did their jobs, and by midnight, every officer in town was on the look-out, a recent school picture of a smiling Bethany Hopkins at their side. Plans were made for a county wide search the next morning, but the two boys discovered Bethany's body before the search could begin. Which explains why the police had been so quick to arrive; they'd all been assembled in the Food Lion parking lot, still going over the details of the upcoming search.

The coroner's report for Bethany Hopkins cited strangulation as the cause of death. There were no signs of sexual abuse or torture. Someone simply choked the life out of the little girl and left her there in the bushes.

The police did their work tirelessly, but there were no leads.

After a while, people stopped whispering and life returned to normal.

3

Until the next body was discovered—in almost exactly the same spot.

This time by a home-for-the-summer college girl who was jogging along the worn dirt path that snaked through Hanson Woods and looped past the water tower on its way back toward town.

The old water tower was as much a part of Edgewood as Main Street or the Campus Hills Movie Theater or Tucker's Field, where the annual Summer Carnival and Fall Pumpkin Festival were held.

The aging tower stood up there on its hill, overlooking the town, looking like one of H.G. Wells' spindly alien invaders marching over the horizon.

Long ago, when I was a kid, before the trees and thick bramble overtook the slope, we used to sled there on snowy mornings when school was cancelled. I remember playing flashlight tag and kick the can there on countless summer nights, fireflies dancing around our heads, our young, excited voices carrying in the darkness.

Once the woods took over, and the years marched on, the old water tower became known for a different kind of playing.

Instead of sledding, kids snuck up there to party or have bonfires or shoot their father's .22's. Too often, the ground was littered with empty beer cans and broken bottles, forgotten shoes and shirts and even brassieres. There were stories of drunken fights and carnal abandon and even Satan worshippers in the summer and fall of '76.

There were a number of complaints from the older folks who used that stretch of land for daily strolls or bird watching or getting to and from their favorite fishing spots on Hanson Creek, but none of them made a difference until the local newspaper ran a front page editorial about the issue. That did the trick, and soon after, warning signs were posted and the local police added the area to their daily patrol routes.

The bonfires and drinking went away— moved somewhere else, of course; kids will be kids—as did most of the litter and trouble. Most, but not all. Things still happened there from time to time. Bad things. People move away, people forget; but I've done neither. I remember...

A local husband, distraught after he discovered his wife was cheating on him with her best friend's husband, jumped to his death from the water tower in 1986.

A decade later, someone climbed the tower in the middle of the night and spray-painted satanic graffiti all over the damn thing. Goats heads. Pentagrams. Inverted crosses. Pretty much everything but a big red 666. It took three weeks and two budget meetings before the town got its act together and painted over the atrocities.

A few years later, a middle-aged, black woman—a stranger—was found hanging from one of the tower's criss-crossing metal support beams. Neither her identity—nor an explanation—were ever discovered.

Of course, when a series of dark and mostly unexplainable events occur in the same spot over the course of many years, and most especially when these events occur within the confines of a small town, the spot is inevitably said to be cursed or haunted—and the old water tower was no exception. Stories spread. Legends grew.

The land around the old water tower was unholy ground; it attracted evil. Ghosts and demons roamed there. It was a backwoods meeting spot for drug runners and gang members traveling on I-95 from New York to Florida. An old witch, her face burned and disfigured, lived somewhere back there in the woods; her cabin hidden amongst the bramble.

A local high school boy even wrote a term paper a number of years ago that spotlighted the area's dark history in great detail. He contended that there was once a slave house that stood on that lonely hill—long before the water tower ever existed. The slave house was burned to the ground one night by a drunken and enraged master, and everyone inside had perished. Then, during the second world war, while the tower was being built in that very spot, it was reported that a half-dozen workers had died or been seriously injured during its construction. Workers also reported dozens of dead animal carcasses were found on the property; an explanation was never found. As a result, the tower was said to be cursed from the very beginning. Then, there was the story of the newlywed bride who, while on an early morning walk the day after her joyous wedding celebration, was bitten by a mysterious two-headed snake while resting in the tower's shadow. The woman died of her wound later that evening, and the snake was never found. There was even a lengthy section discussing the long-rumored worship of devils and demons on the grounds, and a handful of witness accounts claiming the area was haunted by the ghosts of murdered slaves.

There was more, much more—29 pages in all.

The fact that there were very few truths to be found in this young man's report did nothing to diminish its impact. The boy received a "B+" (he was said to be a terrible speller) and became a hero of sorts to his fellow students.

And, with the passage of time, as so often is the case, the many stories became truth, the legends became fact.

I would know. Many of the other old-timers moved away or forgot, but not me. No, sir. I've been here since almost the beginning.

My Lord willing, I'll turn eighty-four years old when this chill October rolls around, and I spent just over forty of those years hauling the mail around this town. I've seen it all, and I've heard it all. Trust me, people like to run their mouths, and the only person likely to hear more rambling words than a mailman is the bartender down at Loughlin's Pub. But I've learned that drunk people mostly tell lies and folks standing in their sunny front yards holding onto their mail mostly tell the truth—or at least the truth as they believe it.

Lot of folks around this town think I'm just a friendly, old man. They say their polite hellos and offer up their polite waves and keep right on going when they pass me on the sidewalk.

And they might be right, you know it.

But, don't you forget what I said: I have seen things.

4

The second body was discovered in plain sight. According to police, the whole thing looked staged.

Our resident home-from-college girl, a bright young lady named Jennifer Ward studying to become a teacher, came jogging around the bend—and stopped dead in her tracks. Her iPod tumbled from her hand down to the ground, yanking her headphones right out of her ears. Justin Timberlake broke the morning silence.

Everyone in town knew Gina Sharretts. She taught math at the local high school and coached the field hockey team.

Gina's limp body lay propped against one of the water tower's rusting metal legs, her hands folded neatly in her lap. She could have been sleeping if it weren't for her hideously bulging eyes and the dark bruising around her swollen neck.

Jennifer snatched up her iPod and headphones and took off at a sprint. If campus life had taught her one thing, it was that safety was in numbers. Out on the road, she flagged down the first approaching car, and told the driver to call the police.

The patrol cars arrived a short time later, and once again the police tape came out, and the picture-takers and the lookie-loos, and this time around, it was a distraught brother and sister—Gina was thirty-seven and single on the day of her death—crashing the crime scene.

Once again, in the frantic days that followed, the police did their jobs and did them well—but there were still no leads.

Someone had simply strangled the life out of Gina Sharretts... just as someone had strangled the life out of Bethany Hopkins three years earlier.

And left them both at the base of the water tower.

This clear pattern escaped no one's notice, of course—most especially that of the police and the press. But even this discovery seemed to lead nowhere. Just one more dead end street in another dead end investigation.

5

This time, it took longer for the town to return to normal.

People were angry and paranoid. Old grudges and suspicions gained new life. New grudges and suspicions were born. There were more drunken fights at Loughlin's Pub on Friday and Saturday nights. More arguments and mean-spirited gossip between sunburned moms at the community pool.

Interestingly enough, it was adults responsible for most of the bad behavior. It was summer break, and most of the teenagers chose to hang out at the quarry or the Dairy Queen or over in Fallston at the new shopping mall. They seemed to feel safer together, and whether they were a fan of Miss Sharrett's math class or not, there was an unspoken agreement that they had lost one of their own.

It was a strange time to live in Edgewood, with the constant police presence, the daily newspaper headlines and the local television updates. There was no new information, so the news folk chewed up the old information to tiny pieces and spit it back out.

Most days were too hot and humid for an old man like me to spend outside, so I sat in my glassed-in back porch, drank iced tea and read my paperbacks. Old oaters, mostly, with the occasional spy novel thrown in for good measure. I used to like mysteries and thrillers, but I was a younger and braver man back then.

On mild evenings, I liked to walk down to the park and sit on one of the benches and watch the town wind down for the day. I'd watch the shop owners flip the OPEN signs to CLOSED (or in most cases nowadays, they turned off their glowing red electronic signs). I'd watch the lovers stroll down Main Street hand-in-hand or arm-in-arm. The mothers and fathers hurrying after their racing children to stand in line at the Dairy Queen. The tired factory workers shuffling into Loughlin's Pub to drink their paychecks as the streetlights blinked on behind them.

To a stranger, it may have appeared to be a Norman Rockwell scene of small town serenity; the kind of golden-tinted picture that makes city slickers wish they could pull up roots and move to a place like Edgewood. But if you stopped and looked closer, *really* looked, you could see the lovers holding onto each other a little tighter than was necessary; the moms and dads hurrying after their children, not with relaxed smiles on their faces, but expressions of worry and concern; the workers looking more defeated and angry than tired; and what kind of stores closed up for the night at 7pm, before it was even dark outside? And then there were the patrol cars making their way up and down Main Street with a much higher regularity than anyone would believe necessary for such a small town.

I saw all this—and more—from my park bench. Most evenings, I spent in solitude; a silent observer. But some nights, folks would do more than just flip me a wave or mutter a hurried "hello." Sometimes, they'd stop and chat briefly, and once in a great while, someone would even sit down next to me on my bench and chew my ear for a time. Usually it was Mrs. Brown from the library or Frankie from the barbershop, but it was real nice to have company on those nights.

Company kept me from letting my gaze wander…over to the western outskirts of town…where the water tower stood like some kind of dark sentinel.

Company kept me from thinking too much, and remembering…

I used to sled there as a child. I shot my first squirrel in those woods. I used to play kids' games there at night, the air filled with the laughs and screams of happy children. We used to climb the tower's lower beams and dangle from our legs like toy monkeys on a playground. Kids were kids. Knees got scuffed. Bodies got bruised. The occasional bone got broken. But no one died. Not when we were kids. I never had an inkling that the place was bad.

Until many years later.

I moved away from Edgewood when I was eighteen years old. Six long, miserable years in the Army, and back home I scurried just as fast as my legs could carry me. My momma was still alive then, and my baby sister, Amelia, too. I settled back into my old bedroom and took a job at the shoe factory, which was a blessing because that's where I met my Beth Anne, God rest her soul. It would be another four years before I started delivering the mail; that didn't happen until sweet old Ralph Jenkins passed in his sleep, leaving the job opening for me to step in and fill.

It was probably a month—a happy month, too, believe me—after I came back from the Army that I found myself standing at the base of that water tower staring up at its expanse. To be honest, and despite seeing the tower outlined in the sky every damn day on my way to and from work, I had mostly forgotten about the thing and the times I had spent there.

But that evening, I was on my way to Hanson Creek to try my luck for catfish when I stumbled upon it. I stopped and glanced up, and then, I slowly turned and looked around me at the woods and the wild bramble—and the tiny hairs on the back of my neck went all tingly. I've read about that kind of thing happening in countless paperbacks, but I never believed it until that night.

I spun in a slow circle, looking all around, suddenly sure that someone—or something—was hiding there, watching me. I started to hurry away, but something else stopped me. I stood there, trying to figure it out: was there a smell? Was the light somehow different? Why was it so quiet all of a sudden? Where were the damn birds?

And then it struck me—there was something wrong with the air. I know how that sounds, but I swear to you it's true. There was a thinness to it, almost like being two places at once, like there was another world underneath this one.

I stood there and I swear on my momma's family Bible that I could almost see glimpses of movement in the shadows; that I could hear whispered snatches of words in the empty air beside me.

I thought of the Ray Bradbury stories I loved so much as a young man, tales of faraway worlds and the mysteries that existed right next door to all of us. It could have been a magical experience...but this was different.

I realized I was frightened.

This was a bad place, and I had just had my first real glimpse of it.

I remembered all this sitting there in the park at dusk, but I didn't want to. Lord, no, I didn't.

I have seen things in my lifetime.

And I have done things.

6

Reverend Parker never made it to the church last night to give evening prayer services. There aren't a lot of secrets in a small town, so most people knew that Reverend Parker was a drinker. He would occasionally be a few minutes late to Sunday worship or Wednesday night bingo, and on rarer occasions you might even catch a whiff of whiskey on his breath when he passed you on the street—but he had never missed services before.

Still, most of his parishioners weren't overly concerned. Sure, that old bitty Clara Lotz was put off by his absence and told everyone within earshot exactly that; she had better things to do than wait around for someone who didn't even have the decency to show up to do their job. And poor Hannah Pinborough was visibly worried that she might go to hell without her usual Thursday night worship. But most folks just shrugged their shoulders and went on their merry way.

If it wasn't for Sophie Connolly, the church secretary, and a renown worry wart, the police probably wouldn't have been notified until long into the next day. Instead, after repeated calls with no answer, Sophie drove to the Reverend's house, used her key to open the front door, and upon finding the house empty, called the police to report the Reverend missing.

She happened to glance at the kitchen clock when she hung up the phone and noticed that the time was 7:13pm.

According to official reports, the police discovered the Reverend's body at 7:29pm.

They had obviously wasted little time before searching the woods surrounding the water tower—as if they expected to find something there.

And they did.

Reverend Parker was tied spread-eagle to the four foundation posts of the old water tower with four lengths of thick robe. His eyes and mouth were open obscenely wide, a smudge of dried blood crusted his nostrils, and there was severe bruising on his neck. He was still dressed in his preaching clothes, but the gold crucifix he always wore was nowhere to be found. His Bible lay on his chest.

The press had a field day. *Why hadn't the water tower been staked out? Why were there no leads? Was it a serial killer? Why in a place like Edgewood? If the Reverend wasn't safe, who was?*

Stores started closing their doors even earlier. The police and town council were considering a curfew. The Dairy Queen laid off two of the summer help because there weren't enough hours to keep them working. A front page editorial in the newspaper called for the sheriff's firing.

In the end, the town council called for a Town Meeting on Friday night "to clear the air and inform the townspeople of the appropriate measures which were being taken." Those were the mayor's word, not mine, let me tell you.

Friday night was almost a week away, and most folks weren't buying the "appropriate measures" story. They knew the sheriff was just trying to buy time, and who could blame him?

Something very wrong was going on in our town.

Something very bad.

I had a good idea what it was, but there was no one I could tell.

There was no one who would believe me.

7

I told you before...I've seen and done things.

Things I'm not proud of, nor fully understand.

I thought I'd forgotten most of it; that the passing years and the burning shame and guilt had erased it from my memory, leaving me a simple old man living out the rest of my days in the town that gave birth to me.

I kept to myself all these years, read my books, minded my business, prayed every night. I tried to be a good person and live a good life. I didn't dare pray for redemption, only peace.

I knew I wasn't that man anymore.

That man who had been infected by whatever evil dwelled in that miserable stretch of land beneath that damn tower.

That man who had been cursed to hear its calling...and proved too weak to ignore it.

That man who had not only heard its calling, but *listened* to it...

Finally, luring a stranger there under the pretense of liquid and carnal sins—only to bludgeon her soft skull until it cracked like an egg from my momma's coop. I buried her that night in the soft, dark soil behind the tower and went home to my own bed.

Only to awaken and complete this horrible act again...and again...and again.

But not without remorse; not without judgment.

I dreamed many nights of killing myself. Or leaving this town and never coming back. I even considered turning myself in to the police. Once, I went so far as to write my own confession, but I burned it to ashes before I could find the courage to turn it in.

I realized I didn't control my own thoughts anymore than I did my own actions.

These thoughts—and I—belonged to someone else. *Something* else.

Until my Beth Anne somehow saved me.

I did not—could not—confess my sins to her, but she knew I was struggling; she somehow knew I was in a battle for my soul.

I don't know why my prayers were suddenly answered or why the voices suddenly vanished. I can only believe it was the immense goodness in my wife's heart and her undying faith in her Lord and in me that was responsible. Beth Anne lead me back to God and saved me; she saved my very soul. I have no other explanation.

I only know that the things I saw standing there in the *thin* air surrounding that wretched tower were not of this world; not of any world that contained even a sliver of goodness.

It was an evil, *hungry* place.

In the years that followed, I prayed more than ever before and did my research. I found no record of a slave house or any other building having existed atop that hill. Two men did die during construction of the water tower, and a third worker was killed during an argument with another worker. There were also many credible reports of animal carcasses being found on the property. Not surprisingly, most of the devil worshipping stories turned out to be nothing but rumors and campfire stories; nothing was substantiated.

I believe now it is the ground itself that is *wrong*. It acts as some sort of mysterious conduit, perhaps even a portal to another world or dimension. I believe it allows whatever it is that dwells in that other world to control its chosen one in this world. Why it demands blood? I do not know. The tower itself remains another mystery to me. Does it act as a lure to attract people there, so there are higher numbers to choose from? If so, why was I selected? What did it sense inside me?

I don't know these answers—and that is a blessing.

8

Can you guess now how this story will end?

There will be another body soon, of course.

And they will find it sprawled beneath that old water tower.

I see the tower silhouetted against the western sky most mornings. I watch the setting sun paint it a golden shade of orange most evenings. But I haven't placed a single foot in its shadow for close to four decades.

Someone else has been chosen; I know that now.

Stranger or friend, I do not know, nor do I wish to.

I pray myself to sleep every night.

I pray for the lost soul of the chosen one.

I pray for the lost soul of this town.

And I pray for the deceased.

But most of all, I pray that I don't wake up one morning and feel the urge to slip on my walking boots and pick up my cane and make the long walk up that hill again.

Ancient Spin
Steven R. Southard

Tears flowing into his beard, Eullil wept as he trudged amid the rubble. Stone blocks lay strewn everywhere, many crimson-stained. The structure had fallen that morning, but even now in mid-afternoon, a gray dust lingered in the air like fog, obscuring sight and hindering breath.

Eullil cried for the structure that had stood here, the great tower that had stretched to the sky. He had considered it *his* tower, for he had conceived and designed it, won King Nimrod's approval for it, and supervised every detail of its construction. His culminating lifetime achievement, the soaring edifice had dwarfed all other buildings in the city of Shinar. People called it the architectural marvel of the world upon its completion three days before. Now, the wondrous building had collapsed, destroying his reputation and causing the deaths of hundreds.

Beyond the edge of the debris circle, the dust thinned and Eullil saw people moving about. Most gathered their possessions and heaped them into donkey carts, preparing to leave the city. *Where,* Eullil wondered, *will they go? If they scatter to distant lands and settle far from Shinar, will they become different from each other? Will their descendants even speak the same way?*

Those Shinarites who knew him glared and shouted curses. Eullil walked on, burdened by his responsibility for the disaster. He felt the weight of guilt as if the massive blocks had fallen on his shoulders. After walking farther, his thoughts shifted from the recent disaster to his own future. Running his hands through his beard, he pondered various ideas, shaped them, and constructed a plan.

Eullil reached the house of Ludarat, his brother. Shorter and younger, Ludarat had never aspired to great construction projects. He served as one of the city's scribes, writing down the King's pronouncements and the priests' orations. In the years since they had left their parents' home, the shaper of stone blocks had grown apart from the wielder of words.

"Brother," Ludarat met him at the threshold, his expression sympathetic. "I am so very sorry—"

"You were right, Ludarat," Eullil said. He had stopped crying, but knew tear-tracks must still mar his dusty face. "All those times you told me how your stories could outlast buildings. I did not believe you, but you were right. Your words pass from person to person, generation to generation, and onward forever. Even the hardest stone bricks won't last forever."

"You need food and rest, my brother. Come inside."

"I am here to make a request," Eullil said, without moving. "When you write your story of the Babel Tower, I beg you to leave out some things. Do not mention that I built it too close to the Euphrates, upon weak and shifting ground. Do not reveal that I designed it to use the least amount of materials, to save costs. Do not state that I rushed the construction pace to complete the tower ahead of schedule. Your story should include none of those matters."

"Then, why did the tower fall?"

"You must write this: God made it fall."

"God?"

"Yes," Eullil stroked his beard, "and here is how your story should go..."

The Siege of Ravelin
Ray Kolb

*J**adroth, the northern gate sentry for the night, sat silently*** on his helmet. Both hands were cupped over the handle of his sword, the blade stuck half a foot into the soft ground below. Jadroth's chin rested upon his hands, while his eyes remained locked on the city, Ravelin.

The city's stone grey walls climbed high, disappearing into the starless night sky. Light from the various campfires and the entrenched torches along the edge of the camp weakly illuminated a fraction of the city's drab walls. Jadroth, like thousands of sentries before him and the others posted at Ravelin's other eight gates, saw nothing from the city. Ravelin's inhabitants hadn't been seen in decades.

A few old members of the general's staff supposedly remembered seeing movement from the city, but Jadroth had never met any of them. He didn't believe anyone could still be alive in the city, and he didn't believe anyone had been alive inside Ravelin for quite some time. No city could withstand a properly executed siege, let alone a siege of one hundred years.

Jadroth looked around, and then, reached beneath his hauberk and into the pocket of his tunic. He pulled out a flask and took a long swig. The cheap alcohol burned as it went down, but Jadroth knew it would keep him awake. As he always did after a few gulps from his flask, Jadroth cursed his situation. He wanted to be back at his village, tending the family herd, finding a good woman to marry, and settling down to raise a prosperous Garmeldian family before he was too old.

~

The war between the Cessians and the Ravelins had continued for generations. They fought over a two mile stretch of dry, arid land. The land, *Natajeich*, was the fabled birthplace of the entire continent, where Nataj the Warrior-King had founded his empire. Owning that piece of land meant owning the right to rule the continent.

Jadroth had been to the edge of Natajeich, just like every other male who turned fourteen. It was *the pilgrimage*, after which boys became men. Jadroth had seen it and been disappointed. It struck him then, as it did now, as stupid to fight over something so worthless.

The siege began as a point of honor. Cessia had gained the upper hand in the war and pressured Ravelin to surrender. Ravelin's high council echoed the feelings of its citizens, pronouncing they would never give in. Cessian pride took over, the city's leaders claiming they would siege Ravelin for one hundred years if necessary to break the will of its citizens.

~

A point of honor. Jadroth cursed. What point of honor was there in guarding a dead city?

Despite the liquor, Jadroth could feel his eyes closing. He shook his head, fending off the urge to lie down and sleep.

He looked up at the city walls. His eyes glazed over, making the shadows dance crazily in the dull moonlight. Like clouds, the shadows began to form strange and comical shapes. Jadroth saw an arm rising in the air, a huge double-edged axe in its tightly clutched hand.

The shadow arm moved swiftly in a descending arc, headed for Jadroth's head.

Jadroth fell backwards, off of his helmet, and onto the cold hard ground below. He looked to where the shadow had been. He saw nothing. Only the featureless grey walls of the dead city of Ravelin.

But now, he was definitely awake.

~

At the break of day, Jadroth was relieved from his post. His groggy replacement dutifully asked for a report on activity during the night.

Jadroth decided against mentioning his adventure with the shadows. Besides, he was finished. This was his last sentry duty ever. It had been a long, senseless siege, but it was coming to an end.

Tomorrow would mean the end of one hundred years of waiting patiently at the feet of Ravelin.

Before he could return to his tent and sleep, Jadroth had to report to the sentry commander. As was always done, each sentry would make an accounting that nothing had occurred during the night. Jadroth would do the same.

After reporting, Jadroth started toward his tent. As he made his way through the maze of tents, campfires, wagons, and people surrounding Ravelin, a hand grabbed his arm.

Jadroth jumped, surprised to find himself so on edge. He turned to see Lugeren, last night's sentry for the western gate, looking anxiously at him.

"What is it?" Jadroth demanded, somewhat irritated. He could feel sleep calling him.

"I need to speak with you," Lugeren said, his voice barely above a whisper. He let go of Jadroth and looked around to see if anyone was near enough to hear.

"Later." Jadroth turned away, intent on returning to his quarters.

"Now," Lugeren said. He grabbed Jadroth's arm again.

"Leave me alone." Jadroth casually put a hand on the pommel of his sword.

Lugeren released Jadroth's arm.

Jadroth smiled and began to walk away.

"It's about Hasnell," Lugeren called after him.

Jadroth stopped. Hasnell was his younger sister's husband. Young, eager, and stupid. Hasnell had volunteered for service, even though he had a waiver from military duty since he had a wife and a child.

Jadroth turned around, his arms folded before his chest. He looked crossly at Lugeren. "Go on."

"He was sentry on the south-western gate last night."

"You're wrong," Jadroth said, feeling a bit smug. He had talked with his brother-in-law only yesterday. And Jadroth distinctly remembered who had been the sentry for the south-western gate. "That was Dunkrin's post last night."

"Dunkrin became ill," Lugeren said. "Hasnell took his place."

Jadroth, irritated he had been shown his error, continued gruffly, "So? Hasnell was the sentry."

"He hasn't reported yet this morning."

Jadroth tensed, fighting away any unpleasant thoughts of the past night.

"What's wrong?" Lugeren asked. He stepped toward Jadroth, a look of concern on his face.

"Nothing," Jadroth said, recovering. He returned his thoughts to his brother-in-law. "Hasnell probably just left his post without reporting in. You know how lax these boys are? They've nothing to guard. I wouldn't be surprised if he's passed out drunk in some tavern."

"Normally I'd agree with you," Lugeren said. "But—"

"But what?" Jadroth felt he already knew the answer.

"Something happened last night," Lugeren said. "On my watch. At least I think it did."

"What happened?"

"I can't really explain," Lugeren said. His hands were waving in the air, trying to visually describe something, but focusing on nothing. "Just strange occurrences in the night from the city."

In his mind, Jadroth saw the shadow axe plunging down toward his head. Involuntarily, he jumped back.

"You saw something, too," Lugeren said. He put his hands on his hips, his face now covered with assurance he was right.

"Don't be a fool," Jadroth said. "There's nothing to see from the city. It's been dead for decades."

Before Lugeren could continue, Jadroth hurried away.

∼

Jadroth sounded off as his name was called. He stood at attention, just one of the twenty men in his unit. Three men away to Jadroth's left stood Lugeren. The two hadn't spoken since their encounter the day before.

Dallo, Jadroth's unit commander, inspected his men, as the remaining commanders did with their own units. Dallo's unit and nineteen others made up one battalion. His battalion, commanded by Piceri, along with nine other battalions, made up the seventh legion. The seventh legion, one of twelve surrounding the city, was commanded by Orbindal.

Jadroth grunted with disgust. Orbindal was a political appointment placed in control of thousands of men from the city of Cessia. He knew nothing of warfare, and his incompetence showed.

The army was disorganized and lax. Jadroth hadn't wanted to enlist and had, in fact, been *volunteered* by one of his village's leaders. But once he became a part of the Cessian army, Jadroth had decided to do a competent job.

Not that it mattered, Jadroth thought. It would only take one man to capture a dead city. And thank the gods for that. Because if this rag-tag array of ill-trained men actually engaged in battle…

Jadroth straightened up as he heard the horns blow, signaling the army's march into the city was about to begin. He strained to look at the southern gate, where his battalion was situated, trying to glimpse the huge battering ram he knew was about to be employed. All nine of Ravelin's gates were ready to be burst open.

Despite his conviction all of this was a waste of time, Jadroth felt his pulse quicken. Whether or not they encountered anyone would not lessen the excitement of engaging in activity. After having waited idly for so long— Jadroth himself for nearly seven years— this army was finally going to engage the enemy, be they alive or just a dead city.

≈

The ramming of the city gates went well. Each opened easily, without shattering any of the huge double doors, almost as if they hadn't been bolted from within—not that anyone had time to check as the legions rushed in, soldiers screaming excitedly at the top of their lungs.

Jadroth's unit near the rear of the battalion had to stand in place as the slowly moving force of the army crawled into the city. From within, Jadroth could hear cries of joy. Unconsciously, he began bouncing up and down on his toes, forgetting his disinterest in capturing a dead city, anxious to get inside. From the exclamations coming from within, Ravelin was a city of great wealth, and it was there for the taking.

What he could do with riches in his small village of Garmeld. He could live like a king—or at least an overlord. The Garmeldian council would be at his feet, eager to please one so capable of increasing the village's wealth.

Jadroth's daydreaming of riches was interrupted by a rough shove from behind. He turned quickly, the blood racing to his head, his sword half way out of its scabbard.

"Move, you fool." It was Dallo, his unit commander.

Jadroth turned back to the city. His unit was moving forward without him.

~

Jadroth couldn't believe the beauty of Ravelin. He stood among his unit, his face staring up into the sky, admiring in silent awe the majesty and richness of the towering spires of the city. Every conceivable shape—conical, square, pentagonal, hexagonal, and many others—had been used to build dazzling streets and rows of soaring edifices.

And the colors.

Banners and streamers every color in the rainbow, plus dozens of hues that bespoke nature's beauty. The streets were a vivid crimson, lined with white or sky blue. The buildings, whether they housed shops or tenants or taverns, were decorated with exquisite tapestries, brightly painted murals, and shining ornaments hinting of gold and silver.

Jadroth laughed out loud. He couldn't believe the beauty of Ravelin. He held out his arms, soaking up the sun peeking through the towers. Even the heat was a pleasant companion.

He felt sorry for the soldiers forced to stay outside the city's gates, standing guard in case of a surprise attack. As Jadroth could plainly see, there was no one to sneak up on them. Ravelin was beautiful, but it was dead. Not a single living Ravelin soul was to be found.

~

The celebration started as soon as the confirmation came from high command that there was no one alive in the city.

Only one ugly scene had been found.

Thousands of skeletons, still clothed where the bugs hadn't eaten the fabric away, huddled together near the granary. The bones were bleached white from years under the scorching sun. A few other skeletons had been found here and there, but it was apparent the citizens of Ravelin had died waiting to be fed.

But to the victors went the spoils. And the army of Cessia was enjoying itself. The whores, the wine, and the entertainment that had been left outside the city during the raid had been brought inside. It would be a night of triumph and festivity.

~

Jadroth sat on a back bench in a tavern called *The Lucky Buffoon*. He grunted merrily, thinking how appropriate the tag fit his legion commander, Orbindal.

Jadroth had already downed several pints of quality ale and now had his eye on the lovely woman, barely clothed, who danced upon his table. He withdrew a silver coin, one of many he had found in the tavern's back room, and threw it at the dancer's feet.

The dancer lowered herself suggestively, picking up the coin with her teeth, allowing Jadroth a long look at her curvaceous figure. She slid off the table and glided to Jadroth's side. Eagerly, he reached for her, stumbling over himself as she darted away.

Enjoying the chase, Jadroth staggered around the table and headed for the back rooms, where the dancer had disappeared.

"Jadroth."

It was Lugeren. Jadroth didn't know where he had come from, or how he'd managed to find him, but he didn't care.

"Go away, Lugeren," Jadroth said.

"Something's wrong."

"Yes, something's wrong," Jadroth said. "You're in my way."

"No," Lugeren said. He waived his hands in broad gestures. "This. It's all too easy."

Jadroth squinted through bleary eyes at Lugeren. "It's supposed to be easy when the enemy is already dead."

Before Lugeren could answer, a loud banging noise, coming from outside, shook the tavern.

The banging repeated itself, again and again; nine times in all.

The dancer forgotten, Jadroth followed Lugeren outside, two among the milling crowd, anxious to see what was occurring.

"The gates! The gates!"

It seemed everyone was screaming those two words. The liquor made the words hammers on the side of Jadroth's head. With Lugeren at his side, Jadroth ran toward the nearest gate, winding through side streets and frantic people to do so.

Upon reaching the southern gate, Jadroth stopped, his eyes locked on the doors of the gate. They were shut and several people, mostly soldiers, were pushing, punching, and kicking against them.

The doors did not move.

The screaming beyond the doors began. It was horrible, wretched screaming: the screaming of men terrified, panicked, and in agony. Then, the screaming turned to gurgles, like men choking on their own blood.

~

Already knowing what they'd find, but having to see for themselves, Jadroth and Lugeren ran from gate to gate. Each was closed, and each refused to give way. Behind the closed gates could be heard the wailing of men close to dying. Mixed amongst the pained moans were occasional cries for help.

~

Their trek ended near the granary and its skeletons.

Jadroth was sober now. Between the shock of the gates being closed and the running and sweating he'd done for the last hour, Jadroth's head was clear. He wished he was still drunk.

"We're locked inside," Lugeren said.

"By who?" Jadroth pointed back to the skeletons. "The people of Ravelin are dead."

Lugeren shook his head. "The shadows."

Jadroth spat on the ground. "Nonsense. Whoever closed those gates has to be flesh and blood. A shadow can't move earth and wood. And a shadow can't make a man suffer physical pain."

Jadroth looked up, his eyes searching the night sky.

"What are you looking at?" Lugeren asked, trying to follow Jadroth's gaze.

"The watch tower," Jadroth said, pointing to the highest tower of the city, its top nearly invisible in the darkness. "I want to see just who *has* closed those gates."

∽

With Lugeren following, Jadroth made his way to the campanile. They reached the long row of steps winding its way against the city walls and up to the tower. Jadroth and Lugeren pushed by several men who had obviously come for the same reason.

When they reached the entrance to the watch tower, it was surrounded by soldiers, but no one was going inside.

"Move," Jadroth said, shoving men aside. His actions were greeted by grunts of annoyance, nevertheless everyone let him pass. Lugeren followed close behind. Jadroth turned to a soldier. "Why is everyone standing outside?"

The soldier shook his head and swallowed hard. "There's something unholy in there."

Those around the entrance murmured in agreement.

Jadroth moved to go inside. A soldier put a hand on Jadroth's chest. "Don't go."

Jadroth brushed the hand away, unsheathed his sword, and entered the structure. Lugeren followed.

It took a few moments for Jadroth's eyes to adjust to the sudden darkness. Unlike the rest of the city, there were no torches lit within the tower. Jadroth searched but could find none stuck within a crevasse of the wall. He retreated to the doorway and called for a torch. After a moment, a shaky hand passed him one.

Inside the tower, a set of stairs located in the middle of the structure wound up and vanished into a dark ceiling. Jadroth held the torch above his head and climbed.

Shadows danced on the walls and ceiling from the flickering torch as the Jadroth and Lugeren swiftly moved up the steps. Jadroth made an effort to avoid watching the shadows' movements. He kept his eyes on the stairs.

It was a long climb, seeming to go on for hundreds of steps. Drenched in sweat, Jadroth had to stop and catch his breath several times. He looked back at Lugeren, saw he was also covered with sweat.

Jadroth was glad Lugeren was with him.

As they reached the top of the stairs, Jadroth poked his torch into the gaping black hole into which the last step disappeared. The torch did little to illuminate what was above.

Jadroth took a deep breath and continued up. As he stepped onto the floor of the top level of the watch tower, he held the torch above him. The chamber was more than fifteen feet high, topped by a domed ceiling shrouded in darkness. At eye level, along each wall, were several portholes through which watchmen could see outside the city. He was surprised it wasn't darker outside. Hearing a noise behind him, Jadroth turned, and saw Lugeren inside the chamber.

With his friend by his side, Jadroth headed for one of the portholes. Something wet struck his cheek. He stopped, touched his fingers to it, and held them under the torch.

Blood.

Another drop hit his shoulder.

Jadroth looked up, raising the torch as high as he could.

Shoved into what would have been the sky porthole of the dome was a figure, the head and upper half of the body hanging down.

Jadroth steadied himself. He looked closely at the figure.

It was Hasnell.

"By the gods," Lugeren whispered.

Jadroth didn't know how long he stood looking up at the mutilated body of his dead brother-in-law. The tower's silence was broken by a noise, low and rhythmical, coming through its portholes.

Jadroth thought it sounded like the chanting of a spell. Through the portholes, he could see a flood of torches surrounding the city. In every direction, as far as the cloudless night allowed him to see, Jadroth could locate no end to the fire. The torches lit up the surrounding sky as if it were high noon on a summer's day.

As behind him Lugeren beseeched the gods for mercy, Jadroth moved forward for a closer look. All he could see beneath the torches were shadows—dancing shadows, with axes in hand.

Leaving the Tower
Rie Sheridan Rose

I've been locked here in this bloody tower my entire life. Until last week, I'd never seen another human being… except for *her*. Not even myself, except in the wavering reflection of a water bowl—*she* won't allow me a proper mirror.

She's stooped and wrinkled, gray of hair and eye. I know I must be more comely than that. At least my hair is golden as the sunlight…I can see it as it falls in waves about my feet. And spills across the floor. And creeps everywhere—in my food, catching in cracks, pulling me down.

I've begged her to let me cut it. *She* refuses.

The room I am kept within is twenty paces side to side—it used to be forty—but now that I've grown, it has shrunk. There are two windows. One directly across from the other. They let me see a tiny slice of world…the world I have never walked upon.

Each day, *she* comes with her basket and bottle, bringing me food and drink, but no real nourishment. *She* stands at the bottom of the tower, and she calls, "Rapunzel, Rapunzel, let down your hair!" And I, fool that I am, do.

What sort of name is Rapunzel, anyway? I do have books. No one is named Rapunzel. No one but me. I would rather be Bethany, or Sabrina, or even Kate. Yes, I quite like Kate.

Last week, something happened that will change my life. And I must tell someone. *She* had already been here and gone.

I was reading of a world I expected never to see when I heard a soft call outside the window. "Rapunzel, Rapunzel, let down your hair."

I froze. It was a strange voice, deeper than hers, yet somehow stronger. An unknown timbre.

I went to the window and peeked out.

On the ground stood a figure with trousers instead of skirts. Boots instead of slippers. Interesting bulges in places where she did not possess them.

I had seen illustrations in my books. This must be a man. Young, by the look of his thick chestnut hair and muscular shoulders.

"Who are you?" I called down.

"My name is Grantham. I have heard whispers of your beauty, but nothing prepared me for the reality of your splendor."

That caused me to raise an eyebrow. I was well-read, after all. I knew false flattery when I heard it. Still, this fast-talking fellow at the foot of my tower was a welcome diversion.

Why not?

I threw the weight of my hair out of the tower, as I had done so often before, winding it around the hook set into the sill. It spilled in a flood of sunshine down the dismal gray stone.

Grantham wound it around his fist and climbed the tower just as she had done ever since my hair reached the ground.

For the first time, I wondered how she had reached me as a child?

But then he was clambering over the sill and into my room. His weight had pulled harder than hers ever did. My scalp ached as I reeled in the tresses. That wouldn't do for many visits.

"Hello," he said breathlessly. Climbing the tower must take a lot out of a person.

I was suddenly shy in the face of a stranger. All my fancy words flew from my head. "You're tall," was the only thing I could think to say.

Grantham laughed—a hearty, vibrant laugh that filled the room with happiness. That laugh stole my heart.

He's come back to me every day since, waiting until *she* is long gone. And we have devised a plan.

Yesterday when he came, Grantham smuggled a pair of shears beneath his waistcoat. He has cut my hair. Think on it! Long enough to reach the ground it has been, and now, it fluffs about my face in flyaway curls, like a dandelion in my books.

We spent the rest of the afternoon braiding the length of it—with a cunning cord woven into the strands. It makes a thick rope, and even braided, it still falls to the ground. Hooked upon the windowsill, it makes a ladder that was strong enough to hold Grantham as he departed.

Today, when *she* arrived and called her hated litany, I threw down the braid, but did not wind it round the hook. I held the end of the cord as she began her climb, muscles straining against her weight, waiting for the right moment. When I judged she was halfway up the side, I let go the cord.

Her scream was the sweetest music I have heard to date.

When she hit bottom, I ventured to look over the edge. *She* lay in a graceless heap upon the ground—her basket scattering bread and cheese upon the grass, and the bottle spilling wine as red as her blood.

I slowly drew the cord back up, and with it, its precious ladder. My heart was in my mouth lest it pull free and leave me trapped in the tower without even *her* hated company.

But, after one snag upon an uneven stone, it slithered over the top of the windowsill like a snake. I made it fast.

My bag is already packed with the few garments I own, and my books. Nothing breakable within—she never allowed me anything with which I might harm myself. I've tossed it out the window. Now, I follow. To freedom.

Leaving the tower…to what?

Does it matter? My feet will walk on grass for the first time. It's enough.

And now, I shall be Kate.

They Warp the Fabric of the Sky
Kelda Crich

*F**uelled by cheap synthetic Rioja, Barat, the Brems' chief*
negotiator, had become talkative. My brother was drinking
in his stories like space nectar. I sat beside them both, barely concealing
my irritation. I resisted the urge to drum my fingers on the table. The
deal wasn't concluded yet.

"You may be interested in the saga of King Serit the Vanquisher,"
said Barat, his lipless mouth opening and closing around his sibilant
words. He wore an elegant, diamond-dot robe. The same material was
draped in swathes over the walls of his ship. The Brem liked to display
their wealth.

"Perhaps we could return to the negotiations," I said. I took a sip
of my juice—no alcohol for me until the negotiations were complete.

Arnos held up his hand to interrupt me. "Wait a minute,
Penelope. Wasn't King Serit the founder of the Praster clan?" Arnos'
ability to grasp the nuances of the Brems' tedious lineage was both
astounding and irritating.

Barat's lizard mouth twitched. "That's correct, sir. King Serit
was, indeed, the founder of my own clan. It's gratifying to see an
outsider with such an appreciation for our heritage."

I glanced through the metal-glass windows at the world that
hung like a plum in the sky. Arom-ka the Brem called it. It was almost
mine for the taking. I could taste it.

Barat began to recite the saga of King Serit. It sounded very much like the other sagas he'd recounted during the evening's endless meeting.

"Very interesting," I said, when the story concluded.

Perhaps my tone had slipped into condescension, because Barat turned to me and I thought I could see the dislike in his eyes. "If you do buy our world, you must stay away from the anterior lands."

"Why so?" I asked politely

"Those lands are poisoned. Some say," Barat paused to take another sip of his Rioja, "that the anterior lands are cursed. They say that they are inhabited by spirits."

"Spirits?" asked Arnos.

That was all the encouragement Barat needed to launch into a tale of the Brems' mythical older race. He became maudlin, speaking of hereditary duties and ancient broken contracts. I'd heard similar stories countless times before. The legacy of the ancients: the galactic monomyth.

"We too, have such a heritage," said Arnos. "In fact, my sister and I were raised as seekers. Are you familiar with the religion of the seekers?"

"Why, no," said Barat. "I'd be honored to hear your account."

"The seekers were founded after Earth's discovery of an ancient artifact," said my brother. "The so-called wave-fluid cube. Provenance and, indeed, dating of this artifact has remained a subject of intense controversy." Arnos relaxed into his chair, making himself comfortable. The history of the seekers was a long and convoluted tale. I couldn't stand to listen to such nonsense any longer. I made my excuses and returned to our ship. Arnos stayed behind eagerly sharing his credulity for the ancient and the untrue.

∽

"What do you think you were doing last night?" I asked when Arnos wandered into the engine room, disheveled and possibly still slightly drunk. "I could've concluded the negotiations. We *could* have been owners of a planet, by now."

"Not with that attitude, Pen. You haven't got an appreciation of the fine art of negotiation. The Brems are a proud people."

"A proud people who are willing to sell a planet for the price of a broken-down battleship?" I looked out of the window at the planet. The Brems had abandoned Arom-ka generations ago, preferring to live as nomadic traders circling the worlds of the local red-dwarf star. "I can't believe that they'd sell a world,"

"It seems strange," agreed Arnos. "They do own it, don't they Pen? It's not some kind of con?"

"They own Fed-assigned deeds to a cluster of worlds in this system," I said. "I'm not a novice trader, you know, Arnos. I've been doing this for a while. We're just fortunate that they haven't encountered human technology before." The battleship that I'd towed half way across the galaxy was a treasure trove of innovative and new technology to the Brem. "If you ask me, they're fools to even consider selling their planet."

"That's exactly the attitude that will lose you this deal." Arnos waggled his finger at me. "That's why you need me."

"If you say so, Arnos." I turned my attention back to the engine. "We needed a new recursive modifier. If this deal doesn't come through, we might be stranded in this system."

"What's the matter with it, Pen?" Arnos leaned over my shoulder and peered into the bowels of the engine.

"You see this?" I pointed to the fibrous strands of material that marred the steel and metal glass of the recursive modifier. "That's the radiotrophic melanin fungus that grows all over the outside of the ship."

"Is that bad?"

"Yes, I'd say so." It was as if he'd suppressed all the space-eng lectures we'd sat through as children—the lessons he'd excelled in. My brother had changed in the last ten years. He seemed to revel in his ignorance. It was all an act. "The engine is a delicate tool," I said, patiently. "It doesn't need to be clotted up with strands of fungoid tissue."

Arnos reached into the engine and broke off a piece of the fungus, "Mmmm," he said, holding it up to his nose. "It smells tasty."

"Oh, no." I started to laugh. "You're not going to?"

He popped it into his mouth, "Mmmm. Mushroomy."

"Oh, that is so gross." I laughed again. "You realize that that fungus feeds off gamma radiation. Oh, that is so, so gross."

Arnos rubbed his stomach. "Mmmm. Yummy fungi."

Arnos could always make me laugh.

～

There hadn't been many laughs growing up. Seeker parents abandon their children at birth. They give their babies to a seeker monastery to be indoctrinated. I remember the Parses Monastery as a bleak house, full of whispered secrets, mumbo-jumbo mysteries and rigid expectations.

Arnos had been the monastery's star pupil, until his nervous breakdown. It wasn't unusual for children subject to the seekers' regime of extensive indoctrination to have a nervous collapse.

When he started to babble, speaking in tongues, the nuns at the monastery had become very excited. They gathered around his bedside. They transcribed his words. They believed that his nonsense would give a clue to the location of the ancestors. So you can imagine how angry they'd been when he'd managed to slip out of the monastery one night and hitch a ride off-world on a tourist trawler. Not many kids manage to do that. I certainly didn't.

I'd faked my way through another five years at the monastery. You had to fake it, that's the only way the seekers would give you a ship. Once you're in Fed space, you're free. I was a good liar, good enough to convince the nuns that my only purpose in life was to seek out the ancestors. I'd completed the small missions within seeker territory, mouthed the words until it seemed as if I almost believed them myself. Then, when they trusted me enough to let me into Fed space, I'd abandoned them. I would've loved to have seen the look on the nuns' faces when they realized.

It took me another five years to forgive Arnos for abandoning me. Then another two years to find him. He was a hustling on a Centauri asteroid, spaced out on leaper drugs, running after any two-bit alien that might offer a key to the unknown. I'd set up as an independent trader by then. I'd rescued him, and he'd been happy to come aboard. My happy-go-lucky brother, blissfully unapologetic for abandoning me.

"It's good to see you laughing again, Pen," he said. He was smiling. No one could be that happy all the time. I wondered if he'd ever let me past the shell he'd built up.

~

"What do you say, Penelope?" asked Arnos, as we left Barat's ship.

"I don't know what you mean."

"Say it."

"Okay then. You were right."

Barat had bought a Brem scribe to the meeting, who had patiently transcribed Arnos' history of the seekers. And then, Barat had sold us the planet. It was thanks to Arnos, and he knew it.

"Just imagine, Pen. You and me. A whole planet for ourselves."

"Well, we're not going to live on it," I said. "We're going to strip-mine it then sell it on to some sucker."

"Still, a whole planet. Who'd have thought it, when we were on Parses, that we'd have a planet for ourselves?"

~

Barat had told me to stay away from the anterior lands. That was the first place I'd started exploring. I didn't trust Barat.

Images of the landscape melted into a seamless cascade as the skimmer flew across the sky. I was tele-skimming, exploring Arom-ka from the safety of my ship.

My first sight of the tower was against the backdrop of the diminishing sun. That red-dwarf, vast, ancient, burning the cloudless sky to the color of old blood. I'd encountered smaller towers all over the anterior lands. Their images were random spikes in the flow of tele-skimmed images that zipped into my mind. At first, I thought that the towers were a natural formation. The elongated, hollow towers rising from their globular stems reminded me of the colossal termite nests that overran the Sterile Regions on Parses. The anterior towers were unreasonably tall, rising a hundred meters into the rust-stained sky.

Yet they were dwarfed by the tower I'd found. I saw the sporadic windows and glimpsed carved decorations, the complex convoluted shapes that spoke of meaning. This was no monstrous insect tower, it was something constructed by a sentient mind.

I linked to the ship's web and summoned Arnos. He came into the skim-room wearing his molecular utility suit. He was eager to visit the surface, but I'd told him that he had to wait.

"What have you found?" he asked.

"A tower in the anterior lands. Something made by the Brem."

"Barat said that the Brem had never lived in the anterior lands."

"Not recently," I agreed. "The area's flooded with gamma radiation. The radiation's making the readings very difficult."

"So it's something ancient?" Arnos said the word quite casually. "Perhaps it predates the Brems. We should go down and investigate."

"Maybe." I continued to direct the flyer towards the tower. I wanted to gather more data. The structure was a ruin, gaping uneven lesions marred the walls. "Come and have a look for yourself."

Arnos sat down beside me and linked into the tele-skimmer. He gasped when the images hit his mind.

"Remember what Barat told us," he said, "about their ancestors? Maybe they lived here."

That thought disturbed me.

~

I landed the tele-skimmer, and prepared to initiate a smaller probe. I needed the probes to get closer to the tower to study the inscriptions. My first thought had been to strip-mine Arom-ka for rare-elements, but looking at the carvings, a new and altogether more profitable venture became a possibility. The Fed, the seekers and any other number of cultures, you might care to mention, were in the market for old-world relics. Everyone seemed to believe that there might be old treasures, old weapons lying latent in the ruins of the ancestor civilizations. If these ruins were the genuine article, we could be looking at a significant profit.

It took me longer than usual to establish a connection with the scanner portals of the probe. I checked and re-checked the linkage while Arnos bristled with impatience.

"You're taking too long," he complained. "Let me do it."

"I can manage."

By the time I'd established tele-linkage, the sun had completed its long, slow descent. The double moons of Arom-ka cast convoluted, contradictory shadows over the tower.

"Computer, what was that?" I asked. "Was there someone or something moving at the window?"

"Negative," replied the computer in its silk-synthetic voice. I thought I'd seen a movement, a pale face at a tower window. That was impossible. We'd scanned the planet for life forms.

"I didn't see anything," said Arnos.

I smiled, "The Brems' myths must be influencing me."

"That's not like you, Pen. You don't believe in anything."

I said nothing and directed the probe to make a close inspection of the tower, beginning with an examination of the unexpected glyphs carved into the exterior walls, but the gamma interference was too strong to get any decent reading. "We better go down and explore."

"Yes," said Arnos, punching his first into the air.

"Do you have to be so peachy keen?" I asked. "Show a little

explorer's ennui, why don't you?"

"This is the first world I've ever owned, Penelope."

～

We left the pod and walked towards the tower. We both wore utility suits. The gamma radiation varied between 3 and 10 MeV. The gamma rays would have penetrated our flesh, causing diffuse and lethal damage, if not for the protection of the layer of radiotrophic fungi on the surface of our suits.

I felt uneasy stepping into such a poisonous atmosphere. The clouds of dust which swirled in the air creating drifting wraithsand, the weird shadows cast by the double moons, did little to calm my nerves.

"We should have waited until morning," I said.

"It's beautiful here at night," said Arnos. His voice was tinged with awe. "Perhaps we could clean up the atmosphere and make this place into a tourist attraction."

It was an impractical suggestion on many levels, not the least of which was the fact that we were on the cusp of known space." This isn't Centauri," I said. Still, I had to admit that the tower presented a certain gothic grandeur. I scanned the atmosphere. "The gamma radiation seems to be emanating from the tower."

"Are we safe?" asked Arnos.

"The suits will give us about an hour of protection."

"Are you sure that you don't want me to do that?" asked Arnos when I started to activate the mobile probe.

"I can manage. We should be able to get better readings, now that we're closer."

"I'm going to explore then."

"Fine." As he walked away, I said, "Don't go too far, Arnos." Even though we shared a tele-link between the suits, I felt nervous.

My fingers were unusually clumsy as I set up the probe. My head pounded with a nervous throb of anticipation.

I launched the probe into the sky and initiated the link to my mind. The probe slid up the shaft of the nearest tower. It sent the images of the carvings into my mind. The tele-skimmed glyphs swirled in my mind, and I knew that they were old, perhaps older than anything that had ever been discovered. As I stared at the glyphs, the words of the seeker nuns came to my mind.

"An old people, dead, but undying. They are our ancient ancestors. They wait for us. They are trapped by guardians who will, one day, grow weary of their duties. Disbelief will accrete. The old ways will be forgotten. The undying ones wait until the day their children will unleash them. Then they will resume their rightful place."

"Hey, Pen. Are you okay?" The sound of Arnos' voice broke into my memories.

"You better come here," I said.

"What's wrong?"

"Nothing." That was a lie. I was trembling. Something, everything, was wrong with this place. I hated how the words of childhood come back to you. No matter how far you travel, they are always there. It was so quiet. We were the only people on Arom-ka, a lonely desolate place. I saw a movement, high in the tower's windows.

"Arnos, come over here quickly," I shouted, as pale shapes emerged at the feet of the towers. Ten elongated ethereal figures, then twenty, and then uncountable shapes materialized. What frightened me most was my recognition; the words into being; the old ones; the ancient ones, who had been waiting for me. I had been so wrong, all my life. I had been so wrong, but it didn't matter, because I was here now. I was what I always should have been: a seeker.

I gazed at the pale shapes. My presence had reawakened them, and, as a gift in return, they had reawakened their memories in me. I lived in the memories, the forms penetrated my mind, changing and shaping me.

"What are they?" whispered Arnos.

"Don't you know them? You should. You have searched for them all of your life."

"Are these are our ancestors? They don't look right. Come away, Penelope. Let's get back to the ship."

I watched as they advanced towards us, slowly as if floating through the sea of ages. "Why should we leave?" I only wanted to bathe in the presence of the old ones and learn their secrets.

Arnos took out his scanner. "They're not here. They're just images. They're just patterns in the gammas."

"Do you really believe that, Arnos?"

"No," he whispered.

The swirling group of revenants opened their voices in a song of welcome.

"Why do they shriek?" asked Arnos. "Their voices tear into my mind."

I watched them dancing the sacred dance.

"Why do they move like that?" asked Arnos. "It's unnatural. They warp the fabric of the world when they move."

The old ones stretched out their arms. I began to unfasten my suit. They would be reborn in me.

"What are you doing?" asked Arnos. His voice was fervent. I remembered how he used to sound when he spoke in tongues. Some truths are too much for a person to bear. "Can't you see that they want to consume us? They want to consume the whole world. They're poison to us, Penelope. They will make the galaxy into their bone-house."

It was the truth, and it was glorious. The inexorable hand of fate had pulled me to this world. The cloisters of my childhood had set me on the pathway home. The old ones had waited a long time for my arrival. I would release them. I only need to open the channel. The old ones would be free after countless centuries. The blood sang within me, the memories that will unwake them, passed down, generation after weary generation. I raised my hand to the throat of my suit.

"What are you doing, Penelope?"

Arnos tried to stop me. The stories of our ancestors had not touched his mind. He was afraid, but all I could see was the glory of their ascension. They would return within me and rebuild their civilizations. A galaxy-spanning civilization that had touched every culture and left its memories.

Arnos tried to stop me. I was still linked to his mind through the neuronal connections of the suit. It would be easy to over-ride the protocols and send a jolt of electricity into his brain, whispered the voices. He had abandoned me. He had betrayed me, as he now tried to betray his ancestors. Arnos, my brother. Arnos, the betrayer. Arnos who would eat a piece of space mushroom to make me laugh. Make me laugh. There hadn't been many laughs growing up and if the ancestors came back...what then?

Arnos the betrayer eating the space mushroom and making me laugh. That image kept moving through the whisperings of the ancestors. It seemed more important to me than anything.

He stood at my side, as the ancestors floated around us. His face was painted with fear, but he did not leave me, he did not abandon me. "Come with me back to the ship, Penelope."

Some things are eternal, and some things are poisonous to the flesh and to the mind. Some things are eternal and dead and should never be reawakened, despite the endless wishes of their misguided descendants.

I turned away from the ancestors; there are ties of family that are more important.

"Penelope," said Arnos. "Are you all right?"

"I'm all right," I reached for my brother's hand. "When we get back to the ship, I'm going to nuke that haunted tower. Maybe I'll nuke the whole world."

"That's right, Pen." I saw a flicker of something within my brother, something that I'd feared had been lost. "We'll nuke them all."

We walked together, hand in hand, back to the pod. When my ancestors hissed their fury at me, I shrugged them off. They were nothing to us, just the irrelevant ghosts of our past.

The Tower of the Sea Witch
Peter Schranz

*A*s *she scraped barnacles off of her feet, the witch Ruth* glanced out at the ocean and thought about her lost husband Ezekiel. She sat on the balcony most mornings to look at the waves and dangle her legs from the bare face of the tower. But today, Ruth kept vigilant watch.

While she watched, she didn't mind scraping away the unwelcome creatures that clung to her. The task provided a moment away from the endless thoughts of her Zeke, the whaler captain, who had on their wedding day promised her eternity.

No ship had passed through this part of the ocean, not for as long as she waited there. But Ruth had grown at ease with such emptiness. She worried that should a vessel pass by, her hope and her despair would make one another worse. A ship would entice her with the thought that Ezekiel might be among its living crew, but when that was proven false, she'd be reminded he was dead.

Ruth thought of the long night before. She had traveled miles and miles, not in a ship, but on the shell of a leatherback turtle, to meet with the other witches.

Though they seldom offered her new hope, Ruth came, though her attention never strayed far from the horizon. Her old hope to find Zeke had never died.

That last barnacle, the one Ruth had failed several times to coax off of her foot, always moving to others in frustration, finally dropped into the ocean. She hoped a whelk waited there to chew it to pieces.

She stood on bleeding feet and tottered under the roof at the column's peak. In a tank by the bed crept Ruth's familiar, Warren, the conch. She bet that Warren had outlived any other conch that had ever been born. She had learned to communicate with him a long time ago, and was happy to have gleaned the skill. He kept her company, such as it was, and told her things she could never guess.

It occurred to Ruth to ask Warren how long she had been in the tower. Ruth bent over Warren's smooth glass tank and whispered, "Warren, dear, how long have I been waiting here with you?"

Warren heard with his conch's ears through the dash of water Ruth had brought him up from the sea. He extended his siphon and spit little bubbles up to the surface of the water. The bubbles, by Warren's demonic prowess, collected neatly on the surface in the shape of the number *seventy* and then popped, all at once.

"Seventy years?"

Warren withdrew his siphon, and felt no compulsion to clarify himself.

Ruth started when the bubbles popped, and glanced out upon the lonely sea. *Seventy years.* She could not believe it.

Ruth's hair was long and gray, and her skin couldn't hide the shape of her bones. She knew she had grown old, but Warren's message shocked her. She remained spry, and the spell which had given her eternal life assured that she could climb the shell-ladder on her tower, and jump a hundred feet into the sea, never feeling fatigued or breaking a bone.

She dropped onto her bed, hunching over with her chin in her hands, and watched Warren roam around his tiny tank. She tried to recollect all the time she'd been here in the tower.

~

The most ancient crone in the coven had offered Ruth eternal life to wait while the crone discovered Ezekiel's fate. In exchange, Ruth promised her unwavering allegiance to Hell. She knew not to hope for much, only the bitter closure of her husband's fate, so she waited.

She let her head collapse against the stony wall above her bed, remembering.

Zeke had captained a leaky whaler, the *Egyptian Rat*. He'd told Ruth he'd killed ten whales himself. His voyages had been lucky, other than the time he'd come back without a hand. The second mate put a harpoon through it after rum ruined his aim. Worse still, the man's drunkenness saved the whale he'd meant to pierce.

Ezekiel had wrapped the wound in a leather pouch while he remained at sea. When he returned, he found a surgeon in the port town where they lived who cut off the rotten parts and fitted the rest of his arm with an iron hook. Zeke never got used to it, asking *what kind of hand has only one finger?* At first Ruth had such deep sympathy for him, but slowly she grew to love his hook more than the hand it replaced—though she never said so.

Zeke wasn't lucky on the last voyage either. After a heavy squall, only the second mate with the taste for rum washed ashore, floating on his stomach. Ruth waited just long enough to learn there would be no search for the other members of the crew. Then, she sailed to sea on her own, in the little skiff she and Ezekiel went fishing in when he was home.

She hadn't found Zeke. Instead, she met the witches, and found the strange tower where she now made her home.

She remembered again the last night she traveled to the coven. She knew when those nights came, when the floating white moon began to wax, but was not quite full, or when it began to wane, but was not yet a crescent.

She recalled the leatherback turtle hundreds of feet below peering up at her, as always, waiting there with its shiny black shell and eyes. Ruth jumped from the balcony. She had hoped to die, and to cover Zeke with kisses in Heaven.

But she bobbed back up to the surface, wet and living, with hair clinging to her face. A jet of brine had burned its way up her nose, and her violent snort to expel it only made it hurt worse.

She climbed on the turtle's back, and he sped through the water as though at full gallop. He kept obediently near the surface, though Ruth knew how much deeper he wanted to dive.

She never looked forward to coven nights. The turtle's shell was uncomfortable, and the meetings began late and seemed to last forever.

And the question she had asked at her very first meeting, seventy years ago, had not been answered yet.

She waited on the turtle's back, her feet in the sea. There were several witches facing each other in a circle, floating in a seemingly arbitrary place in the ocean, the place her turtle knew to come. They varied in appearance, but there was always something the matter with each of the witches. Salt in their eyes or barnacles on their feet; none of them was perfect.

The oldest witch was a gangly crone who came in a dory from whose prow swung a flaming lantern. She bore a giant conical seashell on her head. Her neck quivered under its weight as she spoke softly.

But Ruth wasn't interested in what the old woman said. She only listened when the witches asked the crone for favors.

Ruth always asked for nothing, still waiting to discover Zeke's fate. All these years gone by, all these meetings, and the crone still said nothing about Zeke.

Ruth ached to bring it up, but was afraid. For several meetings, a witch whose name Ruth didn't know, pestered the crone about her earlier request for a vial of pearl dust. For the witch's impatience, the crone punished her with lampreys, which came up from the frothing water to drink her blood. Long afterwards, when it suited her, the crone furnished the requested dust.

Ruth hoped at each coven meeting the crone would reveal the solution to the mystery of Ezekiel's fate to her, but years passed without a word. Sooner or later, the other witches all received what they asked for, and Ruth prayed her turn would come—though she did not wonder to whom she prayed.

For at the close of each meeting, with enough left of the night that they could all return to their dwellings before dawn, the witches would chant for Lucifer to reveal that he, too, had been present. Sometimes, not always, a small, bright light, miles below the witches' circle, might glow in reply. Then, satisfied the he'd heard their summons, they would hasten away.

Suddenly, Ruth came out of her reverie. She was *not* out at sea with the other witches, she remained on her bed, only a little after Warren had told her how long she'd been at the tower. It was still day; her feet still bled.

She shook her head and smelled something other than salt. Warren had hardly moved during her daydream, but he had extended his siphon once more, trying desperately to reveal something to his deeply distracted witch. When she finally noticed him, she stood from her bed and paced over to the tank. The bubbles on the surface spelled "*ship*."

Ruth gasped. She sprinted outside and saw what the mollusk foretold—a ghostly ship drifting in the distance.

It drifted closer. Once she was able to read the words "*Egyptian Rat*" on its hull, she felt as if fangs had pierced her heart. She paced around her tiny bedroom, sure of what to expect, but unsure of all else. Her agitation increased, and then she plunged so deeply into despair that she only returned to herself when the ship knocked against the tower and shook it. Ruth clambered to the edge of the balcony and peered below, where the ship floated.

The mast, nothing now but a wet stake, jutted crookedly from the deck. The vessel had trawled up kelp like a meadow of moss, and a great hole the shape of a whale head obliterated the spot where its keel once had existed.

Ruth plunged aboard. This time she worried the fall *would* kill her.

She landed hard on the deck, and its feeble wood groaned. She took her time to stand on her cockleshell-cut feet, but aside from a splinter wedged under her fingernail, she was unharmed.

Ruth approached the crooked cabin door, where a captain might once have quartered, and wrenched it open. The door sloughed off its hinges and fell into the cabin, leaving the knob in her hand.

Ruth's stomach twisted. She knew the crone with the conical shell on her head had sent the ship to her, and she'd held onto that thought from the moment she'd spied the ship wandering alone through the sea. She was certain of it when she stood in the cabin, where she spied in the corner, a pile of sloppy bones and that iron hook, nothing now but barnacles and rust.

Kiss of Death
Jeremy Zimmerman

*A*rmand swallowed hard, hoping his face did not betray his fear. He glanced over at the withered face of Lucinda, the Lich Queen, trying to gauge her emotions from her body language. But her face remained expressionless, her posture still and serene.

"I am sorry, I was lost in thought. Could you repeat that?"

Lucinda chuckled, a dry and dusty sound. "I had asked if you would like to relocate your residence to my tower."

"Ah. Yes." Armand cleared his throat and stared out the window at the moonlit landscape beyond. He could dimly make out the silhouette of his village across the valley. Sweat streamed down his spine in the summer heat, leaving the folds of his flesh feeling sticky. He tugged at the front of his tunic, hoping to fan himself with it. His face felt flush, but he knew that wasn't due to the weather. "That would involve a good deal of logistics."

"Oh? What sort of logistics are worrying you?" Her teeth clacked together as she spoke. Armand wondered how she could speak without lips, but had never broached the subject. It struck him as gauche. He was certain he possessed a tome on the subject.

"Let us start with food," he said, feeling more confident with specific points to make. "Since you no longer eat, you often forget that I still require sustenance."

"This is about the ham, isn't it?" she said, sorrow creeping into her voice.

Armand felt ill at the memory of the ham that had gone bad while she saved it for a special occasion. "It is not just the ham. There exists an entire continuum of logistics involved in getting food delivered to your remote tower in the midst of a blasted heath instead of my cozy manor in town."

"But I have gotten better about feeding you. I've cooked for the first time in five hundred years just for you, love. And if you are living here, you can be in charge of all the food arrangements. Perhaps you could hire an acolyte to obtain food from the market and pay him with lessons in the dark arts?"

"And what of the privy? Or, rather, the lack thereof."

"You said you were fine with the chamber pot."

"I was fine with the chamber pot when I only visited occasionally. To live here full time having to use a chamber pot is… untenable."

"Armand, you currently spend as much time here as you do at your own home. More, even. I do not see that it will be a drastic change for you. And even then, we can have a privy added on."

"There are your visitors."

"My visitors?"

"At least once a month you have some scoundrel trying to break in, or some knight on a quest, seeking to slay the scary undead woman."

"And they never make it far. You've said yourself you enjoy watching them die."

"That does not reassure me. Plus, there are the space constraints," he said, trying to ignore her counterarguments. "My manor is full to bursting with my equipment and library. They would not fit here."

"We could remove duplicate items…"

Armand gasped and clutched a meaty hand to his chest. "I have spent many years assembling these tomes and supplies. To simply cast them away—"

"What is your real fear?"

"I do not know what you—"

She placed a skeletal finger on his lips and shushed him. The earthy smell of her desiccated flesh, barely detectable over the smell of the chemicals in her laboratory, filled his nose and caused his heart to pound in his chest.

"I love you and want to have you closer."

Armand's mouth gaped open. She had not mentioned love prior to this. He could feel all of his delicate organs seeking to pull up into his body cavity.

"Ah. Here we have the crux of the matter," she said. Armand started to stammer as he formed a response, but she cut him off. "This is not the first time I have run afoul of this. What you need is time to decide how you feel about it. And us."

Armand silently berated himself. He could not understand why he hesitated. It made sense for them to share a dwelling. They could pool resources, collaborate on research, share knowledge and, best of all, spend more intimate time together. And yet here he stood, as stammering and bashful as he had been when he was twelve and saw his first dead woman. The memory of the pale flesh roused his passions, but he shook his head to clear his mind. He needed focus.

"You are right, Lucy," he said, hoping his discomfort didn't show. He focused on the empty sockets of her eyes. He could stare for hours into those eyes. "It is best we not rush into these things."

She cupped his jowly cheek with a bony hand and he leaned into it. Armand reached forward and pulled her towards him, her bare ribs pressing through her robes and into his hands. He nuzzled the dried tendons of her neck.

"Shall we sleep on it?" she whispered into his ear. No breath reached his flesh with her words.

"I thought you'd never ask."

His eyes burned from exhaustion as he stumbled into the public house. In the days since his conversation with Lucinda, Armand had been unable to sleep. The loss of several degrees of independence terrified him.

This brought him to the local tavern, seeking the man who could best advise him. His own collection of peers, grave robbers, alchemists and undead minions would be of no assistance in matters of love.

He hauled his bulk onto the barstool, gasping for breath after his hurried walk across the town. Behind the bar, the barkeep shelved tankards. When the man didn't respond to Armand's presence, he cleared his throat.

The bartender glanced over his shoulder in annoyance. His eyes focused on Armand and widened in response. He spun around and pulled back against the shelves. The tankards rattled.

Armand gave a small wave.

"C-can I help ya?" the bartender asked.

"I find myself in need of your services."

"So… you want a beer…?"

"No, good sir, I seek your advice." Armand drummed his fingers together in agitation. He already regretted this choice.

"My advice?" The bartender relaxed a little. "Aren't you the fella that sits in the corner and meets with all the weasely types?"

Armand bit the inside of his cheek and stared hard at the man. He used this tavern to meet with the grave robbers who provided his materials. He should have picked a different tavern for this mission.

"I do tend to sit in yonder corner and meet with business associates. The spurious accusations by the mayor are false, I assure you. But this is unrelated to the matter at hand."

"What can I do ya for, then?"

"I am given to understand you are a common point of contact for the local citizenry in matters of love."

The bartender stared at Armand before recognition dawned in his eyes. "Oh, ya mean ya got lady troubles?"

Armand could feel the muscles in his face collapse as his will to continue this conversation evaporated. A part of him noticed how quiet it was in the establishment, but he could not detect anyone out of the corner of his eyes eavesdropping on him.

"Most fellas are just lookin' for someone to open up to," the bartender continued. "So I mostly listen and ask a couple questions. They usually figure it out on their ow— Wait a second. Are you saying ya have a lady friend?" The man's face turned green as he said that.

Armand clenched his jaw and narrowed his eyes, regarding the gap-toothed, sour-smelling heathen before him. He had had quite enough of this.

"I beg your pardon. Perhaps we should just part ways here." He dropped from his seat and turned towards the door. As he did so, it registered that he was the only patron. "Isn't it usually busier this time of day?"

"Yup. But a bunch of them knights with the church—"

"The Templars?"

"Yeah, them folk. They came in saying they were looking to hire warm bodies to help in some siege outside of town."

Armand's pulse pounded in his ears. There was only one threat nearby that would draw the church, so he knew the answer to his next question. "To whom are they laying siege?"

"That dead witch that lives in the tower — the Bitch Queen or whatever they call her."

"The tower that lies five miles out of town, left at the tree struck by lightning, across the dry creek bed and right past the abandoned mill?"

"I guess so?"

Armand rushed through the door as quickly as his fat legs would carry him.

∾

Armand's existence had become one of sweat: drops of it streamed down his back and into the nether portions of his body. The sweat caused the rolls of his fat to stick to one another. The smell of his perspiration might overwhelm him, but the stench of military latrines overwhelmed his ability to detect it.

On leaving the tavern, Armand had used his magic to contact Lucinda and ask about the siege. She confirmed it was happening, but did not seem concerned. She was ancient and had faced threats like this before. He had only heard a few of her contingency plans in the past, but he had the sense there was no end to her scheming. He found that irresistible.

Lucinda had assured him she didn't need his help and she would prefer it if he spent his time considering her proposition. She repeated that assurance the next five times he contacted her.

"At worst," she said, "this form would be destroyed. But I've safely hidden my soul in a phylactery. I may lose some things, but I will live to fight again."

He decided to take her at her word and let her handle this herself. After ten minutes of pacing and letting his imagination run wild with all the things that could go wrong, he contacted her and said, "I am coming, regardless."

His skeletal servants had loaded his travelling armory into his cart: Chests filled with animated skeletons, bottles filled with bound specters, vials of alchemical concoctions. He rode out to face the armies in the name of love.

And now he sat stewing in his own sweat. He shifted to loosen up the clothes that clung to his perspiration-soaked flesh.

His eyes were blind to the area around him, instead seeing the world through a flickering construct of shadow and ectoplasm he had conjured and sent flying over the encampments.

The Templars surrounded Lucinda's tower. Through his construct, Armand saw the play of arcane energy pooling and rippling through the area. The soothing violet of the Lich Queen's necromantic workings surrounded the tower in a maelstrom of energy. The baleful white of the army's channeled prayers circled the tower like a noose. Unable to starve her out, Armand suspected the Templars were trying to wear away at her energy. With effort he could identify the meditating monks that anchored the prayers, their seated forms obscured by the aura of power. Surrounding each of the monks was a vanguard of Templars, swords drawn.

In the border lands between the dark and the light, Armand saw the shattered remains of the undead. Their unnatural life had been blasted from them by the priestly magic. He felt impotent looking upon the sight. All of his usual preparations would disintegrate under the onslaught of those prayers.

A finger poked Armand in the side. He cried out, his heart pounding, as he reached back for a bottled specter and released the visual connection to his construct.

In the direction of the poking finger, a scrawny and filthy rat of a man backpedaled away from the cart, his face pale and his eyes wide with terror. Armand recognized him as Jean, one of the grave robbers that provided the necromancer with raw materials.

Armand gasped for breath and clutched at his chest. "You, sir, should not sneak up on a man like that."

"Sorry! I just figured I could be friendly since I saw you and all."

"And what, pray tell, are you doing out at this horrible daytime hour?" As he spoke, he leaned down to return the bottle back to its crate.

"Oh, I'm working for the Templars."

Armand froze, his hand still on the bottle.

"Oh? And what manner of work are you engaged in on their behalf?"

"Diggin'," Jean said, staring at the bottle Armand held. "Mostly. I'm no good in a fight. So they got me carryin' stuff, hammering at some walls, and diggin' a lot."

Armand did not respond.

"You ain't gonna throw that spook bottle at me, are you?"

He stared at Jean through narrowed eyelids. He didn't trust the man farther than he could throw him. That in itself was not very far, as Armand was not a physical man. But if he could turn this situation to his advantage it may be worth the risk.

"I can refrain from killing you outright if you can direct me towards any nearby graveyards."

∼

Armand began a widdershins circuit through the tall grass, tossing powdered herbs and reagents to either side of himself as he chanted in the chilling language of the ancient dead. Each word sent a refreshing surge of grave-cold energy coursing through him, pushing back the sweltering heat. His flesh itched from the drying sweat.

The curve of his walk brought the rubble of the former church back into view. This wasn't an ideal venue for his work. The dead here were long buried and he would be lucky to have any complete skeleton. Outright cadavers were all but impossible. But, Armand reasoned, at least the land was no longer consecrated.

His circle drew opposite his starting point and he could see the earth beginning to churn, the loamy smell of fertile soil thick in his nostrils. He wrinkled his nose, but continued chanting. He hated the smell of the outdoors.

Like corks bobbing to the surface, bones boiled up through the ground and assembled themselves into mostly human forms.

Armand reached his starting point and shifted to the left, turning his circle into a spiral, continuing to chant and scatter his ingredients onto the field.

For hours he continued his work and a growing army of the dead built up around him. The cloying smell of the earth replaced with the moist and moldering smell of rotting bone.

While talking to Jean, Armand realized an army of the dead would be useless in a direct assault against the Templars, but it could lure them away from their encampment. Several villages lay nearby and marauding bands of skeletons were certain to draw off some of the religious army and weaken their siege against Lucinda.

He reached the center of his circle and stopped walking before ending his chant, tying off the webs of dark power and sealing the enchantments into the bones. The sun lay low in the west, casting long shadows from his skeletal force. Over a hundred pairs of empty sockets and shattered skulls looked towards him, awaiting his command.

Armand leaned against the nearest one and took a deep breath. The skeleton lacked key parts and its bones floated in rough approximation of where they should be. But it was still strong enough to support his weight. He wondered if he would have time to go back to sleep in his own bed, or if he would need to rough it in the back of his wagon and wage war against mosquitoes all night.

The pounding of hooves caught Armand's attention. He looked off towards the sound and saw mounted soldiers round the curve in the road and head in his direction. The warriors were clad in the gold and white colors of the church. The necromancer's mouth worked for a few seconds, words failing to form. Finally, he mustered enough will to command his servants.

"Attack them, my minions! Protect me from harm!" As one, the skeletons turned towards the approaching force and shambled forward. They stretched their bony hands outward in preparation to attack while Armand ran in the opposite direction towards his wagon.

He only made it a few steps before he began breathing hard, sweat pouring down his flabby flesh. In another few steps, the air burned in his lungs and aches began to spread through his abdomen, but adrenaline pushed him on.

His foot slipped on something uneven and twisted hard. Pain exploded from his left ankle and he fell. He stretched out a hand in an attempt to break his fall. His palm scraped across the grass; his wrist and elbow screamed out as they bore the force of his fall.

He glanced back in terror. He could make out the Templars through the bones of his army. His foot looked uninjured, but he soon spotted the culprit: the nub of a gravestone he had stepped on and twisted his ankle.

Armand scrambled to get his feet under him and nearly fell again. His ankle did not want to support his weight, and only terror kept him from collapsing and crying. He was certain it was just a sprain, but that did not make it hurt any less.

He reached his cart and pulled himself up into it, only to find his motion halted. He looked back to see an angry Templar clutching the back of Armand's shirt with a mailed fist. A squeal escaped his lips. Armand locked his fingers around the bench at the front of his cart and held on for dear life while the warrior sought to pull him down. His breathing wheezed in his throat.

His fingers weakened and his grip slid down the bench. Desperate, he flailed out and grabbed hold of one of his bottles. With a blind throw he tossed it back at the Templar. The glass shattered harmlessly on the Templar's helmet, but the specter that blossomed out surrounded the man's head. The Templar fell to the ground, screaming and swatting at the misty shadow that held onto him.

Armand pulled himself up into the cart again before turning to look out at the conflict. Half of his skeletons had been destroyed and the rest did not look like they would last long. Which meant the he needed something more to keep the Templars distracted.

He threw more bottles in the direction of the conflict, each bursting when they hit the ground and releasing a shadowy figure that prowled the field for souls to devour. Then, Armand threw open his chests and set loose his elite skeletons: lacquered, warded, and blessed with an animal cunning. The constructs unfolded themselves from the chests, lifted up their swords and ran forward to meet the enemy.

Armand scanned the contents of his cart to see if there was anything he was missing. Ah, yes. The vials. He had brought a few dozen, with several different varieties represented. He lacked the time to be selective. Instead he opened the carrying case, pulled out a handful and threw them out into the field.

The vials exploded on impact, their arcane effects mingling and spiraling out of control. The horses at the front of the cart whinnied and bolted forward. Armand lost his balance and fell into the bed of his cart, rolling back until he almost fell out. He grabbed onto the side and prayed to whatever powers looking out for the likes of him that he not fall.

The dark gods that might show concern over the fate of Armand ignored his pleas. He fell off the cart and into blackness.

∼

Pain throbbed through Armand's head. Even lying down he thought he might fall over from waves of dizziness. His chest burned, making it difficult to breath.

Someone shoved him.

"Beloved, I am not feeling well," he said. "I just need a few more minutes of sleep."

A hand slapped him, bringing him closer to consciousness. He realized his hands were bound together.

"Really, Lucy, I'm not in the mood for such games right now. You can leave me tied up, but please let me sleep a bit more."

A man's voice growled, "Wake up you simpering cur."

Armand opened an eye and saw the blurry image of a Templar standing over him. He closed his eyes and winced.

"You, sir," the necromancer said, "are not my beloved Lucinda."

"All that dark education has served you well for you to be so observant, wizard."

"Sir, I am far too tired and ill to maintain civility and decorum at this juncture. And so my answer to you must be simply: Fuck off."

Someone kicked him in the ribs and a new man's voice said, "You will show the proper respect to Lord Commander Marcellus."

"My most humble apologies," Armand mumbled. "Fuck off, *Lord Commander.*"

This earned him another kick.

Armand heard the sound someone running towards them and yet another new voice said, "Lord Commander, the monks report the necromantic wards are weakening and request advice on the next stage of the siege."

"Very well," Marcellus said. "You, wizard, would be well advised to consider a modicum of cooperation or else your bones, too, may litter this field by morning."

"Duly noted, Most Holy Bastard," Armand said, sleep creeping up on him.

A kick struck him in the abdomen, breaking the tenuous self-control that had held back the nausea. He vomited, but did not have the energy to pull away from it. The acrid smell filled his nostrils.

The men walked away, leaving Armand alone with his vomit.

"I'm sorry," Jean's voice said.

The necromancer opened his eyes again and looked over at Jean, who was tied to a stake several feet away.

"For what are you sorry?" Armand tried to assess the symptoms he was experiencing. The pain in his side possessed an obvious boot-shaped source.

"The Lord Commander thought I was a deserter and questioned me on where I had gone. I tried to keep your existence secret, but they threatened to cut my hand off, so I broke."

"I am disheartened to hear I am less valuable to you than your hand." If Armand had struck his head when he fell from the cart, it would explain the headache and nausea.

"But it was my left hand. I do all my favorite stuff with that hand!"

"I am certain that justifies it." But the burning in his chest was peculiar. It didn't seem likely, but Armand worried the priests had implanted some angelic parasite in his chest that would eat away at his soul.

"It's not like I *wanted* to betray you. I have three women and six little mouths to feed. If I die, they may have to turn back to the streets."

"There exist teas that can end simple problems involving unborn children. Perhaps you should consider them the next time some doxy tells you your seed has taken root." The necromancer didn't dare channel much energy this close to the monks. Not only would it alert them to his powers, but it was likely to be painful as well. But a small amount of energy might work.

"I don't know what that means," Jean said. "But I feel insulted."

"Let me make it simpler: The next time one of your women tells you she is with child, find the tallest set of stairs and shove her down it." His skin itched as he used his magic. Armand hated priests. Tendrils of his magic sunk into his flesh, and probed towards his heart. The answer he found surprised him.

"That might hurt the child."

"That is the point, you buffoon!" The arcane nodule lodged next to his heart was necromantic in origin. It was a cage that held someone's soul. *Lucinda's.*

"I take it you don't like little ones."

Armand broke off from his examination of the magic to turn towards Jean. "You sold me out to the people who most want to kill me. It is my greatest hope, should I escape this predicament, that I will hunt down all six of your larva, boil them alive, render the flesh from their bones, and sell their animated dancing skeletons to traveling carnivals in hopes that every peasant with two coins to rub together will see the fate of your ill-conceived spawn!"

Jean stared, pale-faced, at Armand.

"Now, leave me alone. I am engaged in other matters."

Armand took a deep breath and turned back to his examination. The cage his chest contained was Lucinda's phylactery, to which her mind would return should someone destroy her physical form.

Despite her encouragement not to assist, he had brought her soul to her enemies. Having the phylactery bombarded by the monk's prayers likely weakened her magic. Armand closed his eyes and silently cursed himself for being such a fool.

He gnawed on his lip for a few minutes, pondering what he could do. He whispered a chant, directing his power towards the phylactery.

"Armand?" Lucinda's voice said. Her voice sounded strained and distant.

"My beloved. It appears that I have been a fool."

"But brave and loving as well."

"I imagine all fools are considered brave and loving. But I may have a solution to our predicament. Is it possible for us to combine our power in order to better fight off these zealots?"

Silence.

A moment later, "Perhaps. Give me a few minutes to get something ready."

Armand waited, drifting close to sleep. He was brought awake by a blinding light and the roar of thunder. The tower had exploded in a ball of green and purple flames. Cries of fear and pain came from the Templars. Armand could almost make out soldiers limping around and clutching wounds from flames and flying debris.

And then, the power came, flowing into him as though a pitcher had been upended over his head. He felt awake and alive, filled with energy—with it came a sense of Lucinda's presence.

He looked down at his wrists and watched as the ropes binding them moldered and rotted away to nothing. Violet energy coursed around him as he stood up. The aura expanded into a bonfire of necrotic power, lashing out and tearing through the scattered armies of the church. Their flesh withered and their eyes blossomed into flame before they crumbled to ash.

In the midst of all this, Armand found Lord Commander Marcellus. The Templar was trying to rally his scattered knights and drafted peasants. Armand was surprised to realize he was looking down at the knight from a great height, buoyed up by a pillar of dark flame.

The leader of the Templars looked up at Armand with fury in his eyes.

"What sort of monster are you?"

"Monster?" Armand asked. His voice sounded distant and tinny. "I am but a man in love."

"Oh, Armand," Lucinda's voice whispered in his ear. "That is so sweet of you."

"You are in love? What? With that thing from the tower!" said Marcellus.

Armand noticed a Templar run up and attempt to strike at him with a sword. The man touched the aura and exploded into black flame. Armand would have to ask Lucinda how to do that trick.

"That *woman*," Armand corrected, "is the light of my life, and a better person than you could contrive to be." The necromancer paused, hesitating before he said the words on his lips, though he knew in his heart they were true. "There is no limit to what I would do for her, and I hope to spend the rest of my days with her."

The knight screwed up his face and threw his sword at Armand. A hand pushed Armand out of the blade's path, but it still raked the side of his thigh. The pain was distant but still present. The aura about him flared out and consumed the knight commander, reducing him to ash.

"I have to admit I was surprised at your proclamation to the Templar," Lucinda said in his ear. "Does this mean you're comfortable living with me?"

Armand smiled and said, "Yes, I think it does. Chamber pots, ham and all. If nothing else, I won't run off to do any more *heroic* acts. I also imagine this is the closest I will get to making vows in a church."

"Trying to make an honest woman out of me?"

"I wouldn't dare."

Soul for Sale
M. J. Ritchie

Nicholas Marsden burrowed deeper into his navy blue parka, feeling nervous as he sat in the last pew. Churches were alien territory to him, but as safe a meeting place as any.

Organ chords reverberated, the notes of *Silent Night* descending on the fifty or so sinners gathered for early Mass, scheduled to begin in fifteen minutes. He scanned the marble interior, eyeing the other people in the pews. Most dressed like normal Chicagoans; others looked like members of the growing urban homeless population, and were probably seeking shelter more than salvation.

The air was redolent with vestiges of incense. People occupied pews, heads bent, while others made their way around the perimeter of the church, contemplating the small sculptures depicting what appeared to be stages of the crucifixion of Christ.

Some people brought their problems to a church, others to a bar; an avowed atheist, Nicholas preferred the latter.

A woman slid into the pew; he did a double take. A classic beauty, she wore a camel-colored coat that had the soft appearance of cashmere with a Burberry scarf at her throat, her long, golden hair lambent in the lighting. Setting an expensive-looking attaché case beside her on the pew between them, she turned to him. "Mr. Marsden?"

It took him a second to recall his name, and why he was here. "Yes."

"I am Andie, the winner of your eBay auction." She gave a nod at the attaché case, stared at him with glacier-blue eyes, and said, "I am here to collect your soul."

~

When he'd placed the ad on eBay, Nicholas felt that he'd nothing to lose. He didn't know he'd be in for the ride of his life. Sitting next to Andie in the back of a hired car, en route to the airport and a private plane that would take them to some ancient Mayan site in Mexico, he wondered if he'd been foolhardy in accepting her bid. She had advised him that travel to Mexico—all expenses paid—would be required as part of his bid acceptance. She also advised him as to what clothing to pack for the trip. At the time, he thought a two-day trip to sunny Mexico sounded like fun. Now, he wasn't so sure.

"Why are we going to Mexico?" he asked.

"We are meeting a shaman there who will conduct the soul retrieval, and subsequent installation process. The first ceremony is to collect your soul, the second, to ensure that it is compatible with my energy."

He shifted in his seat. He hadn't known what to expect when selling a soul, only that it wasn't this. Under his parka, sweat pressed his shirt against his pounding heart. "I'll still be alive, though, right?"

She stared at him with those cold eyes. "Mr. Marsden, how much thought did you give this proposition before placing your ad?"

Not enough, he thought. "I did it to see what would happen. As kind of an experiment."

"Experiments have results that can be positive or negative. Some experiments, such as yours, have serious consequences."

Yeah, no shit. He shrank into his parka wishing he could disappear.

"You humans take so much for granted."

You humans? He jerked up in his seat. "What do you mean *you* humans?"

"I am not human. I am an android, an intelligent robot. My father—my creator—is the CEO of Humanatron, Inc. You may have heard of the company. We offer a broad line of robots designed for various functions. I was a prototype, developed when he and his wife could not conceive, and after numerous in vitro fertility attempts had resulted in failure and heartbreak. He put his artistic and engineering talents to work, and created me as a labor of love. I *grew* over the years, if you will. My father developed subsequent models of me consistent with a child's maturation. What you see before you is the culmination."

She crossed her legs and sat up straighter as she looked at him. "After my mother died, and my father decided to monetize his creation, my father realized the need for me to know my identity. He planned to go public with Humanatron. That is when I learned I was not real. Or, as my father always corrects me, I *am* real, just not human. Which is where you come in. You can give me the one thing he could not."

Nicholas sat back in his seat. *An android. He was going to Mexico with an android, who had just bought his soul. Why did this intelligent, non-human want a soul so much? Had he been wrong about souls?* He had researched religions, even gone to church services, and had found nothing in his twenty-four years to alter his belief in atheism. Hell, he didn't even know if he had a soul, let alone whether he could sell it. *And yet, he had.* The money transferred from the attaché case now padding his backpack proved it.

"What happens, exactly?" he asked.

"We are about to find out."

~

From the airport, they traveled over deeply rutted roads in a Land Rover driven by a man with leather-like skin, whose age Nicholas guessed to be somewhere between forty and eighty. He sported a khaki-colored shirt, jeans, and a permanent grin.

After driving several miles through a jungle of low-hanging vines, tall trees, and vibrant greenery dappled with brilliantly colored flowers, Nicholas gasped as he beheld their destination. The jungle had cleared to reveal an expansive plaza, at the center of which stood a one-hundred-foot-tall tower surrounded by smaller pyramids and buildings.

He and Andie got out of the car and stood gazing at the engravings on the tower and the fierce animal sculpture at its entrance. Andie spoke. "This was once an important Mayan ceremonial site. They came to purify themselves here. It is called *El Torre de la Purificacion:* The Tower of Purification. It is believed classes may have been given here on the healing arts, math, astronomy and religion. It is being renovated, so there will be few tourists. It is perfect for our purpose."

They climbed the seemingly never-ending steps to the top of the tower, where a bare-chested man wearing a brilliant yellow, red-trimmed cape, red trousers, and a red-and-yellow headdress beckoned them into a room. At the center of the room stood a low, stone table about six-feet by six-feet. The room had windows carved in the walls, allowing rays of sun and a breeze to filter in. Nicholas felt sweaty and winded; Andie looked as fresh as when she'd just stepped out of the car. *But why wouldn't she? She was a machine.*

The man spoke in Spanish or what Nicholas guessed was Spanish; Andie translated.

"It is important for you to know that no one can take your soul without your consent. For most people, this rite facilitates the *return* of the soul, which will restore to the owner the ability to have hope, or confidence. It is possible that it will complete a healing process, but it is also possible that it will begin the work of new healing and new growing. We cannot say what will happen in your case. Here, we are *transferring* a soul from one being to another entity. We cannot predict, we can only pray that our efforts are successful."

He directed a question to Nicholas, which Andie translated again: "Do you release your soul of your own free will with no constraints or binding?"

"Ask him if I'll die," Nicholas said.

Andie said something, and the shaman answered.

Turning to Nicholas, she said, "He says you are human; you will die, but not from this. A piece of your soul will remain with you."

Again, the shaman said something.

Andie asked Nicholas, "Do you want to proceed?"

Nicholas took a deep breath, "I guess."

The shaman indicated they should lie on the stone table side-by-side. Nicholas did as he was told, and closed his eyes. He heard a low humming emanate from the shaman punctuated by what sounded like a maraca, and intermittent *phh*, *phh*, *ptah ptah* noises as the shaman went into a trance.

A soft breeze swept through the room, and Nicholas relaxed.

≈

Nicholas awoke with a shiver. He didn't remember where he was at first. Then, he did. He moved his hand over his heart as if to make sure it was still beating.

Andie was not beside him. He jerked up to a sitting position. His head hurt. Where was she? Where was anyone? He moved to the doorway, and then, he saw her, a level below, talking to the shaman. They appeared to be admiring the sunset.

"Nicholas," she called. "Come on down."

He made his way cautiously down the narrow steps to where they stood.

"How are you?" she asked, concern in her voice.

"I'm not sure. Okay, I guess. Still here."

"I feel wonderful. Truly alive. It's an indescribable feeling. I'm noticing so many things for the first time." She turned and looked at him, grasping his hand. "Thank you."

The eyes that looked at him appeared different—a deep, warm blue.

"You're welcome," he said.

Bidding farewell to the shaman, she said, "We'd better go before it gets dark."

The steps seemed steeper, his body heavier, as he descended.

∾

Safe at ground level, exhausted, he sat on the bottom tower step.

"Are you okay?" Andie asked.

He nodded. "I just need a minute."

"You sure?"

He nodded again.

"Okay," she said. "I'll wait for you in the car."

∾

The fading sun cast the ancient landscape into a stony grayness that gave the place a brooding feel. He felt strange—hollow and heavy at the same time.

Some experiments, such as yours, have serious consequences.

He shuddered.

On the far side of the plaza, the Land Rover waited to transport him and Andie to town, and dinner. Sucking in a steadying breath, he hoisted himself to his feet and walked toward it with an emptiness inside him that was more than hunger.

The Enchanted Tower
Edward McDermott

Kheelan walked through the woods with only a tune to keep him company. A rover, a minstrel, he paid for meat and mead with a song and often found a lonely maid willing to share the night.

Some said he learned his art from the Fair Folk, for he had been snatched as a baby and grown up a beloved son in the courts of magic. Others said he wandered because he found no peace for a broken heart, because the difference between mortal and Fair was too great to bear.

As he walked in the woods, he came upon an ancient crone hobbling on her way.

"Fair Mother," he said, introducing himself. "Let me carry your burden for a bit. I have none of my own and would share yours if you'll let me."

"Ah, Kheelan," she responded, then cackled. "You are one with words. Here is my burden. It's wood for my fire and warmth for my night. Carry it to my home and I will search your future, for I am a daughter of Lilith and know the dark secrets of the past."

Kheelan laughed. "Carry it I will, and no need of fortune or future. If you have a corner I can lie in and porridge that we can share, then I will sing you songs which will make you remember kinder days."

She smiled, but said nothing.

Eventually, they came to her home, a one-room hovel made of wicker and mud with a roof of thatch. It had one door and one window and space only for a fire and a bed. In the winter, when the snow was on the ground, the hovel was warm and comfortable. In the summer, when the heat was everywhere, he supposed she found it cool and easy to clean.

She told him where to place his burden. Then, he took up her ax and trimmed the kindling to a common length, as she tended her fire and prepared a simple meal of pea porridge. Next, Kheelan searched the nearby forest for a fallen tree. Discovering one, he found its trunk was too thick for one man and an ax, but its branches were the right size. He chopped the branches from the tree's trunk and hauled them to the cottage.

Task completed, he looked at his hands and saw blisters on his fingers. He laughed, for he rarely did such work. Playing a tune was more to his taste.

With the setting sun, the crone and the young troubadour settled inside the house near the fire. She had but one bowl, so they both dipped their spoons into the common source and ate.

"Now, Mother, what should I sing of?"

"Kheelan, you know whom you seek. Why do you pretend? Sing *Ah Love, You Have Wounded My Heart*. You know the words."

He sang and the lyrics came easily. Too true they were. He followed that with *A Bird in a Brier* and concluded with *The Butcher's Bride*. This crone knew his heart too well. Uneasy, he wondered if she was more than a mere hedge witch.

"Well played, and better than I deserved for the poor meal I served you."

"My lady," he replied, gallantly, "what more could you offer but that which also touched your own lips? I have dined with lords and not been as well treated. Another song?"

"Nay. Hold still."

She lit a candle. Then, she took a brass bowl, filled it with water and set it on the embers.

"Hush," she said. "Not a sound. I must concentrate to see. Give me your hand. Wait and listen. Be quiet, for the slightest sound will break this spell."

She stared into the bowl, and Kheelan waited. The water grew warm. A bubble rose from the bottom. By candlelight, he could barely see where the water ended and the bowl began. In its depths, Kheelan thought he saw something that should not be there.

"Ah," the old crone began. "I see. The woods are thick and the way is crooked. This is no straight road you follow. To another, I would warn of the wolf and the bear, but you need fear neither, for they are akin to you. Now, what's this?"

She stared intensely for a moment.

"I see a building within the woods. A watch tower that has been abandoned. No, not so. It now has another use. Five years of penance, for the sins of the flesh. Poor girl. What is this to you? Oh, no."

"What?" Kheelan asked.

"Fool. You broke the spell. The vision has passed. All I can say is that if you enter that tower, you're wandering days are ended. Be warned. Be wary of the guiles of women. You should know that already."

Angry with him, she would say no more.

In the morning, the old hag remained angry and ignored his presence, so Kheelan left with an empty belly. To a traveler like him this was not an uncommon happenstance, so he accepted it. As he walked through the woods, he found a mushroom here, an edible flower there, and soon made himself a tolerable breakfast.

The path he followed spilled into a woodland meadow. In the center of the grass, a tower stood. Kheelan recognized it as a cloigtheach by its round shape and the door set out of reach. It stood four stories high, crowned with what might once have been battlements. As he walked around it, Kheelan noticed fresh horse droppings on the ground. Someone had ridden here recently.

He heard a woman's voice from the tower singing these words:

"They buried Willie in the old church yard,
And Barbara there anigh him,
And out of his grave grew a red, red rose,
And out of hers, a briar."

In response, he pulled out his lute and sang:

"Lavender's blue, diddle diddle
Lavender's green,
When I am king, diddle diddle
You shall be queen."

"Oh." A startled face looked down from the window. A woman—not a maiden—but a woman in her full flower. "Who are you?"

"I am Kheelan, a troubadour, a wanderer, a singer of songs and teller of tales, my lady. I heard your voice and thought the song too cruel for so fine a day." With that he continued to play and sang more verses.

"Has *he* sent you to taunt and to torment me?" she asked.

Her voice was sweet to Kheelan's ears.

"No one has sent me, my lady. I came by my own will. Had I known you were here, I would have come more quickly. Tell me your tale and I will give you my wisdom. Let me in and we can sit by the table and sing to each other if you prefer."

"I cannot. The door is locked and I do not have the key. The Lord has vowed that I must stay here and live alone until I grow old, for he said I had enchanted him and stolen his heart. You must leave. Once each day his men ride here to bring me food and drink. If they find you by the tower, they will kill you. You must hurry, for they will arrive shortly."

Kheelan nodded. "I will stay within the woods until they have come and gone. Then, we must talk some more."

While hidden in the woods, Kheelan pondered the situation. She was lovely, and it seemed cruel to treat a woman so. Yet, it was not just her beauty that drew him to her. He watched the guards arrive with a jingling of traces. The woman lowered a rope with a basket. The guards filled it, rode around the tower and left without a word.

Once they were gone, Kheelan strode from the green darkness of the forest into the sunlight and began to pluck a tune.

"Oh, you have returned. You are real then, and not something I imagined," she said, staring down at him.

"Quite real, my lady. If you'd imagined me, then I would be far more handsome. Now, what should I sing?"

"Anything. Sing. Talk. It doesn't matter. For nearly a year I have not heard the sound of a human voice. I thought I would go mad."

"Has not your captor come to see if you have changed your mind? Love can be strange."

"Not he. Thinking me an enchanter who has cast a glamour on his eyes, he fears me. Caring was never in his heart. Love could not be this cruel. And should you wonder what to call me, my name is Rosaline."

They talked. He told her tales such as the one of *Elidor and The Golden Ball*, a story of taming a unicorn and finding a path into the Fair Lands.

"Oh, if I had been Elidor, I would never have returned. I would have lived among the Fair Folk for the rest of my life and been happy to be nothing more than a servant. However, I am trapped." With that she began to cry, and her sobs would have saddened a nightingale.

"Lower the basket and let us see what might be done," Kheelan suggested, for her tears affected him and he thought to free her.

She did as he asked. As he examined it, he saw that the rope was merely a string and could not bear much weight. In the basket, she had placed wine, bread and cheese. He thanked her for the meal, and he ate while she told him of her life.

Even from the lowest window, which was a mere arrow slit, she was twenty feet above him. It made for a crick in the neck, and Kheelan eventually lay down to stare up at her.

For three days, Kheelan stayed and talked with Rosaline. At the beginning of each day, he eagerly waited for her to rise, ignoring his sore body, made stiff from lying on the hard forest floor.

At lunch, he hid from the guards.

At dinner, he sang his love to her, his heart aching with tenderness.

All the time he searched for some means to free her.

On the first day, Kheelan took branches from the forest and bound them together with the strings from his lute to make a crude ladder which would reach the door. For he knew—to climb to the top of the tower was beyond his ability.

But the door was strong and heavy, bound with iron. The hasp was set into the stone and the lock was strong as well. Kheelan had hoped to pick it, but no one would ever open that lock again, for it had been filled with molten lead.

On the second day, he searched to see if the rocks which made up the tower were loose. He hoped to pry out a rock or two and force a new entrance. Alas, the stones were set in mortar that was as hard as the rocks. Even with his dagger he could only scrape out the tiniest amount. Such burrowing would take years.

On the third day, he tried to climb the rock face. The stones were polished with little space between them, so he found no purchase for his hands and feet. His fingers raw, his lute silenced and his dagger dulled, Kheelan sat back and cursed silently.

"Go," Rosaline commanded. "You have made my life so much richer and kinder, but you risk death each day by being here. There is no way to break these bonds. Go and be free for me, love."

Kheelan laughed. "I still have some thoughts on that. When the moon is full, I will leave you, but only for a little while, my lady."

As the full moon rose, the silvery path to the Fair Lands became visible, and Kheelan trod the way that led to the only home he had ever known. He neither ate nor drank while on this journey. He stopped only to take what he needed: a rope of silvery moonbeams which had been spun by enchanted spiders, lighter than a dandelion seed and stronger than steel.

When the moon was setting, Kheelan returned to the forest with his prize. As the sun rose, still holding tightly onto the moonbeam rope, Kheelan lay upon the forest floor and slept.

After Rosaline's noon visitors left, he strolled out of the forest. When he whistled, she looked down from her prison tower and laughed with joy. "I thought you had left forever."

"Was I gone so long?"

"A month."

"To me, only a day passed, but time has a will of its own in the Fair Lands. Lower down your basket. I have brought you your freedom."

She did as he asked, then he placed the moonbeam rope in the basket. Next, she hauled up the rope. As he commanded, she tied it firmly to the top of the tower and tossed the other end to the ground. Kheelan tried the rope. He had no worry that it would fail, only that her knot would not be equally strong.

With the rope, he mounted the walls and climbed to the top of the tower. Once there, he swung over the battlements and stood for the first time, face to face with Rosaline. She stood shorter than he had expected, diminutive, a slight girl. She kissed him and led him inside her prison.

She showed him all of her tower, every room, every piece of furniture. She told him to sit and that she would bring him wine. She kissed him, and then, she left him.

When she did not return, Kheelan went in search of her. He could not find her in the bedroom. The pantry was empty as well. The study, too. He climbed to the uppermost level, but no one was there. Then, he looked down and saw her. She had climbed down the rope and was lying on the grass, feeling the earth beneath her fingers.

"Thank you, my kind sir," she said, almost laughing. "I was a prisoner, and you freed me."

Kheelan tried to clamber onto the battlement in order to climb down the moonbeam rope, but could not. Some force stopped him.

"Oh, do not struggle so," Rosaline said. "You cannot escape. There is a spell upon these ancient walls. The tower cannot be left empty. The curse keeps the last occupant from leaving. I am sorry, but I could never leave without finding a replacement, and you are my replacement. Do not worry, the soldiers will continue to provide for you. They will simply believe any change in voice or visage is some act of magic. Before I go, is there anything I can do?"

"My lute. Bring it to me," Kheelan said. "And the strings too. I used them on that ladder."

He cursed himself for a fool, yet he loved her and wanted her still. She had betrayed him; nevertheless, he could not bring himself to curse her.

It was then he remembered the old woman's prophecy.

"Lower down the rope and I will tie your lute to it," said Rosaline.

He did so, and she tied the lute to the rope and left him without another word. He watched her walk away. He cried after her. He shouted. He screamed. She never turned her head.

For Kheelan, the days passed slowly. He repaired his instrument and played only the saddest of songs. He ate and drank. The food had no taste and the wine could not drown his memories of her. He slept. In dreams, he loved her and she loved him back.

In the study, he found books, and he read to pass the time. Each time the full moon rose, he tried to follow the silver path to the Fair Lands, but the tower's enchantment barred that method of escape, too.

He decided to hammer out a doorway. Since the walls were three feet thick, it took countless hours to make a new exit. Once completed, unfortunately, the enchantment kept him from climbing out the new door.

The riders who brought him food and drink ignored his words. Kheelan the traveler had become a caged bird.

"Truly, I have been destroyed," he said. "No accident. She lured me, knew my feelings and took advantage of them. Now she has trapped me. I was a fool."

In that instant, his love transformed to hatred and his sorrow turned to rage. He stormed through his prison looking for something to destroy.

The nights had turned colder and the trees had lost their leaves when he saw someone approaching. From the forest, the old woman from the cottage came hobbling. She took her time making the trip to the tower, where she thumped the walls with her walking stick.

"What now, Fair Mother? Your warning was true and your vision correct. Have you come to gloat?"

"No," she replied, too bent over to look up at him. "I have come to free you. I've thought long and hard on this, Kheelan. You had no need to show kindness to a lonely crone, but you did. I took advantage of you. Now, accept the reward for chivalry. Lower your rope. I cannot climb, so you must provide the strength to lift me. It should not be difficult, as age has made even my bones light."

He objected, but she insisted, and in the end he brought her to the top of the tower.

"Now, you will go, and I will stay," she told him.

"No," Kheelan replied. Yet, he heard the pathways whisper to him, the distant horizon calling. *Free.* He could be free again.

"No," he continued, "I cannot ask you to spend the rest of your life here in my place. I was the fool, and I must do penance."

She laughed. "I am ancient and failing. I need a place like this, a fine tower with a solid roof where my food and drink are delivered to me every day. Kheelan, to you, this is a trap. To me, it is a sanctuary. Do not be concerned, I won't remain here for long. Besides, this is my thanks to you."

Reluctantly and eagerly, he found himself climbing down the rope, his lute on his back and bread and meat in a sack.

At the bottom of the tower he called out to her. "Why did you say this was your thanks to me?"

"Rosaline was my child. Yes, she is also a daughter of Lilith. Troubadour, you need to learn this lesson. The sons of Adam never find good fortune from the daughters of my tribe. Now, go your own way."

Kheelan left the clearing. He walked in silence, no tune to keep him company. His heart still hurt.

Freak Justice
Brad Hafford

In a circus tent on the outskirts of town a snake danced at the end of a man's arm. It looked for all the world as though it were attached to his shoulder—no mere act, but a living, breathing part of the man himself.

"It really looks like a snake, don't it?" Leroy whispered, sitting close to his friend in the front row.

Tom shook his head. "It's just a sock puppet. Shit, man, you'll believe anything."

"Will not." Leroy sat up in his chair, his head following the undulations of the performer's arm like a charmed snake himself.

Tom wasn't going to fall for it. He was a *man* now and had learned how to make others follow him, fear him. It had to be the partial darkness, the wheezing smoke machine, and the thrumming music that made the snake seem real.

Suddenly, the snake-arm lashed out, striking the air beyond the boxy wooden stage directly between the two boys. The audience gasped. Leroy jerked back, his chair kicking up dust from the dirt floor. Tom flinched, too, but tried his best to cover it.

The music rattled to a crescendo. Clutching at his errant left hand with his normal right, the sideshow actor struggled with himself for control of the snake. He pretended it would bite his own face, the snake's jaws snapping where his left hand should be, and then a tatty curtain fell. A cheap climax, and only three minutes after Tom had paid his five bucks to get in.

"Rip off!" Tom cried, cupping his hands around his mouth for added volume. "Boo!"

Leroy stared at his friend, his pudgy face holding the dumbfounded look it always held. It only made Tom boo and hiss louder. "We want our money back!"

Murmuring, the crowd filed past the two teenagers. Tom remained in his folding chair, still booing while late afternoon summer fluttered in through the open tent flap. Within minutes, a dark shadow fell. Tom looked up. A circus bouncer towered over him, hairy arms crossed over bare chest, square face a scowl of scar tissue.

"What're you?" asked Tom. "Some kind of strongman?"

A low noise rumbled in the man's throat like bits of glass grinding over asphalt. Leroy ducked and ran. The bouncer's face knotted and the muscles on his chest rippled. Tom tugged his tractor cap down low over his eyes.

A hand thudded on his shoulder. Meaty fingers squeezed. Hardened face leaned in, mouth too close to Tom's ear. "If you know what's good for you, you'll get out of here." The breath smelled of peanuts.

"Yeah, whatever."

Tom shrugged off the big hand and shuffled out of the tent, setting what he calculated to be a hard look of defiance on his face.

He found Leroy in the growing afternoon shadow of the fairground tower. The electric sign atop the girded metal spire sputtered an advertisement for the traveling circus. Its loudspeaker gushed stilted music and at irregular intervals a static-ridden voice announced, "Circus, Circus, Circus! Come one, come all!"

Leroy shifted his weight from side to side. His cap sat far back on his head, emphasizing the roundness of his face. He stuffed his hands in his pockets and scuffed his feet as Tom approached. "Darn it, Tom, you're gonna land us deep in it for sure. Mama told me not to hang around you."

"You do everything your mama tells you?"

"You know I don't. But god, man, you can't go 'round stirring up the likes of him." He tilted his head in the direction of the pillar of muscles standing beside the far tent. Beyond him, a hawker called viewers to the day's final appearance of *The Snake Man*. "Only five dollars!"

Other hawkers added to the din, setting a peculiar pace that made the late afternoon swim, and the patchwork shadow of the fairground tower grew to engulf the line of tents in a weave of dark and light.

"This whole damn circus is a bunch of baloney," Tom said. "I bet that dude's muscles ain't even real."

"Looked pretty real to me. And that snake? Man, I swear it was gonna bite you."

"Me? It was after *you*. But that thing weren't no more real than that two-headed calf 'round old man Gunther's farm last season."

"That sure *was* real! Seen it with my own eyes."

"You're full of it. I made me a two-headed chicken once. Didn't live long, but it had two heads a while. Was that real?"

"That was just two chickens you tore up and stuck back together. You're worse than the freaks in them tents."

Tom punched his friend's fleshy arm.

Leroy gave a weak, "Ow," and an even weaker return punch.

Maybe when he got older he'd toughen up and be a real challenge. But Tom knew he never would. Didn't have it in him. He punched Leroy's arm again, one knuckle out for extra bruising.

"*Ow*. Quit it, man. Let's go see another sideshow."

"They're dumb."

"Lions, then?"

"Nah, they're mostly dead. Don't even try to bite nobody." He pulled a metal sling shot from his back pocket and showed it to his friend. "Let's go to the trapezes and see if we can make them swinging dopes fall off!"

Leroy shook his head. "Ain't no reason to go doing that."

"You're just chicken."

"Am not."

"Leroy!" a shrill voice sounded from the end of the long line of sideshow tents. In the distance, through the rising dust of countless feet, stood a tall woman craning her head to peer through the crowd. "Leroy Michael Bayers! You get your bottom over here right now!"

"Aw, crap. It's Mama. I gotta go, man."

Tom grabbed his friend's arm and tugged. "Nuh uh," he said. "Come on. Through here."

He pulled Leroy between two tents, hopping over guide ropes that held squared sides and pointed roofs. "But Tom..."

"Shut up and come on. Ain't you got no guts?"

"Well, sure I do. But Mama's calling. She'll tan my hide if I run."

"Chicken!" Tom made clucking noises and flapped his arms, jumping the remaining guide ropes to the back of the tents. There he spun to look at his chubby friend, who was hesitating between one end of the narrow space and the other. After a final look at the squawking Tom, Leroy fled back to the makeshift street, the wandering crowds, and his mother's beckoning screech.

"Mama's boy!" Tom yelled after him.

He stuck his hands in his hip pockets and scuffed his feet. What now? Without Leroy, he had no one to push around. He picked up a rock and tossed it at the nearest tent, one striped in dusky red and canvas beige. The rock bounced off and skipped into the broken field behind.

Half the fairground sat vacant here, some fifty yards to a barbed wire fence and a wide stand of trees. Beyond that ran railroad tracks and endless pasture. Tom kicked a crushed can and watched it spin away. The dead clank was satisfying, but only for the briefest of seconds.

There might be moles or squirrels to chase, he decided. Always better to kick something alive. Maybe even tag it with his slingshot. Take the life from it. *That* was entertainment. He set out to find something alive.

But hunting wasn't good. Critter holes gaped empty and trails led nowhere, old and faded. As the final amber of the setting sun caused the trees to flare before fading to smoky night, he'd wandered away from the bustle of tents to the edge of the darkening woods.

Canned calliope tunes wafted from the distant fairground tower, the whistling whine of clumsy clowns and flying fools. The big top show occupied the evening, and lights glittered at its entrance. But its distant spectacle held nothing for Tom. He found thrills in extinguishing brightness.

A bird chirped in the woods—incessant, desperate—a hungry baby calling for its mother. Tom smiled. At last, something to engage his need for action.

In the longest stretch between two posts, he slipped through the barbed wire and began searching. He located the noisy bird's tree and stared up into its thinning, late summer branches. Grabbing the pale, narrow trunk, he pushed and pulled. Drying leaves crackled and fell, a flutter of yellow and brown.

He shook again, harder this time. A few more leaves, some twigs, and finally, something solid. It landed with a cracking thud and Tom bent to stare closely at it. Interwoven twigs formed a bowl and within sat three small, blue eggs—and one baby bird.

Tilting its head to the sky, the bird chirped. It was dead ugly— spurts of feather, more like patches of hair on a bald thing, jutted from its body. Its eyes were large with leathery skin stretched across them, and its wings were nothing but stubs.

It opened its beak, begging for food. Tom hated this needy little thing, how it screeched and begged and whined. Weakness. Something Tom's father had beaten out of him long ago.

He picked up the chick, feeling its bony body and prickly flesh against his fingers. He pinched the flabby skin of its back between thumb and forefinger and held it squirming near his face. "You want to fly, you little creep?" he said, sliding his slingshot from his pocket.

He set the bird in the leather seat at the end of the rubber straps and pulled with all his might. The chirping of the helpless creature reached its peak and then its head lolled, near lifeless in the squeeze. Tom grinned. He let go.

The baby bird sailed into the night. Tom laughed and his arms tingled with excitement. He turned back to the nest and brought his booted foot down on it. Twigs scattered and two eggs crunched.

In the same instant, a nearby tree shuddered, a branch swayed. A dark spot moved toward him. His heart skipped and he drew a sharp breath. Another flutter in the trees and another quick movement. A screech. A cry.

It was only a bird, he realized. Why had he jumped in the first place? Just the darkness, probably. A memory.

But he wasn't afraid of the dark. Hadn't been since... He picked up a rock and slung it at the rustling branch, missing by miles. That was when the bird decided to come full at him, a flurry of black wings. It was small, but it was fast, and on a collision course.

Tom fell to his knees, dropping his slingshot. The starling passed over his head, flailing and screeching. Tom rolled across twigs and leaves to the half-smashed nest and grabbed the remaining egg. "You want this?" he shouted. "Go get it!" He hurled it at the receding bird.

The starling tilted, wheeled and flapped to pick up speed in Tom's direction. Scrambling to his feet, he ran. Twice he fell to the ground; twice the bird swooped and scratched at his back; twice he got up and ran again. After his second fall, he found himself along the railroad tracks. The lights and sounds of the big top raged in the distance and Tom ran toward them along the rails, the bird chasing him all the while. It dipped and climbed behind him, swooping again and again, far too near for comfort, too energetic and angry for a simple bird.

He reached a set of boxcars on a side track and swung beneath them in a scatter of dust, flattening himself against the gravel bed and wooden beams. He heard the bird slap against the car above, scratching at the peeling paint until bits of it fell near his face pressed against the ground. Gravel pushed into his cheek and sweat clung to the band of his tractor cap leaving an uncomfortably slimy trail across his forehead. His breath came in short puffs. The smell of creosote and oiled steel invaded his nostrils, and the incessant scrabbling and screeching of the bird filled his ears.

He couldn't take it, had to get away. He rolled to the opposite side of the train and into the ditch beyond, breaking dry weeds. Up and away, he ran several cars down the line. Finally flattening himself against a boxcar door, he collected his breath.

"I'm not scared of no bird!" he reminded himself aloud, heart pounding.

Tom closed his eyes and pictured himself squeezing that bird to death, wringing the life out it. In his mind, the starling made a funny sound, a squawk of ecstatic pain that raised a spark deep within Tom's chest. Power surged down his arms until his fingers tingled, squeezing tighter around the imaginary body.

BAM! Something struck the boxcar door only a few inches from Tom's ear. He let out a screech and recoiled. The something struck again, sticking briefly in the wooden door, rocking to free itself. It looked a lot like a snake's head.

The thing dislodged itself and immediately, a man tumbled out of the boxcar, apparently chasing the thing that had tried for Tom. He'd seen that man before. The bad actor from the sideshow. *The Snake Man.*

Tom clutched his arms against his chest, trying not to shake, not to show his fear. "Look man," he said, "I know it's an act and it don't scare me. Cut the shit."

The snake guy was thin as a rail, except for the sock puppet arm. His tank top fluttered loosely as he stumbled and grunted, continuing the struggle of arm against arm. "Get out of here, kid," he said, "if you know what's good for you." His voice was a strained hiss.

Tom snorted. "You must think I'm stupid, huh? I bet you got booze or something back here and don't want to share."

Finally, the man got the sock puppet under control. It wobbled in the air in front of him, a strange way for an arm to move. "Are you leaving or not?"

"Hell, no. I ain't going nowhere just 'cause some dumbass with a sock on his hand tells me to."

The arm approached, silently shifting in the night. The closer it got, the more Tom shifted his own weight, swallowing hard and feeling a rising pulse in his ears. That thing *really* looked like a snake.

At last it floated directly in front of him, bobbing, swaying. A thin, black tongue like a miniature slingshot flipped out and shook, then returned; did it again. Damn, that was a convincing sock puppet.

It opened its mouth and fangs sprung into place, glistening. There came a light hiss followed by an earthy smell. Transfixed, Tom could only watch that creature, the movement of its head, the swishing of its tongue.

The snake drew back and wrapped around the Snake Man's neck, hanging there for support. That was no damned arm. No damned puppet. That was a goddamned snake.

"What in hell's going on?" Tom asked.

"I'm Danno."

"That don't tell me shit."

"That blood on your hands?"

Tom flipped his palms in front of his face, searching. "Where?"

"Believe me, kid, I see it."

"I ain't no kid. I'm Tom."

Danno snorted, and then, nodded as if he'd expected a visitor all along. "Well, Tom, if you're not leaving, you'd better meet the inmates."

Tom followed Danno's lead, shaking his head in amazement. A snake for an arm! Leroy would never believe it.

Wood smoke and a murmur of voices gathered as they rounded an old railroad watering tower. The last boxcar sat beneath the draw spout as if ready to be cleansed of its antique filth. Beyond it a cluster of people were gathered around a campfire. A mash of shapes and sizes, their shadowy forms seemed inhuman to Tom. He wondered if they all had snakes. What he wouldn't give for one of his own. That would show anyone who called him weak.

The murmur stopped and a single, clear voice rang out. "Ah, crap. Not another one."

"We all knew it would happen," A second voice said.

Danno addressed them. "Shut up and listen. This is Tom. He ain't a kid, or so he says. And he doesn't want to leave. You know the drill."

Tom rushed forward to ogle the freaks around the fire. A woman stood to block his path. He looked her up and down, but was disappointed—she seemed normal enough. Two eyes, two arms, two...

"Tom," she said, skin glistening in the firelight. "We have to convince you to leave. Trust me. You don't want to be here."

Tom's gaze remained riveted on the woman's breasts, fascinated by the firm flesh bound in a swath of decorative fabric, moving softly with every breath. He'd lost interest in snakes for the moment. "Wow. Are those real?"

"Just listen, Tom. This isn't the place for you."

Eyes still locked on the smooth curves that swelled into patterned wrappings, the boy grinned. "Like hell it ain't."

The woman sighed and returned to the fire. Tom took the opportunity to check out her ass. But she didn't have an ass so much as a...tail.

Wide, long and bumpy, it narrowed slowly as it emerged from her skirt and made a serpentine arc to the grass, finally reaching a blunt tip. The end, segmented in armored scales, brushed against Tom's boot.

"That's Ellie. They call her Gator Girl," Danno said. He stood near now, his good hand coming to rest on Tom's shoulder. The snake curved in from the side.

"Damn!" Tom said. "Are all y'all super freaks?"

"Tom, you aren't listening. We're giving you the opportunity to turn around, to go home and live a good life."

"And miss this freak show? You gotta be kidding me. Come on, start wrestling or something."

"We're not here for your entertainment."

"Oh, I get it. You want my five bucks. Well, I done paid that."

A bald man approached from the fire. Danno shook his head slowly and addressed the newcomer. "They'll never learn," he said.

"This can't be real," Tom said, touching Danno's arm, brushing the point where it transferred from gaunt, fleshy shoulder to tightly scaled serpent torso. The scales were smooth and intertwined like finely woven strips of leather. "That's so cool! I want one of them."

The snake twisted in midair. Danno put his right hand around its neck and pulled it back. "Watch what you wish for, kid." He stepped back as the man from the fire held out his hand. "Meet Ed."

"What's up with your face?" Tom said. Ed's nose looked like it had been hit with a cartoon sledge hammer but had never snapped back. The tip thrust upwards to his forehead and his nostrils faced out rather than down. His eyes were two bulging slashes running either side of that upturned triangle of flesh like rowboats approaching a mountainous island.

He opened his mouth to speak, but his jaw didn't set like normal, it just kept opening. It dropped and dropped, and as it expanded, row after row of spiked teeth jutted from within.

Tom's jaw dropped too. "Damn!"

The pile of teeth named Ed spoke, a drowning, labored voice from within, "They call me Sharkie."

"You see," Danno said, "what has happened to us is far from entertaining. It is our penance."

"We are doomed to this existence," Ed gurgled, "unless we can convince others to repent their vicious ways, the ways we once held."

Ellie spoke from the shadows. "No one's been freed yet. But we try harder each time. Please, Tom. You don't want to be like us."

"You kidding? I'd be able to scare folks shitless with teeth like his!"

Without warning, Ed Sharkie lunged at Tom, rows of teeth rolling outward, snapping, breath a rush of hot brine. Tom fell backwards, landing on his backside on the damp earth, catching himself hard on his elbows. Sharkie advanced, still snapping those horrible jaws, salty spittle flying, teeth ever closer. Tom's shoulders shook. He looked away, couldn't stop the scream that formed deep within him.

The gnashing stopped, and when Tom looked again, Ed had retracted those teeth into his broad jaw and forced thin lips down over them.

"What'd you go and do that for?" Tom tried to hide his shaking, hide the moisture in his eyes.

Danno's snake struck next. It sank its teeth through the fabric of Tom's T-shirt and into the flesh and muscle of his chest. Sharp slivers pushed deep and held firm. No pain at first, just a long, seizing inhale. His eyes opened involuntarily. He couldn't blink, couldn't see. Only stars.

"This isn't an ordinary freak show," Danno said, ghostly and far away. "It calls some people. And it changes them, whether they want to change or not."

Tom's body convulsed. He couldn't let go a breath and he could no longer hear his heart in his ears.

"You have a choice, Tom."

Another convulsion, and air rushed from Tom's lungs as the snake released its hold. Two darts of pain like molten glass remained throbbing in his breast and his muscles spasmed. He coughed and cried out, "You're nuts! Why you hurting me? I ain't done nothing!" Tears welled despite Tom's attempts to stop them.

There came a mix of warped voices from warped faces all around. Tom pushed to his knees and wiped his eyes, then raised a fist toward the cloudy images above. "You're a bunch of freaks!" he cried. "I'm gonna get my daddy's shotgun and I'm gonna—"

"Tom," Danno said, a strong voice from a skeletal body. "We can do no real damage to you. But you *can* hurt us. You must choose not to."

"You're crazy! I'm leaving."

"It's too late for that." Danno tossed a long dagger to the ground. Its sides were curved like waves in the surf. The blade picked up the light of a million stars and reflected it in a bluish glow. Tom's attention went from the knife to the milling freaks and back again.

He snatched up the dagger and leapt to his feet, the ache in his chest gone and the elation of power filling his soul. Fireworks. That's what it was. Like explosions in his arms and in his head. Now, he was strong. He slashed the air and approached Ellie. She took a half-step back, then stood firm.

He threatened Ed next, but old fishface kept his teeth in and stood there, as if ready to die. No fun in that. Finally, he moved to Danno and slashed at his arm. Surprisingly, he hit it. He'd expected it to shift, to dodge the blow. He knew it was fast enough. But it sat there and took the hit, a long gash opening and spilling darkness into the air.

"Gimme a snake arm or...or you'll get more of that," he said, waving the knife.

Danno shook his head, disappointed. "Give him a stone."

"We've got to try again," Ellie pleaded.

"He's made his choice. Give him a stone. He'll see."

"Shut it, all of you!" Tom screamed. "Gimme what I want, and maybe I'll let you alone."

A squish came from Ed's direction and his mouth gave way to teeth once more. His tortured voice let out two words, "Follow me."

Tom traipsed behind Ed Sharkie to the darkened boxcar beneath the lonely water tower. They climbed a tiny set of stairs to reach the door in the back. Tom had his wavy knife at the ready, just in case.

Inside was blacker than creosote and twice as smelly. "Don't play no tricks on me, Fishie."

Ed didn't reply. Instead, a light slowly formed in his hands. It was purple...or blue... It glowed but it didn't glow, more of a presence, a feeling that took shape. Silhouetted in that non-glow stood Ed, holding a box, opening it away from himself, toward Tom. The wider the box opened, the more the glow leapt into arcing lines, spitting and bouncing like rubber lightning. Tom backed up until he stumbled on the short stair behind him. He caught himself on the doorframe.

Ed's deep mouth remained open, though no words bubbled forth. His teeth were lit in frightening ways, non-light flickering across wicked rows, as if sharpening them before flowing back into the box.

"What's in there?"

"What you wanted, Tom. What you said you wanted. We don't know where they came from, but each one calls to us. Just like you. Now, they hold us here. Make us suffer."

"It'll give me a snake? It'll make me strong?"

"It'll show you who you are."

"I know who I am. And I know what I want."

"Then, take one of the stones and put it to your forehead."

The box was directly in front of him now, open as wide as Ed's mouth. From it, tendrils of hazy non-color writhed. Tom reached in and pulled out a small stone. Glowing arcs danced in his palm.

"Don't do it, Tom," Ellie said from somewhere. A hand gripped his shoulder. Tom reacted, rotating to his right and thrusting his hand, clasped about the hilt of the knife, behind his hip. He felt the blade sink in. The hand at his shoulder let go and Ellie screamed.

Tom turned to stare at her, fallen at the base of the low stair. The stream of blood running from her side, just under that light halter top, made her midriff look all the more appealing. He held the knife up in the bizarre light of his opposite hand and saw the dark fluid run along its edges. Together, metal and blood twisted and morphed into something seemingly alive.

"You don't have to do this," Ellie said weakly, clutching her side.

Tom hesitated, watching the knife, watching Ellie.

Finally, he laughed, imagining himself as a fearsome creature. "I want lion claws and snake fangs!" he cried and slapped the stone hard against his forehead. Tendrils of softly curving off-light streamed around his hand and into his eyes as the stone stuck to his head like a wet penny. Tom felt only the force of collision, no biting pain, but he was certain the stone was eating into his head. He could see wobbly fingers feathering over him, shifting reality as the stone sank into his brain.

He tried to scream, but the sound choked back against his throat.

A giant hand reached for him. He couldn't get away, though he tried, running helplessly in circles and waving his arms. The hand closed about his neck and he let out a meager squawk. It tightened and he could no longer make a sound, could no longer breathe. He looked along that huge arm, up into a glowering face. It was the face of blatant cruelty, the mouth pulled back in a grimace that showed yellow teeth, eyes hard and glassy, nostrils flaring in delighted hatred. It was his face. His face as he had never seen it.

The hand tightened again and twisted. His vision blurred and his heart pumped fiercely. The sound of cracking bones ended his sight and the tendrils of time moved.

He saw himself again, older now, unshaven and haggard, eyes blank. He knelt over the body of a dead woman, his hands about her ruby raw throat, but that distant man felt only the familiar contempt Tom had always felt when hounding the animals of his back yard. And he knew he'd done this many times, killed for the sake of killing. His hands were twisted and bloody, his soul bleak and unworthy.

His jaw fell open. He coughed and spoke a single word, "No." It didn't sound like him. He dropped the knife.

On the ground he saw Ellie once more, thought of what he'd done to her. Thought of what she was feeling, lying on the ground, bleeding.

Her body jolted like bacon on a flapjack griddle. She clutched her forehead and radiant arcs of light appeared there, engulfing her hands. Finally, a small gray stone worked its way out from above her eyes and fell to the ground in a heap of hazy light. The ridges on her back smoothed and her tail heaved, slowly fading, losing scales and shrinking back into her hips.

~

Tom sat alone in the darkness behind a ratty curtain on a boxy stage. Outside he could hear the hawker's cry: "Come one, come all. See the latest addition to the sideshow stage—Bird-Head Boy!"

The Sorcerer Climbed Her Tower
Jeff Stehman

The sorcerer climbed her tower, gathering strength with every tread. The one hundred thirteen steps were part of a ritual for her most fell magics. The room at the top had four large windows from which Anoush could survey the surrounding kingdoms. Tonight, she looked to the east.

"King Dalvos, for your slight you must be punished. A third of your kingdom is forfeit. What shall it be? Fire? Blight? Plague?"

The barest hint of fabric on fabric behind her. The corner of her mouth twitched as if to smile. She suppressed it.

"You presume much, thief."

Anoush turned. A gray-clad man perched on the sill of the western window.

"I would risk much for you, most beautiful and terrible of women." Lood pulled the scarf from his face. He did not smile. "But you would punish the man by punishing the king? Punish him, but leave the kingdom alone. His people have done nothing to you."

"They have done nothing for me."

"They never will. They care neither for you or their king. They just want to live their lives in peace. Please, let them."

"Thrice I've taken you into my bower. You think that gives you standing to petition me?"

"Thrice? You make it sound like part of a ritual."

He'd said it in jest. Anoush recognized that. She allowed a smile, just a little, and raised a brow, also in jest. Doubt crept over Lood's face.

"What do you suggest?" she said.

Lood stepped from the sill and spread his arms, presenting himself with a grin. "Punishing the rich is what I do."

There it was. Anoush's gaze lingered over his smile, and she could not suppress her own. Yet he must be kept in his place. "You would steal into my bed again?"

"I would steal into your heart."

Anoush lost her smile. Still, "Very well, thief. Punish him."

～

Lood plucked the great jewel from Dalvos's crown, leaving a score of smaller ones. With this he would ransom the people of the kingdom. Anoush was not cruel, just isolated. His love, even if unrequited, would help her understand, help her empathize. Of that he was confident.

He stepped over the sleeping guards on his way out of the treasury. They would awaken shortly, none the worse, save for a headache. As he crept back into the great hall, he struggled to keep his thoughts from Anoush. Even the smallest of missteps could be his undoing, and a distracted thief would eventually misstep. Indeed, a niggling wore at him that he already had.

He crouched against a wall. Lanterns blazed. Men with pistols and swords charged into the room, surrounding him. Their company parted, and Dalvos stepped forward.

"You must be Lood, pet to that witch."

Lood gave a theatrical bow and removed his scarf. "Your majesty, I am many things. Tonight, I am savior to your kingdom."

There were thirteen pistols aimed at him, and the king held one at ease. Lood had several tricks up his sleeve, but none to win him clear of this.

The king snorted. "Tread carefully, thief."

"You have angered the lady, oh king, putting your kingdom in peril. She was going to destroy a third of it. I urged her to go after your pride while harming no one. She agreed to be placated if I stole this." He held up the jewel between thumb and forefinger. It sparkled in the myriad lights. "A little humility in exchange for the lives of your people."

Dalvos's nostrils flared. "Hand it over, and you will die quickly. Drop it, and I will take my time."

"I see." Lood's chin lifted. "You called me her pet. Would that were true. But in the little time I've spent with her, I have learned a thing or two. If this is to be my last decision, then I choose the lives of your people." He could not deliver the jewel over to Anoush, but it was punishment she sought. Lood would deliver. He focused as she had taught him, whispered words of power, and blew on the jewel. It crumbled to dust and drifted away on his breath.

$\sim$

Sitting in her bower, Anoush watched Lood die under the fusillade. She allowed the mirror to darken to match her heart, which Lood had stolen upon first finding his way into her home.

The sorcerer climbed her tower, gathering strength with every tread. The one-hundred thirteen steps were part of a ritual for her most fell magics...

The Long Road Home
Andrew Gudgel

*I*t *was bittersweet coming down the docking tube that* extended from the ship, through the skylight and into the building, as it was my first time back in Babel since the accident. I fingered the tiny, silver Amitabha Buddha pendant that hung by a chain around my neck.

The pendant had belonged to Moustafa. He had given it to me when he'd asked me to marry him. I'd meant to say no, but rather than hurt his feelings the very day of our dive, I told him he'd have his answer afterward. I came back. He didn't.

I tightened the pack straps on my gear and started walking the mile or so to Maggie's tent—the place where all tower dives started. Behind me, Steve and his gaggle of shiny new tourists *oohed* and *aahed* and yabbled excitedly about how their datapads had all suddenly gone dead, even though they'd been briefed en-route that no electronics worked inside the building. I heard the click of spring-loaded camera shutters. Disgust filled me. Babel should be for divers in search of artifacts, not lookie-loos who've paid a wad of cash to wander a dead beehive.

I dropped my gear outside the tent.

"Maggie!" I said, ducking my head as I stepped inside. Maggie was the foundation stone of the tower-diver community: part of the government team on the first successful entry and exploration of Babel; discoverer of the ramp that spiraled down the building behind the apartments. She'd also been the first one to find an artifact—a thirty-centimeter-long bar of metal that couldn't be analyzed by any known method and which had no balance point. The government returned the bar to her after giving up on trying to understand it. Maggie had sold it to a Chinese oligarch. It made her rich—rich enough to set up permanently inside Babel and have resupply ships bring her the things she needed.

Maggie looked up from the blanket she'd been weaving. "Haimei! Good to see you again!"

She disconnected the loom from the leather belt around her waist and set the bar on the floor in front of her, then stood and held her arms out. "Come here, girl!"

We hugged. "So good to see you again," she said. "How long are you going to be down?"

I let go and stepped back. "Six weeks. I'm trying for a whole floor, solo."

Maggie nodded. "And how deep?"

"Above Mallory."

A decade ago, George Mallory had burned in on a dive, breaking his neck on one of the pillars that separated the floors of the building. The suspension lines of his bright blue 'chute had wrapped around the pillar and his mummified body now hung in mid-air between two floors. Divers used the spot to mark the point roughly two-thirds of the way down the central well that ran the height of the building.

Maggie went over to her desk and flipped open the log book, the unofficial "official" record Maggie kept of every tower dive since the very first civilian dive—hers. She ran an index finger down the half-empty right-hand page, then stopped. "Your number is 1483." She picked up a pen. "When are you leaving?"

"Tomorrow."

Maggie wrote my name, and in the next column, tomorrow's date. The last column remained empty until you returned and checked back in. There were three gaps in that column just on the two open pages. 'Chutes malfunctioned. Return balloons burst or leaked badly enough to not rise. The ground floor of Babel was flyspecked with bodies and broken gear. Including Moustafa's. I tried not to notice the gap by his name.

"Here's your cone," Maggie said, reaching under her desk and pulling out a sixty-centimeter-tall, red plastic cone. She wrote "1483" on the side with a marker, then handed it to me. I was supposed to put it at the edge of the well on the floor where I landed, preferably even with the ramp entrance, so another diver could see the floor had already been visited.

"Do you want to pray together before you go?" Maggie asked. She was a Sherpa. Her people believed every great mountain back on Earth was the abode of a goddess. Maggie had decided to dedicate Babel to Panden Lhamo, the "Glorious Goddess." At the back of the tent, there was a shrine with a hanging *tangka* and a single butter lamp.

I wasn't religious, but it was never a good idea to mess with the traditions of a place. I nodded. "Of course."

Her smile broadened. "Good. I'll make you breakfast, then I can watch you step off."

⁓

I'd been in my own tent all of an hour when there was a cough outside.

I set down the magazine I'd been reading. "Yes?"

"Haimei, you got a minute?"

It was Steve.

I sat up, unzipped the tent door and climbed out.

"Good to see you again, Haimei. Sorry to hear about Moustafa."

I nodded. It was the sort of insincere platitude I'd gotten used to in the past year. "Thanks."

"I, uh, gave my clients their briefing about Babel, but there's not a lot of meat there, you know."

I nodded again. Babel was a mystery. Nobody knew who built it on this dead planet or when—there were no bodies or records left behind. Just ten thousand doorless "apartments" on each one of its ten thousand floors. Nothing powered by electricity worked inside the building, yet somehow each apartment had a tiny fountain of continuously running water. "Yeah, I know."

Steve ran his hand through his short, sandy hair. "I was wondering if you had a minute to come over and chat a bit with my clients. They'd like to meet another diver, maybe ask you some questions."

I snorted. "*Another* diver?" I pointed at the pack sitting beside my tent, which contained my parachute, supplies, and return balloon. "I didn't see any gear in *your* hands when you came off the docking tube. How many years has it been since you last stepped off a ledge?"

Steve took a deep breath. "Look, I know you and Moustafa didn't approve of what I do, but I've got bills to pay. So if you're willing to do me a favor—"

Anger rose up inside me. "You're right on that first part: we didn't approve of what you do. I still don't." I jabbed my finger at the cluster of tents a couple of hundred meters away where a knot of tourists were talking and laughing and passing around a bottle of wine. "Look at them. You take people who have lots of money but no sense, fill them with the idea that they might *actually* find an artifact and then *walk* them down the ramp to a floor that's already been picked over a couple of times. And you still act sympathetic when they don't find anything. They'd have a better chance of winning the lottery, for God's sake."

He bristled. "Look Haimei, there's always the possibility they might find something. And this time, I'm taking them to a floor that hasn't been completely explored yet."

I shook my head. "I can't believe you. There have been three—exactly three—artifacts found in twenty years. It's not about the

138

artifacts. A *real* diver would be doing this even if there was *no* hope of a payoff." I jabbed my finger back at his camp again. "And that is what you charge these people for—false hope. And a good, long walk."

"Haimei—"

The words tumbled out of me. "They have no *right* to be here. And unless you're diving, neither do you."

Steve flushed, stared at me for a long time—eyes narrowed—before speaking. "Thank you for your time, *Miss* Wang. You have a good night." Then, he turned and walked away.

∽

In the morning, I grabbed my gear, leaving my tent for when I got back, and went to Maggie's. We ate breakfast, then prayed to Panden Lhamo for protection. Outside, I climbed into my parachute harness. Maggie did a quick inspection of my gear. I waddled to the edge of the floor and stared straight ahead. I had over a dozen dives under my belt and hundreds of BASE jumps back on Earth. Yet, I was still trembling. I couldn't help it.

"The Goddess go with you, Haimei," Maggie said beside me.

I nodded, leaned, then fell forward. As I went horizontal, I kicked with my feet against the edge of the floor and settled into a stable free-fall position. Periodically, I checked my wind-up watch. At around nine minutes of free-fall, something in the back of my mind shouted *Now!* and I pulled my ripcord. The leg straps of my harness cut into the back of my thighs with the opening shock of the 'chute. I glanced up, made sure the canopy above me was fully deployed, then pulled the handle that released my pack. It fell to the end of its tether, and then, dangled three meters below my feet. *So far so good.*

I steered my 'chute towards a floor. Timing mattered a lot now. Ten seconds out, I began yanking and relaxing my control toggles. That made me swing in slow back-and-forth arcs, like a bell. Time it right, and you swing your gear onto a floor, followed by you and finally

139

your canopy. Get it wrong and your gear may end up dragging you and your deflated 'chute off of the edge and back into the well. That's what had likely happened to Moustafa.

I nailed the landing. My pack slid across the floor. I followed, already clawing at the quick-release buckle attached to my right shoulder. My 'chute collapsed, dangling over the edge and into the well. I rolled onto my stomach, hauled the 'chute up hand-over-hand and rolled it into a ball. It would serve as my bedding while I explored.

Or wouldn't. Habit makes me always recheck my gear immediately after I land. I unzipped my pack, pulled out the smaller kit that contained six weeks' worth of food bars and an empty canteen—I could get water in any apartment. I set my provisions aside, then pulled out my return balloon gear. That's when I saw it. I always push both zippers all the way to the right. Now they were both perched at the very top of the gear sack. My heart began to pound.

The damage was subtle. You'd have had to look right down into the coupling at the top of the hydrogen bottle to see it. The pressure regulation pin had been pulled out. If I connected this bottle to my return balloon and opened the valve, the gas would come out in a single blast and shred the Mylar. My gear had been purposefully—and fatally—sabotaged. And I could guess who had done it.

A mix of cold anger and despair filled me. "You bastard," I muttered, wishing I could think of something better to say.

I don't know how long I sat, mute and numb, but after a while I began thinking about my situation. I was tens of thousands of meters from the top floor. I couldn't use my return balloon. But I had six week's worth of rations and a working 'chute. Yet, Babel was so large, even flat-out walking a single circuit of the ramp and up one floor required three days. It would take literally years to walk back up, and I only had six weeks of food. Well, I could repack my 'chute, jump down to the ground floor, and—I shook my head. The chance any gear that had fallen that far wouldn't be a mangled mess was nil.

"Mallory." The word came out of my mouth unbidden. Mallory had died jumping in. His return balloon would still be in his pack. All I had to do was jump down to his level and retrieve his gear. I slid on my belly to the edge of the floor and looked down into the well. I was almost directly above and not more than three thousand meters up from his bright blue 'chute. I was saved.

~

I took my time repacking my parachute, and putting all my gear—including the ruined gas cylinder—back in the bag. Then, I strapped up, waddled to the edge of the floor and stepped off. Mallory's 'chute grew bigger as I fell.

I misjudged my landing by a floor and pulled up too early. It took almost a week to walk around to the ramp and down a floor to where Mallory's 'chute lay tangled around the supporting pillar. My spirits rose when I saw that mass of blue nylon billowing out up ahead. In a couple of hours, I'd be up on the top floor, waiting for that asshole Steve when he returned with his gaggle of tourists. In the meantime, I'd show Maggie my bottle, and he'd be in the brig as soon as the ship returned to pick us up.

I dropped my gear, ate a meal, then lay on my stomach and slid my head over the edge of the balcony to look down. I stared at the dark brown curls on the back of Mallory's mummified head. I needed something with which to wrap his suspension lines into a compact bundle so that I could pull the body up. One of my own risers would do. I unpacked my 'chute and used my pocketknife to cut away my right riser. Then, I wrapped the yellow nylon strap around Mallory's suspension lines, braced my feet against the back of the pillar and pulled.

Even mummified, the body was heavier than I thought. Buckles on Mallory's harness tinked and clinked as I hauled him up. When the body was almost laying on top of me, I reached one arm down to his shoulders and grasped his harness. I began inching myself backwards across the floor.

When Mallory's legs cleared the edge of the floor, there was a sudden release of tension. I inched back another meter or so, then rolled onto my left side, still clasping the corpse. Nothing happened when I let go. So I stood. When I looked down, my knees went weak. Mallory's lowering line ended in a bit of frayed nylon, probably just where the line rubbed against the edge of the floor below the body. Mallory's entire pack was gone.

∾

I cried, out of frustration, fear, and anger. It was tempting to just walk to the edge of the floor and step off. A couple more of minutes of free-fall, and I could be with Moustafa. I fingered my Buddha pendant. *No.* That would be giving up. If I was going to die, I was going to die fighting Fate to the end.

I unpacked all my gear. I had five-ish weeks of food and one canteen. A full circuit around and up one level would take three days. So I could make it up roughly a dozen floors before my food ran out. I remembered hearing once that a person could go three weeks without food before starving. I guessed that walking would halve that time, so I had an additional week or so once my food ran out. That made for fifteen floors—twenty, max. And I was roughly six thousand floors from the top.

I put the food back in my pack, along with the canteen and my pocketknife to cut open the ration packs. I kept my roll of friction tape—good for mending shoes. I left the rest there on the floor—now it was just dead weight that would slow me down.

I refilled my canteen from the nearest apartment, tucked it back into my pack and zipped the pack closed. Then an idea hit me. I carefully cut open the outer plastic bags of the next two days' ration bars, removed the bars and filled the bags with water. I sealed them as best I could with friction tape and placed them carefully upright in my pack. Extra water meant extra weight, but it would help prevent dehydration. A tradeoff I thought was worth making.

I took a deep breath, thought of Moustafa while stroking my Buddha pendant. *No time like the present.* I lifted the pack, slipped my arms through the straps, and began walking back towards the ramp.

The next few weeks were monotonous. I would walk until I was tired, rest, eat part of a ration bar, drink some water, then continue. When I was really tired, I would sleep. Then, I got up and began walking again. It took three sleeps to get to the next opening in the ramp, where I would refill my canteen and packs of water at the nearest apartment. Then, I would move on. The ramp itself was featureless and curved gently off into the distance and always to the left. When I had to go to the bathroom, I would just squat in the hallway with my back against the wall. I don't know why, but I took to apologizing out loud to the vanished inhabitants of Babel for dirtying their house each time I did.

Four weeks in, I got the feeling that someone was behind me and turned around. A couple of hundred yards away I saw a gray shape, indistinct and roughly half again as tall as I was. Sometimes it seemed to walk, sometimes it seemed to glide just above the floor. My heart pounded in fear. It was at least a day to the next opening in the ramp. Fear swelled to panic. I ran.

When I couldn't run any more, I stopped and turned around. Whatever it was was gone. But I kept walking as fast as I could. I made the next floor early. I went into an apartment to rest, clutching my open pocketknife. Eventually, I dropped off into a restless sleep.

The next morning I convinced myself that what I'd seen was just unconscious fear and exhaustion coming out. I was at the edge of my endurance, burning lots of calories, getting barely enough water for days at a time. I gave myself the luxury of a nap before refilling my canteen and pouches of water. I also spent some time massaging my feet before putting my boots back on and gathering my gear. Then, I returned to walking up the ramp. I made a scratch on the frame of my pack with my pocket-knife—nine floors done and heading now for my tenth. I smiled grimly to myself. *Only five-thousand nine-hundred and some to go.*

I'd been walking for most of the day when I saw the shape again—this time, in front of me, walking in the same direction as I was, as if it had passed me on the ramp. I stopped moving, filled with a mixture of fear and curiosity. *Is it looking for me?* I kept pace with the shape, never walking fast enough to get closer, never so slow that it disappeared from sight. Once again, it seemed that sometimes it walked, sometimes glided above the floor. I trudged along until it was time to rest for the night.

When I woke up the next morning, the shape was standing roughly a hundred meters ahead of me. My heart jumped up into my mouth. I could see it a bit better now: gray and indistinct, bipedal, it had what looked like wings rising from where a human's shoulders would be. It didn't say anything, but I suddenly felt an intense wave of curiosity coming from it.

My fear became confusion, then oddly enough, a matching feeling of intense curiosity on my part. "What are you?" I wondered aloud. "Ghost? Hallucination?" I got no reply. When I started walking, it stayed a hundred meters ahead of me the whole day. When I stopped to rest, it stopped. When I continued walking, it led the way. I felt that I was being examined.

Over the next few days, I took to talking to the shape as I walked. I told it about growing up in China, my tower diving, and eventually Moustafa and the accident. I told it why I'd taken a year away from diving afterward, and why I felt compelled to come back. I admitted I had reconciled myself to dying in the futile hope of climbing to the top of Babel, yet was still afraid of those last minutes. I told it I hoped to get a chance to see Moustafa afterward and tell him I'd changed my mind in the past year about marrying him.

When I ran out of things to say, I'd go back and search for something half-remembered from my past, and begin talking again.

At some point, I ran out of food. I made sure to stay hydrated, but quickly began to feel myself slowing down. I knew I was getting towards the end of my strength when the shape began to take on other shapes. Sometimes it was Moustafa, and I called his name over and over, trying to get his attention. Sometimes it was Steve, and I was sure to catch him any second now and make him pay.

I finally collapsed near an apartment, just after filling my canteen. I was twenty floors up from where I started. I tried to get back on my feet, but my legs were too cramped to move. So I tilted my head back as far as I could. The shape stood not five meters away. I got my first close-up look at it. It *was* gray and misty and indistinct like a cloud, yet somehow also more substantial. It stood on two legs and I could see now that it also had arms. The wings I'd noticed earlier were clearer too—membranous, not feathered like a bird or an angel. The face was a pair of smooth planes divided vertically, with no mouth, nose or eyes. Yet, it cocked its head at me in an oddly human gesture.

"You'll have to go on alone. I can't go any farther," I said to it. It stepped closer. Then, it flapped its wings and hovered above the floor. I felt that same sense of curiosity, of questioning I'd felt before.

"I can't fly," I told it, shaking my head back and forth. "I can only walk. And now, I can't walk anymore." I rolled onto my back, reached up and took my Amitabha Buddha pendant off. My hands were so heavy I could barely raise them off the floor. "Here," I said, extending my right arm as best I could. "Take it. And thank you for walking with me." The world went gray, then filled with darkness.

I woke up with someone gently pouring a slurry of water and crumbled ration bar into my mouth. "Shhh," said a voice. "It'll be all right." I swallowed as much as I could before blacking out.

I came to on my own some time later, wrapped in a parachute. My right hand was cramped so badly that I had to pry my fingers open with the other. My Buddha pendant was gone, but in its place was a small, black ceramic, mushroom-shaped object.

I'd been found by Einar Gunnarson—another diver I'd heard of, but had never met. He'd been testing out a tandem-jump rig so that he could take other explorers or tourists deeper down into Babel. But because he was still working through the idea, he'd jumped in all by himself with an experimental, two-man return balloon. He told me later that as he fell, he'd just suddenly decided it was time to pull his rip-cord. Literally a one-in-ten-thousand chance he'd land on my floor.

Einar immediately scrubbed his plans to do some exploring of his own, and we returned to the top floor that same day. He took me straight to Maggie, who fed me, a bit at a time, until my strength returned. I got back to Earth a few weeks after that. My story went out all over the 'net, and I sold my artifact for a tidy sum. The authorities contacted Steve to discuss the accusation of attempted murder I made against him. Rather than talk, he stepped off the ledge of his seventeenth-floor apartment.

I'm heading back to Babel to live with Maggie. I'm twenty years younger than she is, and someone will have to take care of both her and her work when she starts slowing down. Besides, Moustafa is there—as is my other friend.

Core Craving

N.O.A. Rawle

*T*he castle foundations lay so deep in the earth that the buttresses appeared to grow out of the hill, allowing the battlements and towers to stretch heavenward. Adonis had been working on the reconstruction of the north-eastern tower since the early hours. Below him, the city, a sprawl of clay tiled roofs and church domes, slumbered in the heat. Chimeras levitating across the valley beyond turned the plain of Thessaly into a vast inland ocean. A pair of storks wheeled on an updraft.

Cutting and chipping the stones one by one, building slowly, patiently, he could feel time rolling itself backwards. In ancient times masons made human sacrifices in the substructure in the hopes the ediface would be blessed. Later, only the sweat and blood of master stonemasons was spilled to construct and maintain the fortress defenses against the city's enemies. As chief restoration archaeologist and master stonemason, Adonis's craftsmanship was a willing labor of love; his hands calloused and scarred from caressing the strata, interpreting the desire of its grain, scratched and bloodied from chiseling each block with precision.

An arid wind whipped the ashes from his break-time cigarette. He relit it and inhaled, his gaze tracing the path of the storks' silhouettes against the sky. Another swooped in, circling as if disorientated. Adonis's admiration swelled at their agility. More joined the dance, ascending until a frenzied mass flew up and away from the city. Searching for the cause of their disturbance he perceived clouds of smaller birds taking to the air, getting bearings before absconding en masse.

Alert now, he became aware of the monkeys jabbering and the wolves howling, trapped in their cages in the zoo on Prophet Elias Hill. There was a moment's silence and then nausea overcame him as he stumbled on the ledge. The roar was deafening, unnerving. To his horror the city rippled as if floating on the mirage sea, flimsy apartment blocks wavered and shuddered like tide-swept seaweed. The parapet crumbled, pulling him downwards. The agonizing rumble of the earth rang in his ears long after the earthquake subsided.

~

"I'm thirsty."

Adonis scrabbled up the bank of debris towards the sound. A huge fissure gaped in the section he'd been repairing. The wall was more than five meters thick at the base of the tower and the weight of the buttresses was above him, but fear for the life of a co-worker clouded his better judgment. He entered the darkness of the cavern with the sense that he was entering a vast gaping mouth, the jagged stone blocks like crooked teeth forming a malicious grin.

"Make a sound so that I can find you." He called into the darkness.

The earth rumbled around him. In the remnants of tepid light before the fissure closed, he glimpsed strata upon strata of stone woven through with petrified human remains: eye sockets pierced through with cork-screw stalactites and stalagmites speared limbs, pinning them against the porous rock which had absorbed their sweat and blood as it would his. The earth belched one last after shock and the tower settled on fresh foundations, satiated once more.

Annie the Escaper
Meg Belviso

*T*he tenor bell was silent this morning. That, at least, was a relief. Anne had enough reminders of her impending execution without hearing an announcement of someone else's. She shifted on the floor of her cell—or tried to—the manacles that bound her hands made movement difficult, even as the lice made it impossible to keep still.

"Bastards," she muttered to no one in particular. All of them: the ordinaries who dragged her to their chaotic services to describe to her the hell where she was going after she was hung, the crowds who would jeer at her from St. Sepulchre's Church to Oxford Road. The whining fop who called the police when Anne picked his pocket. The putrid guard who had lain with Anne in exchange for food at the prison, but failed to give her the chance to 'plead the belly' to avoid execution.

Execution. Tomorrow. Bastards.

Anne tried, pitifully, to turn herself around. If she could turn around, she thought, she would somehow also find a way out of her predicament. *Annie the Escaper!* her older brothers used to call her. That's how good she was at getting into trouble and out of scrapes. She used to dream, in secret, of the ballads they might sing of her one day, like Robin Hood, she might be, only a girl.

Struggling would get her nowhere with the manacles. She knew it well, but couldn't stop herself from thrashing. "Let me out! Let me out!" she yelled.

"Shut up in there!" a guard yelled back.

Bastards. Execution. Tomorrow.

She didn't want to die.

That night

There were no windows in her cell at Newgate, no way to mark the sun, but Anne could feel when it was night. The howling chaos of the other inmates that was by day hysterical and cruel, became lonely and doomed. This was not how Anne would have chosen to spend her last night on earth, but who really got to choose their last night on earth? Those with money, she supposed.

She stared into the blackness, listening to the grunts and shuffles of the other inmates around her. Was this what death would be like? Just blackness? Silence? Or would it be the fire and brimstone the ordinaries preached about? Anne was already in hell. Why should she fear it? And yet she did fear hell, and was ashamed.

She shivered on the cold floor. Perhaps there would be no shivering in death. The nicer ordinaries sometimes spoke of heaven. They said Anne might go there if she were truly sorry for what she'd done. But Anne wasn't truly sorry. Surely, God would know that. And anyway, even a heaven with a cozy fire complete with roasted chestnuts wouldn't be worth dying for.

A shock went through her at the sound of a key in the cell door. She hadn't heard anyone approaching, and Anne heard everything. She struggled to sit up and failed.

By the light of the candle the man held she could make out a handsome face with just a bit of beard. The kind of man Annie liked. Perhaps the devil had sent her a fallen angel to keep her company on her last night. If so, the devil wasn't such a bad fellow.

"Anne Cupper," the man said, bending down beside her. He lifted her up so she was sitting with her back against the wall. His hands were strong but gentle. "I've had my eye on you."

He spoke to her in a low, dark voice, telling her things she would not have believed. Things about monsters—vampires, he called them—who lived forever. All she had to do was let the handsome man bite her, and die—but not truly die—and learn to live off of blood.

Anne agreed immediately. Fleas had been living off of her blood for as long as she could remember. They obviously had the better way of it.

She stared into the candle flame as the stranger did his business—not so different than her encounter with the guard, really. She might even have enjoyed it if she wasn't so scared. The stranger said that Annie would wake up when it was over, but she had been tricked before by men less charming and less handsome than him. The whole thing might be a ruse, one last joke on *Annie the Escaper* before she rode off to the gallows. But if the gallows was her destination either way, she had to try.

So she stared into the candle as the stranger did his business and she prayed to whatever powers might be listening to let her live.

The following night

She woke up in the dark. Instead of the human smells of the prison—sweat, urine and disease—her nose was filled with the scent of dirt and wood. A familiar-smelling wood. The smell of the same pine box she was made to stand beside at sermons at the prison; the one she was meant to sit on as she rode to the Tyburn tree. *Coffin!*

Anne kicked out, scraping and clawing, then digging. The wood splintered under her suddenly powerful hands and feet, the dirt came away under her nails. Then she was breathing chill night air and staring up at the lovely moon above potter's field.

"They never do much of a job at burying those they hang," the stranger remarked, offering her a hand out of the grave. Anne fell at his feet and wrapped her arms around his knees. "Thank you. Thank you," she said. She kissed his strong, gentle hands that gave her life.

A month later

"What did you say your name was, darling?" the fat, wealthy man asked.

Anne shifted herself on his lap the way she knew he'd like. "They call me Annie. But I like it when you say, *darling.*"

The man invited her back to his room where the *Stranger* waited. Usually the *Stranger* jumped out almost immediately to dispatch the victim. Tonight, Anne was meant to incapacitate the man herself.

The fat man didn't object when Anne climbed into his lap and buried her face in his neck. Then, it was just a question of holding on when he objected to the biting. *Annie the Escaper* had plenty of practice hanging on for dear life when men or horses or fate tried to throw her off, and blood was so tasty and made her feel so much stronger—she should have no problem.

The fat, wealthy man struggled, weakened, and then, just lay there until his life was gone.

"Well done," the *Stranger* said, stepping out of the shadows when she was finished.

"I'm sorry," Anne said, wiping the blood off her mouth. "Did you want some?"

The *Stranger* laughed. "That's your first kill, Annie Cupper. It's all for you."

As Anne drank down the last bit of blood, the *Stranger* took money out of the safe on the wall for the two of them.

Twenty years later

They called it, *The Grand Tour*. The journey started in Dover and moved through Spain, France, Switzerland, Italy—wherever Anne wanted to go. *Why had she waited so long to see the world?* she wondered, looking out at the moonlight on the Channel from the deck of the boat.

As a child, she had never dreamed of traveling. She hadn't understood how small her country was, how easily known if she had enough time. She'd seen so much in the past twenty years. Everything but the sun, and she could look at paintings for that.

It was only natural her country was now too small to contain her. "Excuse me?"

It was a girl about her age—the age she'd been when she stopped aging. But this was a gentleman's daughter starting her own grand tour, hoping to catch a husband.

"Is this your first trip to the continent?" she asked. "Oh."

Something in Anne's face must have told the girl she was wrong.

"You've probably been all over, haven't you? You look so much braver than I am."

Anne laughed. How could the girl know that what she took for sophistication was only middle age? "What's your name?"

"Suzanne," the girl said.

She had golden hair, like a princess. Her hands were pale and delicate in ways Anne's never would be, even as a vampire. Despite these gentle touches, the girl was throbbing with life. She couldn't wait to get to France, to meet a man, to buy new dresses. Anne could hear her heart beating inside her chest. She was so excited.

She would taste delicious.

"Walk with me," said Anne, slipping her own arm through Suzanne's. There was a place on the far end of the deck that Anne had noticed earlier, a little spot by the railing behind some coils of rope, where she could attack and then, throw a body over the side undetected.

"I'm traveling with my aunt and my brother, George," Suzanne said. "He's fourteen. He wants to be an artist, but he can't actually draw..."

It didn't matter what the girl was saying. Anne couldn't hear her voice above her beating heart.

"I think you'll have a wonderful time," Anne said, moving closer. Her eye was fixed on the vein in the girl's neck, gently pulsing, quickly pulsing. Anne reached out...

...and brushed a stray ringlet of hair off of her shoulder. She stepped back from the shadows, tugging the girl with her. This girl would go to Europe, find her husband, have her children. Perhaps Anne would visit her again in 50 years when she was old, dried up and ready to die. But not tonight. The world would be a duller place without Suzanne in it.

The girl went back to her brother and her aunt with no idea how close she had come to death. Anne turned back to the water. There would be plenty of people to feed on when she got to shore.

At that moment, Anne felt she could drink them all.

150 years later

From her drawing room on Nob Hill, Miss Anne Cupper looked down at San Francisco.

"I'm thinking of going traveling again," she said, sighing.

"I don't blame you," said Lucinda. "So much riff raff in the streets." She sipped daintily from a crystal glass filled with blood. The donor, a prostitute from the mission district, was laid out unconscious on a table in the middle of the room, arms out stretched, wrists punctured.

No one knew how Miss Cupper had begun her vampire life. The most popular story had her as a favorite member of the court of Louis XIV.

"The truth is, things have become boring here," Anne said.

"Come to Chinatown," said Liu Yang. "Tong Wars. Gangs fighting over women, slave girls, money, gambling, territory. Fight on my roof last night leave two people dead. One fly right past my window, screaming. Fight over a woman. Ugly woman, but very loved. Such a puzzle."

"Crazy humans," Anne said fondly. Perhaps she would stay a while.

200 years later

"Please, don't!" the man before her whimpered. "I have a mother...nieces and nephews..."

He tried to crawl away, but loss of blood had made him weak. Once Anne would have drunk him all at once, but lately she had come to crave a little entertainment with her dinner.

He was one of those shut-ins who only spoke to people over a computer. All day in one room. Anne could barely stand being confined to a single country these days. How did he do it without going mad?

His apartment was full of crude attempts to draw wizards and superheroes, painted models and books with titles like, "In Search of Sasquatch."

"I don't want to die," the man said.

"Why not?"

The man started to cry. That, at least, was interesting.

300 years later

The plague was spreading. All the scientists and all the doctors in the world couldn't stop it. The humans just kept dying. Vampires no longer bothered hiding their existence. The revelation was anti-climactic with the world already ending. All those diseases humans had eradicated: tuberculosis, smallpox, AIDS, cancer. And now they were dying too fast to come up with a cure. The virus gave the blood a spicy kick. Too bad it wouldn't be around for long. Time to get used to drinking pigs.

Anne came across the young woman slumped on a bench on Bourbon Street. When she saw Anne approaching, she tried to get to her feet, fell to the ground and crawled.

"You don't actually think you're going to get away, do you?" Anne said.

The girl continued to scoot herself along the side of the road. Anne pinched the cuff of the girl's jeans in two fingers—and got a face full of gravel the girl had scooped up from the gutter, followed by a right hook that Anne barely avoided.

"Don't you know how painful deaths by the plague are?" said Anne. "I'm offering you something better."

"I don't care!" the girl moaned. "Bastard!"

Anne sat down beside her on the ground. "You don't want to die, do you?"

"Of course I don't want to die," the girl cried.

It had been centuries since Anne Cupper thought of her days in Newgate Prison. She hadn't wanted to die then either. The *Stranger* had come and given her life again. All these years Anne had never been moved to do the same for someone else.

"What's your name?" she asked the girl.

"Nancy."

"Well, Nancy, I've had my eye on you."

The following night

Anne had watched several humans turned, gone through the process once herself. So she knew Nancy ought to have clawed herself out of her coffin by now.

The moon was full, like it was the night or her own birth and the night she crossed the channel. She imagined how it would look to Nancy when she emerged as a vampire. Through Nancy, she hoped, all this might become new again.

Perhaps the plague made transformations take longer.

Anne held out until nearly dawn before digging into the grave herself and flinging the coffin lid open.

Nancy was dead. Not undead, simply dead.

Apparently the plague that was killing humans also immunized them against vampirism.

The human world was over. The Age of the Vampire had begun.

50 years later

Fifty years later, the party still hadn't stopped. Every night, for decades, vampires had celebrated the end of humankind. No more hiding their true natures. No more fear of being hunted. No more churches. No more silver. No more Tong Wars, Gang Wars, World Wars. Just vampires and their everlasting lives.

Anne woke up in the basement of what had once been a museum, in a sarcophagus that had once belonged to an Egyptian queen, and stumbled up into the main gallery where vampires were already dancing. There was no music—the electricity no longer worked and no one had bothered to practice playing instruments.

A small bonfire flickered in the middle of the room. Someone had pulled the paintings off the walls and set them alight. Vampires liked to watch things burn.

Anne stepped outside and snatched up a rat. Rat wasn't bad, really. It lacked the richness of human blood, but when one wasn't in the mood for rat there were squirrels, birds, and raccoons. Anne knew several vampires who had toured Africa to taste the lions and the elephants. There were plenty of them, now that humans were gone.

There were more fires outside. One had gutted an apartment house where humans once lived. Could you call it a life when it lasted such a short time? Life was endless, steady and unchanging. Humans were temporary, unstable and unpredictable.

Just think of how quickly fashion had changed in the years humans had been around. Hemlines up and down, new fabrics, corsets, knickers, skinny jeans, all cycling past in the blink of an eye. New movies, new music, new books, new ideas. Anne had completely forgotten to put on clothes this morning and no one noticed.

200 years later

Anne was back in San Francisco, but she couldn't remember for how long or why. She turned the crumbling pages of the book she'd selected at the abandoned library. The story was full of humans doing things that made no sense: fighting, as if there was anything worth fighting over. Wanting things they didn't have. Loving. Longing. Mourning.

Anne had a vague recollection of a story she had liked once, about a girl in a prison who didn't want to die. But she couldn't remember the name of the book or what she had liked about the story to begin with.

She tossed the book onto the fire and went to look for rats.

300 years later

The room had once been a meeting place for ministers and heads of state who needed a private place to talk about the fate of the world.

Once, in the mid-26th century, a government aide had used the room to practice the wedding proposal he was planning for that night. The girl said no.

In the 19th century an ambassador ducked into the room to have sex with a duke. Fifty-six years later on his death bed, the duke's name was the last word he spoke.

In 2018 an MP's teenage daughter ran into the room to have a good cry after her boyfriend broke up with her via text.

Anne sat on the floor, her back against the wall. She no longer bothered with coffins. She'd been awake for several hours, thinking, watching a spider spin a web. She was hungry, but it was a dull, distant feeling. No matter how many webs that spider had to spin, it never seemed to lose interest. Spiders were like humans that way.

Perhaps, vampires could do things, too. Perhaps, Anne could be the first. She could start a war with another vampire, or choose someone to live for. She could take an interest in clothing or music. She could write a book and learn how to print it.

She had a brief flare of something like interest in the project. Then she remembered vampires no longer read. And even if they did, she had nothing really new to say.

200 years later

The vampire wandered down what had once been a city street. Trees grew through the concrete, ivy covered the buildings. Weeks before she had met another vampire making its way through the forest. It had been so long since either one had had a conversation, neither thought to speak.

When she sensed the sun was coming up, she ducked into an empty building if one were handy, or just dug a shallow grave. When an animal crossed her path, she snatched it up, like the squirrel she was currently sucking on. She looked straight ahead, but registered very little besides potential food or things that she might trip over. She'd seen it all before, until it all lost its meaning.

She stopped. *Why had she stopped?* The building in front of her called to her somehow. Perhaps she had slept in it once. In the full moon she could make out a dome with a tower on top. Something had perhaps once stood on top of the tower, but not anymore.

She slipped in through the broken door and wandered through the huge, empty halls, stopping when she reached a spot under the dome. Things were written on the walls, but she could not make sense of any of them. "London shall have all its ancient rights." *What rights? Who was London? What did any human know of ancient?*

She dropped the desiccated squirrel and continued down some stairs. The sun would be up soon.

The vampire found a comfortable spot and closed her eyes. Strange sights and sounds passed through her mind when she did. She saw a stranger with a handsome face and just a bit of a beard. She heard weeping and the clank of chains. She smelled a nauseating mixture in the air, one she could no longer identify as sweat and urine and disease.

She dreamed she was a girl condemned to die. Tomorrow they would hang her. She would not escape.

It was a wonderful dream.

The last night

There were methods to killing vampires, though they took some time to remember.

Anne Cupper walked under the full moon. For the first time in centuries, she thought it was beautiful. She smelled the green things all around her, felt the chilly, damp air on her skin. Now that she was about to die again, she found herself living.

She walked under a great crumbling arch and found a grassy spot where she could look at the stars. She planned to keep her eyes open until dawn, to see the sunrise before it ended her. She wondered how many other vampires had done the same thing in the years since the humans died, when they discovered, as Anne did, that by killing them the plague had killed vampires, too, more slowly.

She felt nothing when the first pink streaks appeared on the horizon. She tingled when the sky turned from black to morning grey. Soon, she was just a pile of ash.

By the time the sun had risen over Tyburn, Annie the Escaper had gotten away.

Dark Ascent
Daniel Beazley

Skah shifted his weight, the discomfort in his lower back easing for a moment. Chief Elder Drahk sat opposite, sucking deeply on a long pipe and letting the thick smoke spiral lazily up toward the tent roof. The sweet smell wafted past his nostrils, but he resisted the urge to sniff. Others would take the pipe before him. He must wait his turn.

Beads of sweat glistened on the smooth head of the man next to him, reflecting the dancing flames that burnt brightly before them. Drakh took one last puff of woodbine and grimaced as he leant over, handing the pipe to the elder beside him.

Outside the wind howled. It buffeted against the leather hides, forcing its way through the door flap and toyed with the fire. The flames swayed, causing the shadows to flicker, and shrouded the edges of the tent in darkness.

Waiting patiently, Skah, watched as the pipe was handed to another who drew deeply before passing it to him. Taking it, he touched his forehead as custom demanded. The elder nodded in acknowledgment and stared back into the fire.

Inhaling deeply from the clay pipe, Skah tasted the citric tang of tobacco as it swirled around his mouth, making him feel lightheaded. He let the smoke trickle from between dry lips and wash over his head, stinging his eyes. With a shudder the knots gripping his muscles relaxed as the dry herb began to revive his body. Passing the pipe on, he nodded that he was ready.

"Welcome Skah, you who are still young of our tribe. I am chief of our people and speaker to the spirits. Tell me of your hunt so that I may share your story with the gods."

Skah let the silence hang for a moment. Drahk was older than anybody he had ever seen before. Yellow tinged the man's skin that stretched across his gaunt frame like a hide drying in the sun. Wisps of white hair sprouted from his ears.

The other elders were watching with an intensity that bore into his soul. None made a sound; there was only the haunting howl of the wind. The previous days played over in his mind, and he contemplated how best to tell of what he had witnessed.

"My Chief and council members," he said, looking at each one in turn, "what I am about to tell you I wouldn't have believed until I saw it myself. I fear it may pose a threat to the future of our people and will leave you with a great burden to bear."

He leant back against a tent pole and let his mind float adrift. After waiting for the council to gather so he could recount his tale, it almost didn't feel real now the time was nigh. With a whisper, he began to speak.

"Whilst hunting in the fens near the Garrison of Mynoth, I saw people digging amongst the foul waters. They were a strange sort, not of our race, smaller in stature and wearing black robes. Curious symbols and outlandish writing was tattooed on their arms and faces, and they spoke in foreign tongues.

"It seemed they were searching for something and it must have been of great importance to them for they were completely oblivious to everything else around. They were so intent upon their search that they did not notice me. For many days and nights, I watched them, and they were relentless with their task, not stopping to eat or sleep and drinking from the murky filth they worked in.

"On the fourth day, they found what they had been looking for, a stone tablet no bigger than my hand with a single strange rune etched upon its face. I cannot explain why, but upon seeing this, an awful sense of dread fell upon me. No sooner had they unearthed the item, then they immediately set off north, and I began to follow them."

Skah paused as he was handed a small bowl of steaming liquid. Taking a sip, he let the fiery brew ignite a warm glow in his stomach, and passed the cup to his left before continuing.

"I thought they would be easy to follow, as they had worked for days without food, but these people seemed possessed, as though death itself pursued them. They didn't stop to rest but continued north, always north, and I was hard pressed to stay with them. After two days of pursuit, my quarry slowed its pace and became more aware of their surroundings, taking care that they weren't being followed.

"In the distance, I could make out the roof tops of a small village from where there rose a tall black pillar. The dark garbed figures skulked and wormed their way towards the village, though who they thought might have been following them, I do not know. My hunting skills made it easy for me to stay out of sight, and it was clear they were not trained in the art of tracking, as they did not even attempt to cover their trail. After they had entered the village, I made my way to a nearby outcrop of rock, which gave me a good view of the settlement.

"The buildings were ramshackle huts and makeshift shelters, where people were clearly living, but there was no sense of permanence about any of it. However, the pillar in the center was perfect. A tall, black obelisk reached up into the sky, glinting eerily in the golden sunlight. It was segmented into seven separate sections, each engraved with unknown symbols and lettering. The more I stared and studied this pillar, the more my sense of dread grew, and a sickness in my stomach began to manifest.

"Another thing I noticed, there were no children in the village. They should have been running in the streets, chasing each other at play, but there were none to be seen and only an uncomfortable silence.

"As the sun sank beyond the distant hills and night cast its blanket across the land, the silvery moon gave the pillar a more sinister aura. I watched as the black-cloaked figures emerged from their hovels to come before the obelisk, carrying with them the relic they had recovered from the fens. Gathering around the pillar they began to chant and moan in some sort of ceremony or ritual. Louder and louder their voices became, like a wailing cacophony that ended abruptly in deathly silence.

"There followed an almighty bang and the air around fizzled with a strange energy as a black cloud enveloped the pillar and the figures knelt around it. The stench of death and decay was carried on this vapour, and it made me gag. When it finally cleared, a ghastly sight was revealed. Some of the cloaked ones lay motionless on the ground, but it was what came out of the smog that was truly horrifying.

"An unearthly beast stood there, twice as tall as a man. It was as though it had stepped out of a nightmare, with black skin that was tainted blood red and sickly yellow. Small curled horns protruded from its head, and the mouth was full of pointed fangs, dripping with spittle. It walked toward the worshipers, cloven-hoofed feet crunching on the scorched ground surrounding the pillar. Stooping low, the beast gathered the fallen into its arms before throwing back its head and letting out a blood-curdling scream. It was so loud, I had to cover my ears to try and repel the terror that threatened to engulf me.

"Then, as suddenly as the beast had appeared it was gone, leaving the reek of death in its wake, causing me to retch and vomit. The remaining villagers seemed completely indifferent to what had happened and continued to chant quietly beneath their black idol.

"That was when I left with great urgency, to return to our tribe and inform the council." Skah's body trembled, the terrifying abhorrence taking more of a toll than he had thought possible.

Drahk held his hands out to Skah and bowed his head, a mark of respect that was reciprocated around the circle.

"You have done well, young warrior, but the news you bring us is dark indeed. The council must sit until the sun's light may enlighten us. Go now, and walk with pride and honor, for you have done your people a great service."

Skah rose and was about to leave when he paused. "What is that place? Who would worship such atrocities?"

A low discord rippled through the gathering, but Drahk waved a commanding hand and hushed them. "How are the young to learn if we do not answer their questions?"

Silence met the chief as he eyed each of his council in turn. Not one uttered another word, and when he had come full circle, he continued.

"The place you travelled to has lain dormant for many lifetimes. It was named by our ancestors as Thashe, the birthplace of a great evil. Many moons ago the tribes united as one and attacked its people, taking the summoning stones and casting them far and wide. It must have been one of those same stones you saw the robed ones find and carry to the dark steeple."

A shiver ran through Skah, the nightmarish image having scarred his mind's eye.

"But where did the creature come from?" he pressed.

Drahk blinked and looked into the flames. "What you saw is only the tip of something truly wicked. Thashe is a tower that rises from the very depths of the bad place. Creatures that are summoned there climb its stairs to our realm. It is said that Okee himself has ascended the tower to unleash his wrath upon the people when the years have been hard and our sacrifices too paltry."

Skah felt the hairs on his neck stand on end at the mention of the evil spirit's name.

"Okee," he whispered, passing a hand over his head to ward off bad spirits. "Why hasn't the tower been destroyed?"

"Because light shines its brightest in the dark. All scales must remain balanced young one, or else there would be no equilibrium to life."

In that moment, Drahk's voice sounded ancient, and Skah wondered how many moons the old man had seen.

"Even so, shouldn't we stand guard over the place and prevent any more of these unholy ceremonies?"

His question ignited a disapproving grumble amongst the gathering. Dipping his head, he stepped back and bowed low.

"My apologies, old one, I meant no disrespect."

Drahk smiled. "There is no need for apology; understanding can be difficult for one so young. You must learn the balance, then it will become clear."

"But he is too young and unready for such a trial!" an elder gasped.

Drahk's annoyance was evident, even without the cold stare.

"This boy has witnessed more than most of you who sit around the fire. Tonight, we will forego with the tradition of our fathers and rewrite history. Skah, blood warrior of the plains people, you will prepare yourself for the most ancient rite of passage there is. When the day is new and the sun shines at its highest point, you will undertake the trial of equilibrium."

Taken aback, Skah prostrated himself on the ground, letting his forehead touch the cold earth. He had never heard of such a rite before and had no idea what it entailed, but the significance of his chief's words and the reaction of the council were not lost upon him.

"What must I do, old one?"

Baying wind filled the silence that followed, and when Skah thought that an answer might never come, he finally heard the voice of his chief rumble like thunder through the skies.

"You will descend into Thashe and walk the seven levels."

The Field Trip
Alex Shvartsman

*T**he obelisk towered over the surrounding ruins, the strange* signs carved into its sides gleaming in the afternoon sun. It was mysterious, majestic, and very, very annoying.

I walked over and joined the other students. The group waited in an uncomfortable silence, sizing each other up nervously and trying to guess if any of the others had better luck in figuring out Professor Quilp's puzzle. The stakes were high. Professor Quilp, one of the Milky Way's most notable scholars of xenoarchaeology, had room for exactly one new intern in his department at the Academy. We five were his top candidates, and this was the final audition.

Earlier that morning we were ordered to meet Professor Quilp at his office, and to bring whatever equipment we might need on a field trip. No additional details were provided, except that the world we'd be traveling to had an oxygen-based atmosphere, and we'd be back at the Academy in time for lunch. The former was great news for me as an oxygen breather; it would give me a distinct advantage over Xkinth and Eetal. On the other hand, this implied a brief assignment, and I always worked better when given sufficient time to thoroughly analyze the problem.

Professor Quilp was already waiting at the office, even though every single one of us took care to arrive early. Also waiting for us were information packets. The packets were brief, with details so sparse they might have been written by a Phys-Ed major.

The planet in question used to be populated by tool-using bipedal mammals who learned to split the atom a little too soon for their own good, a scenario so common in this part of the galaxy that there are entire digital storage units full of examples, and they are all filed under *Boring*.

Bipedal mammals account for roughly fifty percent of the intelligent species in the universe. I am one myself. And that's counting them after almost ninety percent of mammal civilizations manage to destroy themselves somewhere along the slow crawl up the evolutionary tree. It may not be politically correct to say so, but mammal cultures do not tend to create very interesting architecture, either. It's always "pyramid" this or "castle" that. Not like the sentient crystals on Galco III who literally dream their dwellings into being.

But I digress.

These particular aliens blew themselves up only a few hundred years back. That's the sweet spot for xenoarchaeologists—the radiation has abated and nuclear winter has passed, but most of the structures were still intact. Mostly there were your typical remnants of industrial civilization—skyscrapers, suburban housing and a lot of fast-food establishments. In this case, however, there was a large area that just did not fit in. It was full of oddly-constructed buildings, with a big obelisk right in the center. It wasn't housing. It wasn't a manufacturing center. Our assignment was to port over to the planet, study the obelisk and its surroundings, and come up with the best hypothesis to explain its purpose—all in one hour.

The portal delivered us a few steps away from the obelisk, in the blistering heat of a desert afternoon. We scattered almost immediately to pursue our various lines of inquiry. There would be no possibility of cooperation—after all, only a single intern position was up for grabs.

I chose to start with the symbols carved into the sides of the obelisk. I scanned them with a portable translation device. The gadget chewed on the data longer than I've ever seen it take before and gave me back nothing. Modern translation machines are incredibly sophisticated, benefiting from having thousands of language structures in their database. If there is any sort of rhyme or reason to a language, the software can figure it out. Amazed, I pointed the device at some of the signage on nearby structures and it was able to translate those well enough. Pointed back at the obelisk, the gadget struggled a few moments longer and gave up once again. I'd swear there was a little embarrassment in the *No Match* beep, but this model was not programmed for emotions. Either the message on the obelisk was encoded by the most sophisticated cipher I've ever seen, or it wasn't language at all, as we know it.

I spent nearly half of the allotted time meddling with various devices, measuring and analyzing the obelisk within an inch of its granite life. I wasn't having any breakthroughs and, by the looks of them, neither were my competitors. At that point, I realized I wasn't going to find a solution or inspiration at the obelisk and decided to port around for some additional perspective. I spent the remaining half hour examining nearby areas. As the deadline approached, I was beginning to formulate a theory. I rejoined my fellow students with not a minute to spare; Professor Quilp ported in right on schedule.

"Archaeology," he said as we gathered in a semi-circle in front of him, "is art as much as science. Any half-decent researcher will respect and study the masterpieces of past civilizations. A good explorer will figure out an occasional mystery like this one, and benefit from this knowledge. But a truly great archaeologist can count on his assistants to do it reliably for him.

"By now, all of you have had an opportunity to examine the nearby ruins and see that this structure does not fit in with the rest. The question is, *why?*

"I am now prepared to hear your theories. Eetal, please begin."

Eetal looked uncomfortable in the bulky suit that allowed a methane breather to move around in a hostile environment. At least she wasn't getting slowly roasted by the heat. Probably.

"In my estimation," she began carefully, "this obelisk could not have been built by the same people who erected these other structures. Design style, materials, and even the writing on the obelisk differ from anything else in evidence. My guess is this is an artifact of a much earlier culture that was either transported to this location as a trophy, or predates them and they chose to build a settlement around it."

I could not believe my luck. Eetal was one of the strongest contenders, and it wasn't like her to make such a monumental gaffe. Professor Quilp frowned; he was probably thinking the same thing.

"Would any of you care to disprove this theory?" he said neutrally.

"The obelisk was built around the same time as these other structures," Q'orr rushed to embarrass a rival, "as should be obvious to anyone who bothered to run the decay test." He brandished the gadget that assessed the age of structures by examining the degree of weathering on their surface. I had one, too, and so presumably would the other students.

Eetal looked as though she was ready to port out of there. "I'm Atrellian," she stammered.

The blunder made sense now. Atrellian religion claimed that the universe was only about 50,000 years old and its followers weren't allowed to use carbon and decay dating technologies that could prove otherwise.

"Next hypothesis, please." Professor Quilp hurried things along, a kindness of redirecting attention away from Eetal, or perhaps he was as eager to get out of the heat as I was.

Nevri, an exchange student from the Orion nebula, could not speak. Instead, it projected three dimensional images and, when absolutely necessary, written text. It showed the obelisk to be a subject of worship by the natives, arguing that its placement in the center of the settlement supports that theory. I got the distinct feeling he had nothing to go on, and Eetal's calamity served as inspiration for his half-baked theory.

"This does not quite work for me," said Professor Quilp. "If such an obelisk was a standard object of worship on this planet, we would find a lot more of them scattered throughout. If, on the other hand, this one was unique, a place of pilgrimage perhaps, the entire settlement would be laid out differently to accommodate the kind of traffic it would draw."

Next up was Xkinth, whose species is known for their knack for linguistics. If anyone could figure out the markings on the obelisk, it would be him.

"I did my best to translate the writing on the obelisk and came to the conclusion that it is nonsense," said Xkinth, to my relief. "The placing pattern and a lack of repeating characters suggest the builders were trying to evoke an image of an unfamiliar language rather than using a real one to communicate information. Since the writing is fake, I must assume the entire object is a work of art, created for purely aesthetic purposes and not practical ones. This would explain both its prominent placement and its singular nature."

"Not bad," said Professor Quilp, his expression not betraying whether he agreed with this theory or simply found the explanation plausible. It was my turn next.

"I ported around and found a number of structures that do not fit in with anything else we've seen on this planet," I said. "Most of them lack any obvious utility, yet are clearly designed to look visually impressive. Therefore, I would agree with the art hypothesis but build on it to suggest that this entire area is an outdoor museum or an experimental zone of some sort, where natives would come specifically to view the unusual structures as some form of entertainment."

"I like that you showed initiative by exploring beyond the immediate area," nodded Professor Quilp. "What else have we got?"

Q'orr, a gray-feathered member of an avian species, was the odds on favorite. He seemed to excel at every class he took, and was the most dangerous rival by far. He confidently laid out his theory.

"There are many clues here to suggest these aliens lived in a highly commercialized culture," he said. "As such, I find it difficult to believe they'd produce such large and expensive works of art for aesthetic reasons alone. Financial gain had to play a major role. I found some images and other small artifacts among the ruins to suggest these people acted out stories and recorded them for entertainment. My solution to this puzzle is that the obelisk and other outlandish structures are merely props that were used in the production of these recordings."

Both of my hearts sunk as we listened to Q'orr outline in detail the facts supporting his theory. My dream of interning for Quilp was slipping away. Q'orr finished laying out his explanation and triumphantly looked down his beak at the rest of the students.

"Your theory matches the conclusions reached by the xenoarchaeologists who discovered this planet," said Professor Quilp. "In fact, it matches them a little too precisely."

Professor Quilp reached into his breast pocket. "You've done very well on your tests, Q'orr, and while I'd like nothing better than to attribute that to my superior teaching techniques, I grew somewhat suspicious." He took out a small device which we instantly recognized to be a telepathy detector. Its indicator was flashing yellow, activated by an illicit mind reading.

"You've been fishing out the answers from my thoughts, and the thoughts of other professors. We needed you to use telepathy in an area almost entirely devoid of life to prove it, and setting up this field trip presented a perfect opportunity."

With a terrified squawk, Q'orr dashed away from the group and disappeared into his portal. I was pretty sure we would not be seeing him again; reading thoughts isn't just cheating, it is also a serious crime in our culture.

Professor Quilp watched him go, and then turned to the rest of us. "I apologize for the ruse," he said, "but the truth is, there is no intern position opening in my department at the moment. I will, however, consider your performances as earning each of you extra credit toward your grades this semester." With those words he was gone, undoubtedly to report his findings to the dean.

One by one, the other students ported back to the academy. I stood there a little while longer, and stared at the obelisk. Although Professor Quilp made it clear that the official explanation of its origins was the one described by Q'orr, I still kind of liked my own theory better. Perhaps, I might return to this planet someday and study it in more detail. If I can prove I am right, Professor Quilp will be very impressed.

My tentacles fondled a small metal sign I had picked up while porting around in the search for clues. It depicted what must have been the face of a native: large circular ears, a pointy nose, and a big toothy smile. My translation device was able to read its text just fine, and while it did not mean anything to me yet, I thought it might eventually yield some clues.

Someone at the Academy must be able to tell me what a *Disney* was.

Night in Nineveh
Jonathan Shipley

I was a child of the Tigris River, born in the City of the Kings. From childhood, I had been promised to the temple. I was to be different, apart from my fellow women and above them. At the age of ten, I was brought to the Avenue of Temples in Great Nineveh and led to the temple of Ishtar, goddess of love and war. Priestesses of the First Rank, it was known, spent the day in meditation and emerged from their chambers only in the cool of the evening. But the High Priestess, Ama-arhus herself, met with me on a sun-drenched porch to determine my worth.

"Child," she said to me, "what do you seek in the temple of Ishtar?"

The question confused me. The High Priestess herself confused me for she was much too young, only a few years older than I. Yet, at the same time, she wasn't. "I seek nothing, Excellency," I finally said. "I come because I have been promised."

"And what do you know of Ishtar and her priestesses?"

I shook my head. Every child knew that the Tears of Ishtar were the Blood of Eternity, but beyond that, I knew very little. I was doing as my father bid me. Was that not enough?

"No," the High Priestess answered, though I had not spoken aloud. "It is not enough, my little Onya. You must have a reason to serve or you will have little to offer."

"I offer obedience," I said meekly. That had always been a good enough reason in my upbringing.

"For that we have servants and slaves," Ama-arhus responded with a shake of her head.

Now, I felt panic. To be found wanting of the calling I had been prepared for—it would shame my father's house—and I would be married off to a fat merchant as my older sisters had been. I had never thought much about marriage, but now that it loomed real before me, I found it terrifying.

"Speak," Ama-arhus ordered. "You have decided something, I see."

"I would rather read the scrolls than marry a fat merchant," I blurted out, then stopped. I sounded like a spoiled child.

"Ah," she said. "That's a start. Above all else, a priestess must know her own mind. Come, my Onya. Let us see how you fare among us."

And so it began. Only later, did I discover that many girls were turned away by Ama-arhus, and I counted myself lucky. Only much later, as I began to see the difference between one candidate and another, did I realize it had not been luck at all.

I learned my lessons rapidly from the Mistress of Acolytes and slowly became aware of the greater truths that surrounded me. The truth trickled into me so gradually until I finally realized I was living among women far different than I. It was never said; it simply became apparent these Priestesses of the First Rank were beyond my conception. A learned and privileged class, yes, but more than that—they echoed with life and death and eternity.

One reminisced about a king dead for four generations, or another made a reference to the discomforts of old Nineveh—that pile of brick and clay, before the Kings of Assyria transformed it into the magnificent limestone capital of an empire. That was at least half a century past.

I was puzzled, but I could always retreat into the ready answers of the temple. It was the will of Ishtar—that was all I needed to know. And it was a comforting thing to know that Ishtar could work the magic of long life among her priestesses. Not all the gods were so generous to their followers. But at the same time, I sensed this was forbidden knowledge, not the proper realm for a mere acolyte. So I threw myself into my studies, happy that Ama-arhus had allowed me into her temple.

For several years it continued so—many days of study with occasional visits from my family, especially Sidra, my younger sister. We had always been close and tried to hold onto each other, even though we now walked different paths. Suddenly, all that stopped. Sidra no longer visited. I fretted for several weeks, then I heard the gossip. Sidra was to marry. All now made sense. With the flurry of wedding preparations, my little sister no longer had time for visiting, or even a proper invitation. But that I could remedy. I would go to the marriage feast at my father's house.

It was no easy undertaking.

"A feast," the Mistress of Acolytes said coolly. "You want to leave the temple for a feast."

"But it's a marriage feast, Mistress," I ventured. "My sister is to be married, and it would be unthinkable for me not to attend."

"When you entered the service of Ishtar, you gave up your old life. The temple is your family now."

I lifted my head defiantly. "Is the temple also my prison, Mistress?"

"The temple is your sanctuary, child, amidst a dangerous world." But as I continued staring, she sighed. "It is not forbidden to visit your family, though I can see no good outcome. And the time concerns me. An evening feast takes you away from the temple during the dark hours."

And there was the great difficulty of life in Nineveh. For all its beauty and glory, the Queen City of the Tigris was never safe, and became openly dangerous when the sun left the sky. Thieves, yes. Assassins, yes. But mostly it was demons. They walked the night and attacked the unwary.

"Every child knows not to venture out after dark, Mistress," I said. "I will go to my father's house in the afternoon and stay there until the following morning."

Finally, the Mistress of Acolytes consented. A temple guard would escort me, then return in the morning to collect me. And so it transpired.

On the day of the feast, I began the journey in company of a guard in a bronze breastplate, and I had no fear. The distance to the house was not great in a city where the outer walls lay a day's walk from the center, but it was still the better part of an hour. And it was a glorious hour. The golden afternoon sunlight poured downward to be reflected in the many canals. Though we did not dawdle, the sun was low in the sky as we finally reached the house, and the gate was barred for the night. A small brazier of burning cloves sat just inside the court, the sweet pungency a protection against demons. My escort rattled the gate until the steward appeared.

"But all the guests are here," he grumbled, then caught sight of me. "Onya? Child, how you have grown!"

"I have come for Sidra's marriage feast," I exclaimed happily.

"Oh, child," he sighed, but opened the gate for me to enter.

I hurried into the house and found my sister in the midst of her guests. "Good marriage to you, Sidra," I gushed, catching her in a tight hug. "I had to argue down the Mistress of Acolytes to let me come, but I could not miss your wedding night."

She was unresponsive to my embrace. I stepped back with a frown. "What is wrong, Sidra?"

But she turned and left the room, leaving me mortified and mystified. Yes, it had been too long since we had spoken, but how could my little sister deliver such a rebuff?

I wandered the once-familiar rooms, receiving only a cool reception from my family. Even my mother was distant in a way that made her into a stranger. Was it because I was now pledged to Ishtar? Her temple was very powerful in Nineveh, but why should that make such a difference? The words of the Mistress of Acolytes drifted back to me. Had she known my family had no more warmth to offer me? Was it so with all acolytes?

Coming here had been a mistake. The dancing and laughter were from a different life, a life I barely remembered. Perhaps it was I who had transformed into a cold, untouchable priestess of Ishtar without even knowing it. I continued through the house, nibbling on my favorite honey cakes without appetite. The cakes, like myself, were only the pretense of festivity. In the garden, I intruded upon Sidra with her husband-to-be. A fat merchant. Of course, it would be. Sidra's eyes met mine, reading all I was thinking.

"Yes, a fat merchant," she murmured in a low voice that only I heard. Her merchant was too intent upon his wine to notice.

"You are promised to the temple and shall live forever, cold and high, nourished by Ishtar's eternal blood. But I am promised to this." Her face contorted. "I hate you, Onya," she whispered.

I fled the garden. Sidra wanted the temple life—I had not known. But now, all I could do was leave quickly. I would not shame her at her own nuptials. I reached the courtyard, beckoning the steward toward me. "I must return to the temple," I said. "You will escort me."

He was shocked. "Not at night, child. Wait until morning."

To leave was foolish, but to stay was intolerable. "I cannot wait," I said firmly. "I am leaving now—with or without you."

Without him, it turned out. But I didn't care. I followed the street back to the market square, pausing when I saw how empty the usually bustling market was. Only then did I question my choice. *I did not handle this well*, I thought to myself, but resolved to press onward. The distance was not great to the temple district, and I was, after all, a Chosen One of Ishtar. That should protect me from thieves and assassins on the dark streets of the city. The demons I would worry about only if they turned out to be real.

I passed through the main food market and was crossing the Cloth District when I heard footsteps behind me. I hurried my pace and wove erratically among the empty stalls of the market place. The footsteps continued to dog me.

Then, a dark-cloaked man rose up before me. "You are out late, little princess," he hissed. His accent was strange, his beard was not plaited, and his clothing was rough. Not an Assyrian, I was sure, nor anyone from our sister-cities to the south. A barbarian? His eyes certainly held a manic intensity. What was this wild man doing in the Queen City in the middle of the night?

"I am a priestess of Ishtar," I told him. I tried to put authority in my voice in imitation of Ama-arhus, whose words no one ignored, but my voice sounded shrill, even to my own ears.

He gave a dismissive snort. "Acolyte, maybe, but no priestess. You don't have the power, and that makes you mine." His mouth stretched wide to reveal a predator's fangs. The hand that reached for me was clawed.

I stood frozen. *Demon.*

Yet even with my own heart pounding an erratic rhythm through my body, still I wondered, *What power does he speak of? Is it something that comes with the final vows?* But I already knew the answer. It was the power I had sensed among the First Rank. And it would not come to me with vows or in any other way, for I had reached the end of my path here in the Cloth District.

"Back, beast!"

I heard the words, saw the demon step back, then realized another man stood beside me. He had close-cropped hair and stood bare-chested in only an Egyptian kilt despite the chill of the night. A priest, I realized with relief. Only a priest would dress so.

"Go and wait at the next bridge, child," he ordered. "I shall escort you back to Ishtar when I finish here." He stepped forward and the demon shrank back.

I wasn't sure what sort of finish he had in mind. One priest against a fanged demon seemed a very bad ending indeed. But even as I ran for safety, I sensed something greater at work here.

At the bridge just beyond the market, I waited skittishly. I wanted to continue on—the temple district was only two canals away—but decided that was foolish. If I had a willing protector, I should let him protect me, if he could protect himself. The priest arrived a moment later, appearing suddenly in the dark beside me. "He broke free at the last moment," he sighed. "But I have his scent. I shall track and kill him tomorrow night. He shall drink the Blood of Eternity no more." I stared a moment too long, and he broke into a knowing smile. "Ah," he nodded. "You are too young to know the Hunt. I should have realized. But come."

Yes, I was young, but so was he, I now saw. More the age of an older brother than a father. None of this made sense—demons, killer priests, the Hunt. But I didn't want it to make sense, just to go away.

"You are a priest of Egypt?" I asked as we walked. It seemed a safe question that would not lead to demons.

"Once. Thebes. More lately I was a priest of Marduk in Great Babylon. Now that Great Babylon is in ruins, thanks to your King Sennacherib, I am a priest of Ashur here in Great Nineveh."

I mulled this over carefully. King Sennacherib, the rebuilder of Nineveh, was two kings ago. And this youngish priest had been in Babylon before King Sennacherib…and Thebes before that. It had the familiar flavor of the First Rank priestesses who were also too old for their age.

"You are very old, then," I said carefully, suspecting this was forbidden knowledge.

"Not so," he shrugged. "Not even two hundred years. A mere child compared to your High Priestess. She is the oldest in the city, as she was the oldest in Great Babylon before the Kings of Assyria became so mighty."

"Ama-arhus was a priestess of Babylon?" The concept was shocking. Babylon was our rival, our traitorous sister-city.

"Yes, High Priestess of Ishtar there as she is here. And long before that, a priestess of Isis in Egypt. All the priesthoods move as the power shifts. Ah, but you are a child and do not know these things. I should not even speak of them."

"I am thirteen summers, almost fourteen," I said proudly. "My sisters were both married at my age, and I have been in the temple of Ishtar for over three years. I am no longer a child."

"But a child in the ways of the temple," he insisted. "And you shall remain so until Ama-arhus decrees otherwise."

I accepted that. In truth, I had enough revelations for one night. Power, demons, two-hundred-year-old priests—these I would need to think on.

I wasn't given much time. The next day, Ama-arhus herself summoned me to her sunny private porch overlooking the Avenue of Temples. "Sit, Onya," she said. "It is time that we spoke."

I sat on the carved stone bench across from her, noting again how she looked much too young to be First Rank, let alone the oldest in the city, as last night's guardian claimed. And she did not look Egyptian, though she wore heavy kohl around her eyes in the Egyptian style.

"Bezhet says you had an adventure last night," she began.

"Is Bezhet the priest from Babylon and Thebes?"

She nodded gracefully, but her eyes were not happy. "His tongue was careless, but he did well to save you. Now, I must attempt repairs where his wagging tongue has confused you. What did Bezhet say last night?"

I shifted uncomfortably. "That he came from Babylon and Thebes many years ago. That you, Excellency, were High Priestess in Babylon and priestess of Isis in Thebes, that you are the oldest…that I am a child too young to know. But none of this came as a surprise, Excellency. I have seen for years that the First Rank are much older than they appear. I have always assumed the Tears of Ishtar fall bounteously upon them."

Ama-arhus sat silently, contemplating my answer. "It appears," she said finally, "you are no longer a child in these matters. Your own eyes have shown you the truth, even before Bezhet. Now, you cannot move backwards to innocence, even though it is not yet time to move forward to knowledge." Her eyes fastened on me again. "What of your attacker?"

I sucked a breath, not wanting this conversation but having no choice. "It was a demon, Excellency, with the form of a man, yet with fangs and claws. I did not know until that moment that demons were real."

"Inconveniently so," Ama-arhus murmured. "Bezhet will dispatch the demon and all will be well again."

"All will *not* be well, for if one demon is real, then many more are as well." I shivered. "I should never have left the temple yesterday. I never shall again."

"Most awkward, my Onya. Most awkward." Ama-arhus rose and began pacing. "A priestess who cowers behind the temple walls has no strength, yet what else can one expect of a child? There is but one solution to this situation. You shall take up the Hunt and kill the demon yourself. Only then shall you find your strength."

"Excellency..." I began, horrified.

"No, I am decided, my Onya. You and I shall go hunting."

If it had been any other than my High Priestess saying this, I would have protested such madness. I was not yet fourteen, and Amar-arhus, ancient or not, was a mere slip of a girl herself. Yet, the two of us would hunt down a demon. *Madness.* There was no other word for it.

I waited on the porch as Amar-arhus summoned guards and servants, issuing orders in a continuous stream. The gist of the matter, I quickly realized, was not that we were hunting a demon, but rather that the High Priestess was leaving the temple for the afternoon. Apparently, this was not often done. From the interchanges, it would seem the entire temple would collapse without her guiding hand, yet I had never seen her anywhere except her porch, basking in the sun.

Within the hour, we were walking the baked clay streets of the city, heading towards the Cloth District where the demon had attacked. My fears were swallowed up in sheer wonder as to the nature of the Hunt. Amar-arhus bore no weapon. I remembered that last night Bezhet had also been unarmed.

"How are we to fight this monster, Excellency?" I asked as we approached the market. "You have no weapon." I understood nothing about what we doing, especially why we were alone. Ishtar's High Priestess should be traveling on a litter with a retinue of guards and retainers.

"Ah," she answered with a sly smile. "So it might seem. But the great weapon is the mind. There are gifts of the body that will come, but never confuse those with the great gift of the mind. Without that, none of us would be any better than these rogue blood-beasts from the hinterlands. These rogues are little more than rabid dogs. No control, no vision, no sense of eternity. We purge them from the city, yet they keep coming. Today, you shall see how one uses the mind, my Onya. The rest will come in due course."

And that was meant as an answer? I walked on in silence for fear I would let slip her answer made no sense. We slowed as we reached the market square and stopped at the exact spot of the attack. She placed her palm against my forehead and said, "Remember—every detail, every sound, every smell."

Suddenly, it was night again and I was alone. The demon, eyes glowing red, appeared, cloaked as a man, and reached for me with clawed fingers. The sweet odor of decay surrounded him and he salivated as he opened his mouth to expose long, wolf-like fangs. His wild hair was covered with fine, golden flecks that also fell from his robe as he moved. Bezhet appeared beside me in a sudden gust of wind and the odor of decay intensified. I ran…and the night faded to afternoon.

"Definitely a tribesman of the northern steppes," Amar-arhus murmured, more to herself than to me. "And there was chaff in the folds of his cloak. He sleeps in the old granary, I think. It fell into disuse when the new one was built and would make a perfect nest."

I accepted her explanation without question. I merely followed as we cut through the central gardens toward the older section of the city that predated King Sennacherib's rebuilding.

"These gardens are one of Sennacherib's better ideas," Amar-arhus offered conversationally, as though we were not seeking the lair of a demon. "There is much to be said for defeat in battle when it forces a king to abandon the battlefield for more mature concerns. If Sennacherib had been a better warlord, Nineveh would never have been built in such glory."

"But Great King Sennacherib *was* a great warlord," I protested. "He conquered all to the south and the west."

"To the south, yes, though the destruction of Babylon was excessive and unnecessary. To the west, he was less successful. Assyrian historians tell the tale differently, but he lost the greater part of his army at the walls of Jerusalem and had to abandon his campaign. For that we should thank the Hebrews, troublesome though they may be with their stiff-necked independence. Ah, here it is."

The neighborhood where we had arrived was run-down with streets full of beggars. I saw faces turn in our direction as we passed, eyes narrowing at the fineness of our robes and the gold of our armbands.

"We will never leave this place alive," I whispered desperately.

"The mind is a weapon, my Onya. The mind," she replied and pushed into the abandoned granary.

The inside was dark after the golden afternoon sun. I stood a moment, letting my eyes adjust, then hurried after Amar-arhus across the debris-littered floor. She paused at the first grain bin, listened, and moved on. Three more times it was the same. After pausing at the fifth bin, she nodded. "Here."

She stood back and closed her eyes. A power welled up within her and the bin exploded, rotten wood scattering in every direction. I screamed, then stopped. Nothing had touched either of us.

Inside the bin, a dark figure writhed in the dim light that now filtered in. I recognized the cloak as the demon's. What would happen now, I wondered. Would he attack? Though it was not night, surely this intrusion into his lair would rouse him. As I stared, a shard of wood lifted from the littered pieces and came directly to my hand. My fingers fastened around it of their own will, and I was pulled forward to the twisting figure. The stench of decay became overpowering. I saw the red slits of his eyes fasten upon me as I approached, and I feared an assault. The shard shifted in my hand and drove straight into his chest. A piercing scream erupted, then faded as the demon spat blood and crumpled into dust.

I turned to Ama-arhus, who had stood unmoving through all this. This was the weapon of her mind?

"You begin to understand, my Onya," she said. "Forget your fears. Embrace the truth you have discovered today. This was no demon from the Underworld, but a mere blood-beast, easily destroyed by your hand. We hunt these creatures and end their miserable existence. Yet, without the gift of the mind, we of the temples would be little different than they."

I could barely comprehend this new truth, so monumental was the change in my vision of the world. The mind was a weapon—I saw that it was true. Still, I could not see how the temple priests could be like this demon, even though, now more than ever, I accepted the word of Ama-arhus.

Then, she asked, "What do you seek in the temple of Ishtar?"

The question from our first meeting.

This time, however, I had an answer. "I seek the gift of the mind," I said.

Amar-arhus nodded. "Well chosen, my Onya. You have taken the first step to Eternity."

For the Feather Dusters
Briana McGuckin

*I*n his tower, paintings leaned against every bit of wall. A waterfall of paper started on a center table and fed into a stack of books on the floor. The paintings, all, were from admirers. The papers were covered with poetry. He'd looked at the paintings and read the poems—once—and let them lie where you see them. They were the difference between walking to the tower's only window and stumbling there. They gathered dust.

Today, he had received a letter. Now, it seemed he would also be receiving its author. She meekly ruined a scene fit for postcards, leaving apologetic little footprints in the snow. He turned away, his long hair flying around his face like the curtain of a recluse with a solicitor at his door.

Her letter was on the table. The newest thing in the whole room, it shone, startling as an electric light among the ruins of ancient Greece, illuminating the deepest longings of a tiny human's heart. Dirty laundry, in other words, that other men—lesser men—might have sniffed in their perversion. He picked up the sheet as if handling something poisonous and looked it over.

Her presence was louder than any knock her little hands could produce; all at once he knew she was in the room, and here he was holding her damn letter. The sentiments she'd articulated on the page were there on her face, and for a moment he wasn't sure what he was holding: a photograph, a mirror? *An anti-mirror*, he thought, casting the letter down onto the table. *This is what I am* not.

"Why write," he sighed, "if you intend to make a house call?"

"I don't have anything new to say," she replied, not really looking at him. "I'm just here to collect your response. I didn't think you'd take the time to pen one."

He wouldn't have, and the cruelest part of him wanted to tell her this. But he didn't understand his own anger, and suppressed it with the sort of fear specifically reserved for dealing with the unknown. She was not *mean*; why did he feel so meanly toward her?

Just yesterday they'd candied apples at the fair. For her amusement, he had also candied his own finger when the vendor's back was turned.

"Or do you have nothing to say?" she wondered, for many moments had gone by. She sounded almost hopeful, and it occurred to him that her openness was not exclusive of pessimism. She knew she was doomed, and he was sorry for her. *Poor thing*, he thought, *with a heart open so wide that it's indefensible.*

"It's not what you want to hear," he told her.

"Better say it quickly, then," she said, her nod ending in a little bow, so that she offered him her neck. As if this were a gallows.

"You have no idea who I am," he obliged—cutting, but with mercy in mind, to end her suffering.

"I'd like to," she said, still facing the floor. "This is my way of saying so."

"You've written that you love me," he insisted, hacking at her resilient hope.

"If that's hasty, then I love what I think of you." There was new energy to her now that she'd gotten a taste of the pain. His first strike had not been a clean break and she wriggled like a beached fish— aware of the coming loss of everything dear and fighting all the harder because it was too late to stop it. "You're not like the others. You're better. You hold yourself to a standard and, thus, you meet my own."

He held up a hand meant to stop, not offensive language, but imminent self-harm. She might've been clawing at her own neck, the way he looked at her. He was not a placating man, but he did his best, widening his eyes.

"If it's my code of conduct that grants me the—honor—of your affections, then you yourself make our courtship impossible." He was trying, *trying* to be soft, but could only do so much with words necessarily hard: "I have done nothing to earn your love. I have only been myself."

He made himself look at her, to be sure that she was looking back, when he said: "I don't appreciate you. I never have. It mightn't offend you now, but it would—and should—if I were your husband."

When she glanced down he let her, turning himself back toward the window. It had begun to snow again. The rain went where it was sent, no matter how cold the atmosphere; it simply hardened and hoped for the best. He understood that she was crying.

"You think you're safe up here," she said, a fact suddenly understood. "But you're just a stranger to yourself."

Her voice trembled, not with weakness but with restraint. Perhaps she was not so small, and was only folded up to look that way. "Poor thing," she said, "with a heart closed so tight that it's impenetrable."

He did not mean to watch her go. But he did not move away as she passed below the window, trudging through the drifts, punching holes with her boots. The snow was thick in its descent. It bedecked her hair, blurred her lines. It buried her kindly, like an anesthetic, though for whose suffering it was administered—hers or his—he wasn't sure.

She was gathering dust.

The People's Avenger
A Nalo Thoran Story
Robert E. Waters

*F*alco Creed hated Korsham City. A dirty, grimy, smoke-*ridden river town, too gangly and too loud. Its filth and humidity worked its way into every fiber of clothing. Falco scratched away the sweat on his neck and dreamed of the south. The silver and jeweled spires of his Brenian home gave him comfort.

Jandaya was a wonderful place for thieving, pilfering, and burglary. Jandaya was a place where a thief like Falco could ply his craft with honor and distinction. Korsham, by contrast, was a place for the dead and the dying, the down-trodden and disheveled. But he had accepted this mission and was determined to see it through, despite the inhospitable surroundings. *Beware Korsham assassins*, his king had warned, especially the one named Nalo Thoran.

Nalo Thoran. Why, the very sound of it was girlish and frail. If he were an assassin of skill and import, he'd wear a better name. Falco could not decide whether to kill the great Nalo with a knife or a chuckle. *When I face him,* Falco wondered, as he slipped through a sewer grate, *will the sight of him make me cringe, or laugh?*

He moved quickly through the sewer, carefully navigating the dank tunnels, though the stench tested his resolve. He was careful not to attract the attention of any rats. Rats were the extension of Nalo—his ears and eyes. Like a million legged legion of chittering soldiers, their loyalty to the assassin was unshakable.

Or so the songs proclaimed. Falco was not about to prove them wrong tonight.

He had studied maps of Korsham City carefully before accepting the job. They were old and unreliable, but he had studied so many maps in his life he could see mistakes and make corrections. Sewers were often the easiest to negotiate; all the junctions and conduits were neatly laid out, all major lines running slightly down-slope east to west before spilling into the Gold River. Open sewers plagued the poor quarters, and Falco knew if he kept moving forward, left then right at each juncture, he would miss the unspeakable waste of the city's weak and infirm and reach his destination with ease…if nothing got in his way.

Something buzzed across his ear and struck the crumbling stone of the sewer wall. Falco ducked and peered into the darkness, but saw nothing. "So the game is on," he whispered. He crouched low and quickened his pace.

The lip of stone he traveled was slick, but it was better than the foul gutter below. For a moment, he wondered if Tuly's Egg was worth the risk to his life. But as another buzzer shot through his hair, missing his scalp by a mere inch, the answer was clear. *I must risk it all for this. There is nothing more important.*

Someone was chasing him, though he could not hear or see anything. Was it Nalo? Possibly. But if so, it did not fit the legend. Nalo was a choker, one who gets up close and personal. He looks into your eyes as they pop from suffocation. That was his style. This thing in pursuit attacked from a distance and was, dare Falco say, a terrible shot.

Another turn and his flight ended at a stone wall. *Damn!* This was not supposed to be here. *The channel should go another twenty feet at least.* Falco searched the map in his mind. A mistake. He hated making them, and he could not afford any on this run. What to do? Another buzz shot over his head, and then two burst into his side.

He screamed, not because the little darts punctured the skin, but from the surprise of it. He fell to his knees and pulled one out of his side. Thankfully, the leather armor around his chest had prevented the poisonous tip from finding flesh. He screamed again and toppled over.

He curled into a ball and studied the dart carefully. It was a flechette of slender mahogany tipped with a porcupine quill and fletched with feathers of the highland red macaw.

He pinched the dart, careful not to let his fingers touch the poisonous tip. He began to twitch and shake. He even let spittle drop from his lips. He was cornered like a fox. And what does a fox do when cornered?

Then, a figure was standing beside him. He kept twitching, but looked up and tried to make out the shape. A woman, slender, dressed in tight black clothing with bamboo blowpipes tied to her waist. He could not make out her face, but he didn't need to. He fixed his eyes on her right thigh, and waited.

"Huh!" the woman grunted, and knelt down for a better look. "You aren't so tough."

As she turned him over, Falco jammed the dart into her leg. She screamed. Falco jumped up and drove his boot into her chest. The woman fell back, squealing, grabbing her chest, her thigh. He followed, smiling proudly into her doomed face. "You foolish little girl. Why did you come so close? You forgot your strength, and now, you will pay for it."

A swift kick to her chin and she fell into the stinking muck. Falco watched as she tried to claw out, but the poisoned dart did its work and her arms and legs stiffened. A few more desperate gasps, and then, she slipped under the water.

Where to go now? He stood there a moment, his hand upon the small, smooth lump inside his tunic. His thumb brushed over it carefully. It was safe. The fake was still in its nest and waiting its new home.

Relieved, he returned to the last juncture and looked up. Faint moonlight cut through a water grate. He sighed. He did not want to go to the surface yet. He had anticipated at least another hundred yards before ascending. But there was no other way now.

"Damn my terrible luck," he said and climbed up.

Luck had always favored the Brenian Fox. He was a legend in his own time, and more than one leap from certain death had given him a reputation that rivaled any cutpurse in the Kingdom of Brenia. The son of a wealthy merchant and the black sheep of three children, Falco had always found fortune in the jewelry boxes of wealthy widows. At age thirteen he had killed his first man. Killing came easy to him after that, though he preferred keeping it clean and simple. The measure of a good thief was his ability to get in and out quickly, leaving no traces behind. His ability to do that over the course of two decades had brought him to the attention of King Joseph of Brenia, and to the muggy streets of Korsham City.

He stopped and stared out of the drainage slit. A quiet, narrow side street. He could hear a distant clattering of horse and carriage. He waited until the sound dissipated, then pulled himself up through the slit, tearing the sleeve of his tunic. He cursed, looked both ways, righted himself, and slipped across the road to a pool of shadow between buildings. By the map, Artifice Street lay due north two blocks. A left on Artifice Street, three blocks, then a right onto Treasure Lane, and up to the pearl white walls of Korsham's famed art emporium, the Goryr.

He ran. The thick, humid air made running difficult, and Falco's breath grew heavy. He stopped again before an alley. To his left lay the flickering lights of a bustling road of taverns and brothels. *It might be wise to go straight through it*, he considered, *instead of slinking in darkness*. There would be light there, and in the throng of people, Nalo's agents might lose sight of him.

He straightened his clothing, tucked his knife away, checked the fake in the pocket near his heart was secure, and made for the light. He stepped into the street and was immediately swarmed. People moving, pushing, and tugging their way from one display to another. Buyers, sellers, drunkards, urchins, and too many others to count. In the midst of it all, Falco blended in. The commoners were dressed simply in earth tones, and his own attire matched perfectly.

As he walked, keeping his eyes fixed forward, he imagined himself the late, great Brenian thespian, Guy de Porason, or, the Purple Dragon of Agonetta. It was so easy mimicking a Korsham citizen…a creature whose mind was bereft of sophistication and finery. Despite a few inconveniences, this was proving to be one of the easiest runs of his career, and Falco allowed himself to smile.

But as he turned left onto Artifice Street, dirty arms shot out of an alley, pulled him into shadow, and slammed him against a wall.

"What do we have here?" a raspy, whiskey-laden voice said. "A southern tourist, perhaps?"

Dirty, unshaven faces pressed in. A street gang. Mere criminals. Falco's nostrils flared at their foul breath and he tried keeping his belly still against the threat of a rusty blade. But obviously this was no random act of muggery. No. These thugs knew who he was, and had been waiting.

"You'll give us your coin, Brenian, and whatever else you have," said the leader, a tall, starved ghoul whose dry lips twitched, "or I'll gut you."

"Don't hurt me, mister," Falco said in as frail a voice as possible. "They—they're in my left pocket."

Be like the fox. . .

The leader stuck his boney hand into Falco's pocket, and before he realized he'd been tricked, Falco drew a blade and split the man's face.

The man howled and fell back, clutching his bleeding cheeks. Before the others responded, Falco struck a young boy, driving the knife into his chest. The boy whimpered and fell to the ground. Falco booted the thug at his left in the groin, and then, finished him off with a stab through his back. Falco pulled the knife free and slashed the air, but the rest of the gang had scattered down the alley and into the swelling crowds.

Falco wavered a moment in the middle of the bodies. He watched a final breath escape the boy's mouth, checked the fake in his pocket, then turned down Artifice Street.

What's the matter with me? Perhaps it was the dank, muggy environment of Korsham, or perhaps it was the thought of Tuly's Egg. Whatever it was, he was not pleased. It was uncommon for him to kill so many on a run. Unseemly, in fact, for a thief of Falco's reputation, but of course, wasn't that the strategy of his enemies, of Nalo, to keep him bouncing from one engagement to another? To wear him out, physically and mentally, before he reached the museum? Yet, he had dispatched them all quickly enough, so why worry? *If this is the best they can do...*

Artifice Street was less crowded, and Falco made good time. There were crates and barrels, bolts of cloth, and piles of cobbles he could hide behind. Some passers-by gave him looks, others cursed as he pushed them aside, but most kept quiet and went about their business.

As he drew toward Treasure Lane, the air stilled and the street cleared. Falco breathed deeply, and lingered at the corner to see what lay before him.

It was a normal street, cobbled, though wider than most. Falco squinted through the faint lantern light dispersed evenly along the road, and saw glimpses of the Goryr—a massive white structure, the tallest building in the city, its spires piercing the evening fog as it rolled in off the Gold River. *Where did Korsham get the money to build it?* But of course he knew. They'd built it off the blood and suffering of the Brenian people.

How Korsham had gotten the best of Brenia in the last war was a mystery to Falco. Some claimed that it was the poor decisions of the generals; others gave humble credit to the voracious fighting spirit of the Korsham soldiers. Falco did not know the reason, and did not care. The defeat was just a distraction now for the historians. The only thing that mattered to him was to right the greatest wrong, to seek passage into the Goryr, and reclaim, by right of the gods, what belonged to the Brenian people.

But how to get inside? He'd studied crude sketches of the building's interior, rough-outs from the memories of visitors.

Whether they were accurate or not was of great concern, and as Falco moved slowly up Treasure Lane, pressed tightly against the buildings that flanked the road, he tried to imagine the interior by studying the exterior.

The Goryr had rich, ornate walls, angular and garish. Torches lined the museum's front colonnade, and flickered in the cool evening fog like a hundred mad eyes. Around the building stood a tall, wrought-iron fence, with narrow gaps between thick black bars. There were two entrances, one opposite the other, whose iron gates were guarded by men wearing hauberks, chain mail, and steel sallets. Locked tight against their sides were long, thin halberds. They seemed sincere and determined to defend the city's treasures, and Falco admired their resolve. Which entrance to exploit didn't matter. He could jump the fence at the side of the building, but might draw the attention of both guard posts. Having to deal with four halberdiers and Nalo at the same time was hardly an option, so he settled on the closest entrance.

He cupped his hands over his lips and threw his voice into a nearby doorway. *Boys*, the detached, feminine voice cooed. *Want to play?*

The guards heard the soothing voice and looked at each other in confusion. "What was that?" one asked.

Over here, the voice said again, *I'm so lonely.* Falco made the voice coo and moan like a woman waiting to receive her lover. *I'll take you both, if you like.*

Grins on the guards' faces broadened, and one lowered his halberd and began walking toward the voice.

"Wait!" the other guard hissed. "We can't leave our post."

The anxious one shrugged away his partner's hand. "Come on, let's do it. I'm bored, and I could use a little."

They stood there a moment, unsure of what to do, and Falco continued plying them with the soft sounds of an eager woman. Finally, their youthful curiosity and lust prevailed and they moved away from the gate, holding their weapons low.

As they disappeared into the dark doorway, Falco could hardly contain his mirth. Throwing his voice was a trick that he had learned from the Jade Parrot of the highlands. That, coupled with a bit of dark mesmerism acquired from a Subian Gypsy, and these guardsmen were hugging and kissing each other in the darkness, each believing the other was the woman.

Falco moved behind them, slipped out his blade, and drove it into a guardsman's neck just below the leather strap of his helm. He pulled out the wet blade quickly and stabbed the throat of the other man before he could scream. The thief fell back to keep from being spattered by blood and watched the two men gasp and clutch their mutilated throats. They looked at him, eyes wild and scared, knowing that they have been tricked. Falco watched them die.

Looking at the guardsmen, Falco realized this was no longer a mission of thievery. From the moment he had killed the blowpipe assassin, it had changed. *Perhaps it had never been one of theft,* he thought as he turned towards the iron gate of the Goryr, thumbing the fake tucked securely beneath his tunic. Indeed, it was now a mission of revenge, of national honor. *Let Korsham suffer for its crimes, and let them see the cold and violent retribution of the Brenian people. I've passed the point of no return. I'm no longer a thief. I'm an avenger.*

He scaled the gate, taking care not to cut himself on its iron tips. He dropped into the museum yard and ran through the lit colonnade and into the glowing recesses of a hallway whose vaulted ceiling was painted with lively murals of ancient battles. Some of the scenes depicted Korsham knights in golden plate plowing through ranks of Brenian pike. Falco scoffed at that notion. Korsham may have won some battles, but they had never had an easy time against Brenian footmen.

Falco reached a door and turned the handle. Locked. He delved into a pocket on his belt for a set of tiny Blue Lark rib bones. He knelt and pressed them into the lock, twisting and turning the bones until he felt the tumblers fall into place.

Next, Falco opened the door slowly, pushing it against its hinges to reduce creaking. He crawled in, then rose and moved softly across the wooden floor. Faint torchlight pushed against the shadows, and Falco could make out the size and shape of the room. Another hallway, but shorter this time, leading to a broad flight of stairs. In the center of the stairs lay a red carpet, thin and worn, but clean and presentable. Falco crisscrossed the hall, jumping from shadow to shadow, then took the stairs three steps at a time. His heart was bounding, his mind racing.

As his eyes adjusted to the weak light, he saw the paintings and sculptures that adorned the walls and side alcoves of the museum. Splendid spoils of war—artifacts, painting, sculptures—some most assuredly Brenian—taken in sieges of Frothinghall and Mantistein such as Hormer's *Fly of Five Heads* and Billton's famous *The Cage of Many Souls*. Falco's mouth watered as he yearned to steal back such wonderful pieces, pieces that would bring him great wealth and prestige in the Brenian underworld. But none of that tonight. There would be time in years to come for personal rewards.

Then, he felt it. Like the sharp song of a Ruskin Jeweled Grosbeak, Tuly's Egg called to him—over to the right and down the hall. The sensation was so strong he felt like crying, and he leaned against the wall to catch his breath.

He turned a corner, down a flight of stairs and into a small, square room. In the center of the room was a wooden pedestal, and what lay on it was brilliant. Oval, bright white, shining, and smooth. Smooth, except for a fine, jagged crack that encircled the petrified egg at its belly. The artifact called to him, and Falco answered by bounding to the center of the room, removing its glass dome and picking it up. His hands shook as he suddenly remembered the rules governing the handling of Tuly's Egg. Human flesh was forbidden to touch it. To handle it one must have gloves or a cloth. Falco's heart sank at his stupid, childish exuberance in the midst of such history and power.

"Please forgive me, Great God," he whispered as he ripped a piece of cloth from his tunic and wrapped it gently around the egg.

He then pulled the fake egg from beneath his tunic. It was a petrified egg of the same color and smoothness as the real egg. It even had a hairline crack running its center, and Falco held them side by side. At a glance, even he could not tell the difference. The artisan who had crafted the fake had forged it from memory alone, from details of stories heard as a child. That's how strong the feelings were in Jandaya for Tuly's Egg; that's how strong the connection ran. No one outside of Brenia would ever know the difference between the two. But Falco knew. He could feel the difference. The fake egg in his bare, left hand was cold and limp. The real egg in his right—even through cloth— was warm and powerful, and as he looked at them, the real egg began to glow.

Tuly's Egg glowed hot white, and one by one the lamps, fixed at intervals along the walls, flickered to life.

Someone—*something*—was behind him–a suggestion of shape, a sliver that had moved out of somewhere and floated forward without sound, without volume or form. Yet it was there. He knew it. He could smell fresh lemon juice. Falco turned and faced the intruder.

A thin creature stood before him, such a frail, emaciated frame as if it were Death himself, black cloak flowing to the floor like the dark sewer water. A pale face peering, motionless, out of the cavernous space created by the hood pulled forward. The Brenian Fox looked into the vacuum of that face and felt true fear.

The face smiled. "You are a difficult man to stop, Falco Creed. Difficult, indeed. But I'm confused. You wasted a lot of energy and lives out there. Not the kind of behavior associated with one of stealth and secrecy."

Falco answered through his fear. "If the stakes are high enough, Nalo, a thief may adjust his tactics."

The Dark Breath-Stealer considered that for a moment, then nodded. "But so much bloodshed for such a silly little thing." Nalo extended a long, thin arm and pointed at the egg which lay in Falco's right hand.

Falco grunted. "You don't know as much as the stories claim, assassin. This *silly* thing, as you call it, means more to my people—and to *me*—than just about anything else in the world."

The assassin's face twisted.

"You don't believe me, Nalo?" Falco continued. "You don't think that a man of my profession should care so much for matters of state and national pride? Why should a thief care for nothing more than the color of gold, eh?"

Nalo shook his head. "I didn't say that." The assassin moved forward and the Brenian Fox countered by moving back and around the pedestal, keeping the eggs clutched tightly in front of him. "But you must have known the futility of your mission. You must have known that I would never let you leave alive…with the real egg."

With those words, Falco scowled and moved towards his foe, placing the fake egg onto the pedestal. He thrust the real egg forward and said, "Why do you care so much, Nalo? What business is it of yours?"

"I've no personal interest one way or the other," Nalo said. "If it were up to me, I'd be home right now sleeping soundly. But it isn't my choice. You know that. It's the choice of my Guild. Someone doesn't want this trinket stolen, and therefore, neither do I."

"Look at this egg, assassin," Falco said, holding it up as if offering it to the sky. "To you and to your people, this egg is just a spoil of war. To us, to the Brenians, it's the very symbol of our creation."

They circled each other around the pedestal, testing the other's resolve, looking for weaknesses. "We have nowhere to go, Falco, so enlighten me. What is so important about this egg?"

"You aren't worthy of the story," said Falco, "but very well. Tulyraptor, the Brenian Creation God, had wings of gold and he soared over the barren lands in search of a place to rest. But looking down, he realized that the ground was vast and barren, without life, trees, people, and he grew sorrowful. In his grief, Tulyraptor laid an egg, and he took that egg and cracked it over the peak of a mountain and the yoke poured over the land and made the trees, the streams, and the people. This egg—" Falco raised it even higher in his right hand, "—symbolizes the moment of Brenian creation. This egg—why are you laughing?"

Nalo quivered under the black cloak, and more snickering came from beneath his hood. He raised his hand. "Forgive me, Fox. I don't mean disrespect. But the idea that Brenians are descendant from the egg yolk of a tired god…well, that explains a lot."

The Fox snarled and backed away, wedging the egg securely beneath his tunic and leather armor. "You vulgar swine! You're just like this city. Crude, dirty, and unfeeling. Go ahead, make light of my heritage. I knew you wouldn't understand. You have no soul. You can't possibly appreciate kinship and tradition."

Those words touched the assassin. He halted and stared out of the emptiness of his hood, silent and still. "You know nothing of me."

Falco shook his head. "Not true. I know all about you. I know you once had a soul and a long life ahead of you. But you threw it all away beneath a waterfall. You gave it up for Tish, the dark mistress of Kalloshin. That must have been one incredible orgasm." Falco laughed, then continued. "You are the youngest son of Orland and Sabina Thoran, whose bones now grace the old Swords graveyard. And sometimes you go there, don't you, to lay roses on their tombstones. You've been haunting the streets of Korsham for years, longer than you can remember, jumping to and from the shadows, avoiding the light, avoiding anything that reminds you of who you were." The Brenian thief nodded. "Yes, I know all about you. I make it a point to know my enemies."

The assassin seemed paralyzed in place, and Falco ripped open his tunic and drew two slender blades from his belt. He flipped one in the air, caught it on the tip, and flung it straight towards Nalo's chest.

Before the tossed blade had even turned twice, the assassin leaped over the pedestal. The blade flew through the empty space and struck the distance wall. Falco felt a tap on his shoulder.

He turned at the touch and found the assassin behind him, grinning near perfect white teeth. "Not a bad throw, thief," Nalo said, "but maybe next time."

Falco fell back against the pedestal. It gave under his weight and both crashed to the floor. *So the legends are true*, he thought, scooting across the floor away from the agile phantom. Nalo wasn't human, not even close. So rarely were the stories true. There were always embellishments, exaggerations, and lies to tend with. But the stories of Nalo must be true. *This isn't a fair fight. How can I hope to beat an immortal? How can I beat a phantom?*

Nalo pursued. "I thank you for your confidence in me," he said, moving forward again and pulling a garrote from around his waist. He snapped the leather cord tightly then wrapped it around his pale knuckles. "I'm neither a phantom nor immortal, though I have friends in dark places."

"You can read thoughts," Falco said, reaching the wall.

Nalo nodded. "Sometimes. It's a simple skill an old necromancer taught me. It's not that hard, and with Brenian minds, it's easy. Your people think too much, Fox. It's a weakness and a danger that will kill you all."

Falco cowered in the growing shadow of the assassin. He eyed the taut cord as the assassin brought it closer to his throat. Falco brought his left hand up to his neck, feebly covering it as if that would make a difference. In his right hand, hidden at his back, waited the other knife.

Nalo lurched forward, the cord reaching out to find the soft flesh of the Brenian's throat. With a scream, Falco whipped the blade around and cut the cord in half, then drove his right foot into Nalo's knee. To Falco's surprise, the assassin howled and fell over. The thief rolled away from the wall. He rose and stepped back, eyeing the assassin as he rocked in pain on the museum floor.

Falco turned and ran to the door. *Get out now*, he thought, *before the beast can rise*. Now that he had Tuly's Egg, the *real* egg, all that mattered was getting away. He leaped down the steps to the hall and bolted for the door. The light of the torches grew stronger as the cool air of the evening seeped into the hall. Falco smiled as freedom grew large in his view.

He reached the door, but was thrown left by a strong force. A heavy weight crushed him as he hit the floor. His ribs cracked against the egg. His knife was tossed away. Falco screamed and tried to stand, but crude hands found his throat.

"Two can play the fox," Nalo said, spitting the words into Falco's face. "You should have turned that blade against me when I was down. Now is not the time to play safe."

Through blinding pain, Falco drove his fists against the assassin's sides. But no amount of pounding would dislodge Nalo, as he pushed his sharp thumbs into Falco's throat.

The thief gasped for air and reached for the egg. It had slipped down to his sternum, but he was still able to pull it out with a weakening hand and pulled it out. *Forgive me, Great God, for what I'm about to do.*

He drove the egg towards the head of the assassin. But a swift hand reached around and snatched it out of the air and drove it back into his throat.

"Did you forget so quickly that I can read minds?" Nalo asked, pushing the hard egg down.

Falco struggled against Tuly's Egg against his windpipe, but his strength bled away. A few more half-hearted jabs to the assassin's sides, and the thief's arms grew still. Then his mind, then his breath.

He lay there, looking up with watery eyes into the sallow face of his killer. He was not afraid to die, but he thought it would be in a different place, somewhere pleasant, somewhere in Brenia where the Falcon Lilies grew. Perhaps at the end of his days when he was ready to go. All thieves have a sense of invulnerability, he knew, and his sense had been stronger than most. *I'm the Brenian Fox,* he thought. *How can I possibly die?*

Falco studied the smirk on the assassin's face. He found himself smiling, too, despite the searing pain in his throat. *When I meet him,* he remembered thinking, *will I cringe or laugh?* In his last breath, he laughed and thought, *I'm happy to die here and for this cause. See me assassin, one last time, and know that I stand for something that you have lost. You may have won today, but I will win in the end. My soul is at peace. Where is yours?*

And Falco Creed, the Brenian Fox, died.

≈

In the faint light of fire lamps, Nalo Thoran held in his bare hands two petrified eggs above a wooden pedestal. One was fake and one was real.

His mind drifted back to the corpse that lay in the hallway, and he wondered about the words the thief had used. 'I know all about you,' Falco Creed had said, and Nalo considered those words as he studied the eggs. The thief had accused him of having no soul, having no higher purpose, no sense of national honor or pride. The part about having no soul was true enough. Kalloshin's mistress, Tish, had seen to that years ago under the waterfall. *Indeed, it had been a fine orgasm,* Nalo said to himself, letting a smile creep across his thin, pale lips. *My first and my last.*

But he did not linger long on the past these days. His career in the shadows had been so long and, in some ways, fruitful. It certainly wasn't boring. How often does a Korsham citizen get to clap hands with a necromancer and live to tell the tale? How often does a common thug, like the one Falco had killed earlier in the night, tussle with a great thief of Brenia? No, the years had been harsh and savage and disappointing, but not uneventful, and at the end of his days, Nalo would look back on it all and try to find some measure of peace with it, some level of pride. What else could he do?

Nalo looked at the eggs and thought about the thief's last words: '*You may have won today, but I will win in the end.*' He concentrated on the egg in his right hand and studied the fine crack in its center. His hand began to warm beneath it, and warm some more, until the orb glowed white hot. He smiled.

"You were right, thief," Nalo said in the growing light as he placed the fake egg from his left hand onto the pedestal and replaced its glass shield. "You will win in the end. You did indeed know a lot about me, but you failed to learn one important fact. My mother was Brenian, and it's for her, that I will return your egg to where it belongs."

The assassin tucked Tuly's Egg beneath his black cloak, turned, and disappeared into the shadows.

The People of the Town
Kane Gordon

When the last Blue Tiger butterfly landed on the gunman, discarded kimonos caught in the fire winds above Hangjou and played with the burning clouds. Their flaked remains scattered themselves like charcoal confetti across the gardens below; silver grass turning grey. Many of the farmers' heads hung low, defeated by the cooked earth.

We had servant droids deployed to gather the fallen. Stout little machines, mechanical shimobes whose features had been honed, to resemble Bhudda, and were able to hover to great heights or mere millimeters off the ground. Their primary use was in cleansing the inside of the industrial chimneys but for now, they transported the deceased—priests, townsfolk and, as some unexpected afterthought—the scorched remains of the flowering apricot trees.

As a ribbon of floating robotics, they deposit the corpses into The Furnace on the hill one by one. Human kindling.

For every one of those who had fallen, I had taken to ensure the shimobes replaced the dead with an origami kusudama.

My father had taught me to create these geometric replica flowers—roses, hydrangeas, tulips, wisteria. I had made it standard practice, on behalf of all of us in The Tower. A crystal castle of imperious height, able to repel the gases, molded like glass onto the land upon which it stood. We looked upon the flowers as a small way of preserving the memory of the slain.

The shimobes also acted as our eyes and ears.

Through such vision, I witnessed the town's Head Man, the Nanushi, known as Tomi, with an unfurled newspaper lying open across his shriveled legs, as he sat upon a rocking chair. His Montsuki coat worn like a winding sheet, eyes cemented still, a carbonized sensu clasped. The fan no longer able to cool. For the first time since The Event, I shivered.

From the black ink, he appeared to have been reading the words of a journalistic sage. Perhaps not realizing it would be the final thing he would see and would become an unexpected eulogy. I directed the shimobe to scan the words, which I read:

It is September 15. The Tsukimi will have begun. Harvest. We will offer sacrifices to the Moon. Not to a silver Moon but to one bruised purple and green by the afterglow of the factories' ascended waste.

It is the year we were foretold was not far from now but already, it has arrived!

The Never Event we had been informed would not happen, has begun.

The men wearing white suits wearing round glasses and occupying the crystal tower have paid a price for their intellect, for their invention and for their greed. This trinity of desires which the shinigami gods will never fully allow to meet.

A place of uncertainty will always fall between, will always forestall. Damage.

The skies are damning, in their proof.

We have advanced. We have our sentinels of bonded alloys, carved in our own image but the chemicals and metals used to implement these progressions have come at a cost...

The words offended me and would offend my colleagues. I could not defend such thought. We had followed orders. We had offered the people of the town a home within The Tower but none accepted our benevolence. They had been warned of the consequences. Our Executive had declared such belligerence a form of conflict. He said it afforded us the defense to fully trial the chemical *out-gusts* from the chimneys. The Event.

In a town alley, another shimobe came upon the aged washerwoman, Jingu. She was someone I knew, once our family servant; I had taken her to work in The Tower as a thank you. She had retired from service of both wondrous length, attitude and commitment. It had hurt to see her decline the opportunity to live in The Tower.

Through the shimobe, I watched as she abandoned her offerings of steamed buns, gnocchi and rice cakes. Her yard table had been adorned with a hand-sewn Hokusai cloth. The cloth had turned inky, and upon it the blackened remains of bread, sweet potatoes; and beans had turned to pebbles. And the once fresh fruit of pears, persimmon and apples had been replaced by crisp, spherical husks.

Gathering blankets, she knelt beside a dying boy huddled between steaming wash baskets and scalding gutters. "You are shivering, child," I heard her say.

The, boy had wan eyes and was uttering the lines of Chōka: "*Izuku yori. Motona kakarite.*"

I translated them aloud as a dragon's hiss: "*From what place do they come? Night after night, without end.*"

Around the boy's thin shoulders, Jingu draped the blankets. The shimobe moved in close to assist the woman but she brushed it aside, her eyes drawn hopelessly to the cloud tsunamis which had drifted overhead. "We cannot stay out much longer, child. We must hide." The shimobe looked skyward; she was correct in assuming the worst.

Onto her silken wisps of hair, the clouds deposited their vapors.

They set down their fiery snow gases from the distant, brick flutes, which settled on the cobbled streets and minka, and sparked alight these wooden homes.

The shimobe's vision appeared to waver, perhaps remembering the smokestacks and the deadly harvest we had created. The smoke had applied its necrotic touch with appropriate success.

Behind me my colleagues lifted wine glasses, adjusted their white suits and round glasses and, celebrated. Guilt was not within their training. We all answered to The Executive. He had conjured this moment like a magician and we had merely executed the power of the chimneys.

Rumor from the streets was of ancient prophesies having been responsible. We laughed. Along with the others, I agreed we were in fine company to be considered part of such prophesy.

The shimobe turned to glide away. It focused on the distant Tōrō lamps responding with a universal pale glow.

Wandering the streets, like a spectral aria, the dying boy's final breaths echoed, provided a mournful lilt to compliment the evening's exhausted sunset. His words somehow penetrating the windows: "*Mashite shinowayu. Manakai ni. Yasui shi nasanu. Yasui shi nasanu.*" The words, like a soliloquy caused my head to hurt; my breath to thin; I felt weak and I had to stretch out a hand to steady myself.

Regaining balance, I watched as the washerwoman gathered her arms around her frail, shadow. "*The yearning is even worse.*" She said, repeating the boy's lilt. "*The yearning is even worse. Rendering me helpless. Preventing me from resting peacefully. Preventing me from resting peacefully.*"

Around the town, the dead continued to be collected. We employed the shimobes to gather these people and replace them with origami flowers; for Jingu, they had chosen the wisteria.

When they departed, a draft came and plucked them into the air, blew them towards The Tower. I placed a hand to the crystal panes, frowned, curious, and looked at the way the edges appeared fused close. The screams of the fading world beyond tapped like blazing icicles against the panes. Through each eye of the shimobes, the remaining townsfolk dropped, lifeless.

I stepped back, a sudden awareness, a sudden, overwhelming realization that The Tower's weaknesses were its impenetrable vacuum and the glass, air conditioning outlets which would rapidly melt into a solid mass. "We are trapped."

Our reflections told a tale. A predictive tale. Soon, we sweated within our white suits. Behind our round spectacles there was a terror shining from our eyes.

At these heat-sealed windows, we stood. Night, after endless night. Looking out. Watching the affects of our sinister dalliances.

As our number dwindled, the shimobes raised up to place beautiful kusudama on the window ledges beyond.

I wondered what flower they would offer for me.

Giving a Hand
A Charm City Darkness Story
Kelly A. Harmon

*A*ssumpta Mary-Margaret O'Connor hurried down East
Front Street toward the Shot Tower Metro station. She
shouldn't have tarried so long at the museum—daylight had faded fast,
and this wasn't a particularly good area of Baltimore.

The demon mark on her back fluttered, letting her know she
wasn't alone. Her heart thumped, and she picked up her pace, looking
around for the demons.

Just up ahead, the Shot Tower cast the street into near darkness.
A smoothly sloping brick tower, it rose over two hundred feet high
to a crenellated top. Built in the city's early days to manufacture lead
shot for rifles and cannons, the city's residents had rescued it from
demolition long after becoming obsolete. She loved that tower, a
Baltimore landmark, but didn't relish having to walk in its shadow to
catch the bus.

"Idiot." A giggle followed.

The disembodied voice came from Assumpta's left. The demon
mark fluttered again. She had to smile. As far as name-calling went, it
was pretty mild. She'd heard worse from the demons.

"*Bitch.*" A different voice, deeper, harsh.

Her heart beat faster. It wasn't the implied epithet that sent her
heart racing. It was the intended malice she heard.

She hurried, slinging the long strap of her voluminous purse across her body, preparing to run.

The demon mark on her back tightened painfully, squeezing the muscles between her shoulder blades into a tight knot, and she realized the demons were closer than she'd thought. Running might not be an option. She stopped, inching her hand into her purse and grasping the squirt bottle full of holy water she always carried. When you're demon-marked, you protect yourself. She felt a surge of confidence—she was armed, at least against non-humans.

"Show yourself," Assumpta said, scanning the nearby area. This late at night, there was no one around. The other museum patrons had already scattered, and just her luck, none were headed to the same bus stop.

She knew she shouldn't taunt the demons, shouldn't provoke a fight, but wasn't that what they wanted? Getting it over with quickly would get her home sooner. "What's the matter?" she asked. "Scared?"

She would be, if she were a demon. With a steady stream of holy water, she could flay off their skin and reduce them to a puddle of demon goo from thirty feet away—she'd done it before.

Assumpta smelled sulfur, and whirled. They were much closer than thirty feet. If she could smell them, they were near enough to touch.

The demon mark thumped harder, tensing the muscles between her shoulder blades to a painful level. She couldn't wait to get rid of it. The mark was a terrific radar system—but it was also a beacon, alerting every damned demon in her vicinity that she was ripe for the plucking.

Evil laughter echoed through the deserted city street. The hair on the back of Assumpta's neck prickled, sending a frisson of fear down her spine. A sheen of sweat wet her forehead. Her hands shook.

So much for confidence.

This was a new trick by the demons: invisibility. *Why now?*

She caught another whiff of sulfur, then something grabbed her hair from the back, twisted and yanked. Tears burned her eyes. She lifted the holy water bottle over her head and squeezed. There was a screech, the sound of a sizzle, and the grip on her hair relaxed.

Cool water sluiced down her back.

"Whore." It came from her left. More laughter from behind her. *How many of them were there?*

She sprinted toward the bus stop.

An unseen foot kicked her ankle, tripping her. She fell to her knees, slamming her hands onto the rough, cement sidewalk. The holy water bottle rolled into the gutter. She scrambled for it, screaming for help: "Saint Michael!"

Her head jerked back, a claw tangled in her hair, her throat exposed. On her knees on the ground, she felt powerless—could she reach the jar of blessed salt in her purse? She hoped Saint Michael had heard her call.

Hot breath filled her ear. A wet tongue flicked out, touching the lobe.

She flinched.

"Saint Michael's busy," the gravelly voice said. Invisible claws scratched gently across her throat. "Get ready to meet him on his turf." The grip on her hair tightened, pulling her head back further.

Assumpta shoved her hand into her purse and grasped the jar of salt. She struggled with the lid, but couldn't open it one-handed.

Was this the end?

She heard a crackle—the hair on the back of her neck tingled with electricity. Lightning flashed—branching—striking three targets at once—her invisible assailants. It illuminated the large, winged demon about to rip out her throat, and two others wielding spiked clubs.

Thunder boomed, grenade loud. Three piles of ash appeared where the demons had stood.

"*Jesus,*" she muttered. "What the hell was that?" She dropped the blessed salt back into her purse, and sank to the ground, her ears ringing. Then it came to her. Saint Michael, coming through when she most needed him. She closed her eyes briefly, and offered up her thanks.

"You mean, '*Who* the hell was that?'" a man said, peeling away from the antique brick of the Shot Tower and walking toward her.

No, not a man—a figure of black and white, like an old movie—a ghost. She could see right through him. Assumpta looked more closely at his attire. His long-sleeved shirt was covered by a form fitting vest and buttoned tightly at his left wrist. The other sleeve ended in a stump where a hand should have been.

"I need your help," the ghost said.

Assumpta gave him an apologetic look. "I really don't have time for this." *Not while I'm still demon marked.*

She stood on shaking legs, collected her holy water bottle, and walked toward the bus stop. Couldn't he see she had enough of her own problems to solve without getting involved with anyone else's?

The ghost joined her. "The correct response is, '*Thank you, of course I'll help—in any way I can.*'"

She raised her eyebrows, "Thank you?"

The ghost nodded. "The way I see it, I just rescued you from your own personal Waterloo. That deserves a thank you."

She stopped, took a deep breath, and pushed her hair out of her face. "You caused the lightning?"

The ghost nodded.

If she didn't thank him—or help him—would he use that lightning on her?

"I—"

"Besides," he interrupted, "Brona said you'd be able to help." The twinkle in his eye told her he'd saved this bit for last.

She stared at his face, trying to figure out if he'd actually threatened her with the lightning—or if she'd imagined it. His crooked smile decided it—he hadn't—but *still*. She sighed.

It wasn't fair for the ghost to pull the Brona card. She really didn't have time for this, and Brona knew it! If Assumpta died while demon-marked, she'd go straight to Hell. She needed to spend her time finding out how to get rid of it, and yet…

Brona Daly had been the resident ghost at Enoch Pratt Library until Assumpta had helped her cross over to the other side. Having friends in *high* places who owed you a favor was a good thing. Maybe Assumpta could leverage that help to get rid of her mark.

She started walking toward the bus stop again. Her new acquaintance stayed by her side.

"How does a ghost meet an angel?"

The ghost smiled. "I knew Brona when she was just a ghost."

"And after she passed over?"

He shrugged. "Brona likes to look up her old friends and see if she can help them out."

Assumpta didn't know what to think of that. Was Brona making it her mission to help ghosts pass over?

"So, Brona orchestrated all this?" Assumpta swung her hand around, indicating the fight.

"Not the demons." He smiled. "But I have to admit that's the most fun I've had in years."

"And this power only works against demons?" She crossed her fingers.

"Anyone, actually."

Damn. "What do you want?" she asked.

"I want what any ghost wants, to cross over, to join the great collective in the sky."

"And something's keeping you here."

"Yes—for years, longer than Brona — longer than most, not as long as some." The desire to leave was evident in his voice.

She kicked a stone out of her path. "So when the white light came, why did you ignore it?"

"What white light?"

"The light that ushers all newly departed souls to Heaven. They didn't come for you?" Assumpta wondered about that. If the white light hadn't come for—

"What's your name?" she asked.

"Marty," he said, waving his good hand. "Marty Brown."

If the white light hadn't come for Marty, does that mean Marty was doomed to Hell? No, Brona wouldn't push him in her direction if he were destined for Hell.

"Why does Brona think I can help you?"

He grew solemn. "She told me you helped her get to Heaven, and that you can help me. She says you have the tools to figure it out."

They'd arrived at the bus stop just as the bus was pulling to the curb. Assumpta turned to ask Marty one more question, but he was fading from view, waving as he faded. "Meet me in the Poe Room at ten tomorrow morning," he said as he disappeared.

～

Assumpta got home and slammed the door to her apartment, immediately locking all three deadbolts and hanging the chain. She tossed her handbag on a nearby chair, warded the apartment threshold with a swipe of holy water and blessed salt, then collapsed onto the sofa. She pulled her pendulum and a crumpled piece of paper out of her pocket and put them on the coffee table in front of her.

She smoothed out the wrinkled paper. The alphabet was written in large letters in a protractor-like semicircle from bottom left of the page to the bottom right. Assumpta communicated with spirits using the pendulum; the paper helped her determine what they spelled out to her.

She dangled the pendulum over the center of the paper and asked: "What's keeping Marty Brown from passing on?"

The pendulum twitched, and started making a slight back-and-forth motion. As it moved, the arc of the pendulum grew wider until it passed over a letter. "C," Assumpta guessed—it wasn't an exact science, figuring the precise letter the pendulum denoted. At least the alphabet paper got her in the right ballpark. She guessed again. "D."

This time the pendulum jumped, signaling a correct response, then straightened out onto a different path, at nearly a ninety-degree angle over the letters.

"O," Assumpta guessed, assuming the next letter would be a vowel.

The pendulum jumped again, swinging radically and changing direction once more. The path veered toward the early letters of the alphabet.

"B." The pendulum stayed on course. "C," she said. This time, the pendulum jumped.

"Doc…" Assumpta mused, "Document…dockside…doctor…" The pendulum twitched, and instead of changing directions, began circling clockwise. *Doctor* was correct.

"Doctor who?" she asked. The pendulum hiccupped, and veered away on another path.

"K," she guessed, but the path remained constant. She guessed again. "L."

The pendulum changed direction.

Ten frustrating minutes later, she had her name: Dr. Levi Holtz. *Unusual name,* she thought. *He should be easy to find.*

Assumpta jumped from the couch and made her way to the tiny kitchen where she kept the phone books. She pulled the thick *Baltimore City and Surrounding Areas* directory down off the shelf and turned to the yellow pages in the back. When she couldn't find Dr. Holtz, she flipped to the white pages. And when she couldn't find anything there, she shut the book with a *whump* and pushed it away from her.

She tried the pendulum again, but it remained stubbornly silent.

Since she didn't have the funds for an internet connection, it was all she could do for the night.

∾

Assumpta reached Enoch Pratt Library at nine-forty-five the next morning. She hoped Brona would show up. It had been a while since she'd seen her angelic friend, plus she now had a bone to pick— and maybe a favor to call in.

She headed to the Poe Room, the large room on the second floor, housing Edgar Allan Poe's personal library. Assumpta had spent a lot of hours here visiting with Brona. Apparently Marty had, too.

She walked through the room, touching the spines of books she'd read, wondering what her old friend was up to. She heard footsteps behind her.

"Find anything?"

She turned and saw Marty enter through the doorway. He looked nearly solid. *First lightning, now footsteps. What other tricks did he know?*

Assumpta brushed a wayward strand of hair behind her ear. "A name, that's it. Dr. Levi Holtz."

"The doctor who amputated my hand?"

Explains not being able to find him, Assumpta thought. "What exactly happened to your hand?"

"I was pouring molten lead at the top of the Shot Tower when I slipped. My hand plunged into it. I thought the pain would kill me." He closed his eyes, grimacing. "Dr. Holtz lived around the corner, so he was called. He tried to save the hand, but in the end, it proved better to remove it." Marty pursed his lips; he seemed to be considering something. "I've an idea. Meet me on the corner of Fayette and Front Streets."

He disappeared.

Two transfers and twenty minutes later, Assumpta got off the bus directly in front of My Lucky Stars Tavern, one of the many seedy establishments so prevalent on Baltimore street corners. She took a deep breath. *Really? A corner bar?*

It didn't matter that the bar was directly in the shadow of the Shot Tower—that it was somehow connected to Marty's plight. She didn't want to go in—though she knew she had to. As a teen, she'd walked into far too many dark, cramped bars, looking for her drunken father—and she didn't relish repeating the exercise now.

"This used to be Dr. Holtz's residence," said Marty, fading into view. He seemed disappointed.

"Things change," Assumpta said. "Let's see if the doctor is in." She steeled herself with a deep breath, and walked up the two steps and into My Lucky Stars. Inside it was smoky and dark. It could have been any one of the hundreds of bars she'd pulled her dad out of. Even the decor looked the same, dark paneling and beer-truck signs—*old* signs. They looked like crap, but were probably worth a mint.

She nodded to the bartender, and he nodded back without a question. He'd probably seen a thousand women over the years, coming into bars looking for someone. Assumpta looked around for someone, too.

Five or six barflies huddled on tall bar stools near the taps. The small area with tables and chairs was deserted. *Nothing new here.* A couple of drunks already started in on a binge.

"He's not here," Assumpta said, turning to go.

"Don't be so sure," Marty said, nodding toward the back of the narrow joint. "In the back corner."

"I don't see anything."

"He's hiding from the lifers," Marty said. "Saves energy." He lifted his good hand and gestured someone over from the darkest corner of the room. "He'll meet us outside."

Sunshine blinded Assumpta when she pushed open the tavern door and stepped out. Marty faded slightly in the light. A moment later, Dr. Holtz seeped through the tavern door and glided up to Assumpta and Marty.

He reminded Assumpta of a young Albert Einstein, with thick, dark hair long and flowing around his head like a lion's mane. A bushy mustache covered his top lip. He wore a loose suit, with a vest, like Marty's, buttoned to midway up his chest. The suit jacket hung open.

Dr. Holtz held out his hand to Marty and the two ghosts shook. "I'm sorry to see you here, Mr. Brown." Dr. Holtz said in a voice as thin as he.

"Sorry?"

"Seeing you tells me you're trapped on earth, just as I am."

Marty introduced Assumpta to the doctor.

"That can't be a coincidence," Assumpta said. "You're linked somehow."

"Of course we are," Marty said. "The doctor saved my life."

Dr. Holtz shook his head. "There's something I've always felt bad about, Marty. That's probably what the young lady is referring to." The doctor took a deep breath, then spoke softly, a hint of embarrassment in his voice. Assumpta almost had to strain to hear the words. "Shoulda burned it like I was supposed to, but I kept it to examine…and then as sort of a trophy. I truly am sorry."

He walked down the sidewalk around the back of the tavern to the base of a gnarled maple tree, its gargantuan branches spreading high and wide. Dark roots erupted from the ground at the base of the tree and pushed through the sidewalk.

"This way." He stepped onto the grass and walked around to the far side, his ghostly visage suddenly appearing more substantial in the shade of the giant tree. The doctor toed the edge of the highest root with his boot. The root curled around, making a sweeping arc back toward the tree, forming a small protected area, like a cove. "Dig here, on the inside of the circle."

"Dig?" Assumpta asked.

Dr. Holtz nodded.

"I'm not sure about this," Assumpta said. In the daylight, there were plenty of people walking around who might come over to investigate—or call the cops.

"Don't worry," Marty said. "I'll protect you."

Assumpta wondered just what he meant to do if anyone came along.

"More lightening?"

He grinned. "Something less harmful, I assure you."

"Shouldn't take you long," Dr. Holtz said. "By the time I got to burying it, I couldn't do the job very well."

But she didn't have a shovel. She pulled the strap of her purse over her head and set it down in front of her. What did she have that she could use? She rummaged through the contents, not finding anything really suitable, laying the items one by one on the ground: the plastic bottle of holy water, the wide-mouthed glass jar of salt, her wallet. She didn't even have a credit card she could use.

"The salt," Marty said. "Try the lid."

She hadn't thought of that. "But dirt will get all over the blessed salt once we're done."

"Will that destroy its holiness?" Dr. Holtz asked.

Assumpta shrugged. "Probably not." She put everything back into her purse except for the jar of salt. She set the purse aside, unscrewed the metal lid from the jar, then put the salt next to the purse so she wouldn't accidentally knock it over.

"Here we go," Marty said. He placed his good hand on Assumpta's shoulder. She felt a warmth spread through her and watched as her hands faded into ghostly appendages. She could see the grass through them. Except for the curious warmth, she felt nothing, even as the rest of her body faded. Even her demon mark was still.

"I trust this isn't permanent?"

"You're only invisible as long as I'm touching you," Marty said.

Nodding, she put the edge of the lid to the ground where Dr. Holtz noted, and started scraping away the dirt. At least she didn't have to dig under grass. She couldn't imagine having to cut through the roots. The soil was dark and damp, since the tree kept it shaded all the time. The upturned earth smelled fresh and pungent.

Digging the hole wasn't easy, but it wasn't as hard as she thought it might be. When she'd removed about two inches of top soil, the lid struck something hard.

"There it is," said the doctor. "The box is wrapped in oilcloth."

Assumpta scraped away more dirt, using both the lid and her hands, until two corners of the oiled cloth appeared. More tugging and digging, then she grabbed damp material and yanked, pulling the treasure loose. Beneath its wrappings, the polished wooden box was smaller than a shoe box, hinged, but not locked.

"Open it," Marty said.

Assumpta tilted open the hinged lid and gasped. Inside, on a small pillow, rested a mummified human hand.

≈

Marty's grave was located in Westminster Graveyard, the same graveyard where Edgar Allen Poe was buried.

The walled cemetery, located on the corner of West Fayette and North Greene, was too crowded with headstones and mausoleums to bring a backhoe in. So two overall-clad workman wielding shovels and picks, had dug out the grave this morning. Under the coroner's care, they transferred the coffin from the graveyard to the rec-room of the adjoining church—Westminster Presbyterian—commandeered by the coroner's office for the purpose of joining Mr. Martin Brown with the remains of his hand.

And now here she stood, in the harsh glare of the fluorescent lights, along with the minister, some reporters, and the mayor and his entourage—trying to keep out of the limelight. If she had not needed the cash offered for the obligatory *grip-and-grin* photo with the mayor, she would have skipped the entire charade. But Marty assured her that he and Dr. Holtz could make the photos unusable.

Assumpta still wasn't certain why they'd decided to go through all the trouble of exhuming Marty. And she wasn't certain how she rated an invite to the small event. The mayor probably wanted to spin her find into good PR with an election coming up. If her rent hadn't been overdue, she would have declined.

She stood next to two reporters, behind a soft barrier cordoning off the coroner's workspace. She was less than ten feet from the coffin. Marty and Dr. Holtz stood closer, watching like eager school children. It was a good thing no one but Assumpta could see them.

The coroner donned gloves, picked up a crowbar and walked to the coffin—a British version, wide at the shoulders and narrow at the feet, the wood badly decayed and warped. He laid the crowbar to the edge of the coffin and pried. Cameras flashed. The damp wood screeched against the rusty nails as the lid angled up. Several nails broke, jarring the wooden lid and knocking dirt to the drop-cloth beneath the coffin.

The smell of damp earth filled Assumpta's nose as the lid came fully off.

The corner's assistant snapped several photos of Marty's body, then the coroner scraped a scalpel across Marty's fingers.

Marty twitched, shaking his hand. "That tickles," he said walking up to Assumpta. "What's he doing?"

"Taking a sample of your skin," Assumpta said. "They'll probably do tests on it later."

"What kind of tests?" Marty asked as the coroner placed the samples in a small jar.

"Not sure," Assumpta whispered.

The corner and his assistant moved Marty's body into a new modern casket, carefully putting the body to rest on the padded interior. The coroner took a closer look at the stump on the end of the body's arm, and the cuts on the end of the mummified hand.

"I'm fairly confident the hand belongs to Mr. Brown here," he said.

"As if the note I'd left in the box isn't good enough," Dr. Holtz murmured.

Assumpta smiled.

The coroner placed the mummified hand to rest at the end of Marty's arm in the casket.

Marty gasped, lifting his stump. Assumpta watched in amazement as a ghostly hand appeared at the end of Marty's arm.

"It feels wonderful," he said, smiling and wiggling his ghostly fingers. He flexed his hand, then made a fist, opened it wide and turned it over, looking at the other side. He dropped his hand to his side. "Now what?"

"Now they'll lay you to rest," Assumpta whispered.

"I think I already am," he said, his voice filled with awe.

Suddenly, Marty appeared to be standing under a spotlight, the light powerful and golden, the outline of his body fading in the warm glow. He looked up, his smiling face fading into a more serene expression.

"This is goodbye, I think," Marty said to Assumpta.

"The appropriate response is, '*Thank you*,'" Assumpta said with a smile. "Say hello to Brona for me."

"Thank you." Marty faded and disappeared. The white light retracted into the ceiling. Not a second later, a second light appeared for the doctor. He looked surprised, then smiled joyously, waved to Assumpta, and was gone.

The coroner closed Marty's new coffin lid and turned the lock with a click.

To the Flame
Evan Dicken

*T*he tide went out, leaving corpses in its wake. Young girls, small with quick fingers and hard eyes, tread carefully among the bodies. It was considered bad luck to step in shadow—only the dead walked in darkness, and in the Halo only the lighthouse cast no shadow.

Ama stood over a corpse, eyes watering as she squinted at the distant tower. Impossibly tall and straight, it stood like a dark spear rammed through the heart of the world, its beam of life-giving arclight transcribing a slow circle across land and sea. Seeing the lighthouse so close, so bright, Ama could almost forget the farm at the far edge of the Halo, fungal beds left to grow wild, the cabin with white shutters and a lopsided chimney now home to little more than silence.

"Thinking of swimming?" Auntie Haenyo squelched up, sack in hand. Although she wore no uniform, the overseer stood out in that she wasn't spattered with silt up to her neck.

"No, Auntie." Ama blinked, the tower's image picked out like a hot brand against the backs of her eyelids.

"Nice and cool down there in the deeps. Quiet too, I reckon." Haenyo nudged the corpse with her foot. "Fish nibbling at your toes, crabs crawling 'round inside you. That sound nice, girl?"

"No, Auntie." Ama searched the corpse. It might have once been a man, but she couldn't be sure. Sea-bloated and face down in the muck everyone looked much the same. She didn't know if she'd be happy or sad to recognize someone from the village. Although they deserved to suffer after how they'd treated her and Kaito, Ama couldn't bring herself to wish this cold, lonely death on anyone.

She turned him over, wincing as her fingers sunk into the spongy flesh, tongue pressed hard against the roof of her mouth to keep the bile down. Strands of kelp threaded his auburn beard, and fading arclight made dark pits of the hollows where his eyes used to be. There were a handful of tarnished brass buttons on his coat, which Ama cut free with her knife.

"Give 'em here."

Ama stood slowly, hands clenched so tight she could feel the buttons pressing into the flesh of her palm. They weren't worth much, but ribbon men didn't come cheap, and the chance Kaito would even survive a carving dwindled with every arc.

Haenyo backhanded her across the face. Ama had barely drawn a surprised breath before the overseer had her by the arm, shaking her so hard Ama felt her teeth click together.

"This your stake, is it? You own this beach?"

Ama shook her head, tasting blood where she'd bit her tongue.

"Thought not." Haenyo snatched the buttons from Ama's trembling hand. "Don't let me catch you mooning at the lighthouse again or I'll give you another."

She left Ama in the mud, one hand pressed to her swelling cheek. The corpse's mouth had fallen open to gape at her, wet and tongueless. Ama kicked at it, imagining the body wore Haenyo's smirking face instead of a stranger's eyeless surprise. She should've never left the village, should've hidden Kaito from the others even if she had to tie her brother down every night.

The corpse's ribs buckled with a wet snap when Ama kicked it again. It made a noise halfway between a sigh and a sob as trapped gas bled from its distended belly.

Disgusted, Ama stumbled away.

Some of the other girls began a song, walking in time with the slow, mournful beat. Ama didn't recognize the words, but the melody was familiar. Together, they waded across the flat, churning the silt with their feet to expose buried corpses. Their shadows grew long and inhuman as the lighthouse's arc moved across the beach. Ama could almost imagine she was back home cutting strips from the moss patch, Kaito's rich baritone catching the low notes her own voice couldn't reach.

When Haenyo finally called a halt, Ama stripped off her clothes and queued up to empty the meager contents of her satchel into the bucket with her name on it. As the newest girl, Ama was at the end of the line, and the arc had almost passed by the time Haenyo reached her.

"Mouth."

Ama tried to open her mouth only to find her cheek swollen like a corpse's.

The overseer gave an ugly laugh. "Won't be hiding anything in there, I suppose."

Ama squeezed her eyes shut as Haenyo ran rough hands through her hair, then squatted to inspect down below. Haenyo's fingers were cold and hard, and Ama winced at the prodding.

"Don't like this any more than you." Haenyo gave one of Ama's nipples a little flick. "Well, maybe a *little* more."

She hadn't gathered much—a few coins, half a copper bracelet, and a silver earring.

"Miserable." Haenyo pocketed the earring as Ama shrugged back into her rough clothes. "There are girls who would kill to work my beach. I see them back in town—in the alleys, the leech dens, the brothels. You think this is low, but there's always room to fall." She thrust the bucket at Ama. "Do better tomorrow."

Ama trudged home. Dead waves broke on the beach at her back, the air thick with salt and rot. In the distance, the lighthouse shone false promise into a sky full of flat, black clouds.

≈

Kaito had let the fire go out again. The hut was dark but for the waning arclight trickling through holes in the thatch. Ama tried to breathe through her mouth to lessen the sharp odors of mildew and sweat that filled the tiny room. Her brother lay on a pile of matted ferns at the back of the hut, singing softly to himself, one eye pressed to a crack in the peeling mycoboard. His song was high and wordless, more a whine than proper music.

"Stop it," she said.

"I can't get it right." One of Kaito's legs passed through the light as he shifted from the hole. Veins of seawater green marbled the pale skin of his thigh, the flesh so translucent Ama could see the dark shadow of bone beneath. "Will you sing with me?"

"Not like that." The words came sharper than she'd intended, but Kaito seemed not to notice.

He gave a little corpse sigh. "They need to hear."

"Who?"

"The gods."

"There are no gods." Ama made a nest of torn mycelium and struck sparks until it caught.

"Yes, there are—just very far away."

"If there are gods, why don't they help us?"

Kaito ran a thin fingered hand over his mouth. "Maybe they can't."

"Then, they're not gods, are they?"

"Maybe they won't."

"Then, they're not gods, *are they*?" Ama blew on the fire, her stomach so tight she could barely breathe. Kaito's longing was getting worse. Like a moth he was drawn to the light. If she didn't get him help soon, it would be her brother's body the tide left behind.

"There's a ribbon man down by the canal," she said into the wounded silence. "I heard they can carve out all manner of sickness, maybe even the longing."

"Ribbon men don't help people."

Ama stared into the fire, hands cupped to gather the heat.

"Ama."

Tomorrow she'd find the ribbon man, promise him whatever he wanted to carve her brother clean. They couldn't go home, but there were other villages, other farms.

"*Ama.*"

They'd walk the canals like they used to, listening to the chatter of oracular crabs, mouths watering at the smell of roasted mushrooms rubbed with spices from the central Halo where the arcs were long enough to grow proper food. Kaito would buy drilled abalone shells to weave into Ama's hair, hands spread in smiling apology for ever doubting her.

"Ama!" Kaito stood, unsteady as a man coming off an all-night leeching, his arcstruck eyes glowing like tiny lamps in the darkness.

"I need to get closer." He took a shuffling step toward the door, one hand on the wall for support.

"I'll tie you down if I have to."

"I can *save* us." His voice was hopeless and threatening all at once, like their father's had been near the end. Ama's throat tightened at memories of arcs spent waiting to see if their father had made enough at market to leech himself into a stupor, or if he would come home bitter and slit-eyed, frustration bleeding into hard words and even harder hands. Every day, Ama would plead with Kaito not to goad him, but he would only smile and tug her hair.

Better me than the both of us.

"Get away from the door." Kaito loomed over her, the sodden reek of his breath almost overpowering.

"I won't." Ama fought the urge to curl up like a sand beetle, to grit her teeth against the pain, eyes closed and breath held as if that could stop the blow from falling.

He raised a trembling fist, then let it fall, shoulders rounding. "What happened to your face?"

"Nothing." She looked away, embarrassment and relief tickling along the back of her neck. "Now, go lie down while I put the soup on."

"Ama, I'm so afraid. I can't do it alone."

"Go lie down."

He limped back to the pile of ferns and lay down, a shapeless lump in the shadows near the back of the hut.

Ama wanted to run over and kick him, again and again until he sighed that terrible sigh and it was all over. Better now than later, better here than with Haenyo standing over her, smiling.

Auntie would probably want her cut of Ama's tears, too.

Shame made a clammy nest in the back of her throat. It wasn't Kaito's fault. The tower called everyone in the end.

Fingernails scratched across the hut's door, irregular footsteps scuffing a ragged counterpoint to the slow wheeze of labored breath. Faint red light seeped through the seams around the door as doomed men and women staggered toward the sea.

Kaito gave a low moan.

"It's okay, they can't get in," Ama said, one hand on her knife just in case.

"They can't get in, but *we* can. It sings the key." He rolled over, gaze bright as the tiny fire, whining his shrill reprise. The tuneless hum filled Ama's ears, slipping between the gaps in her thoughts to fester and grow.

She winced. "Stop."

"The lighthouse isn't what you think. Somehow we came from it, before the Halo, before—"

"Enough!" She beat her fists on the dirt.

Kaito closed his eyes, head sagging back to the ferns.

Ama watched him until the last of the footsteps faded into the distant roar of the sea. She couldn't let him go, not tonight, not ever.

Only the dead walked in darkness.

∼

The walls of the canal were slick with lichen and dotted with the pale, heart-shaped bodies of oracular crabs. They chittered as Ama stumbled past—lucky numbers and hidden perils, places to go, places to avoid—fortune and doom in equal measure.

Kaito leaned heavily on her shoulder, barely able to keep his feet along the slippery path. Although the light was gone from his eyes, his gaze kept slipping to the horizon, snatches of whispered song dripping from his lips.

They found the ribbon man on a rickety pier by the water's edge, coiled wire feet dangling in the brackish flow. There were holes in his face, bare expanses of rusted frame where people had pried away plates of gold and steel. He'd patched some of them with shells, buttons, and bits of bone, but Ama could still see the seething mass of ribbon inside him, bright and fierce as eels in a ship's hold.

He muttered to himself, feet kicking little eddies in the canal.

Ama chewed on her lip, arms and shoulders burning from her brother's weight. Seeking the ribbon man had seemed like a good idea, but the sight of him made her nervous. There had been a time when ribbon men helped with everything, at least according to the stories, but over time everyone forgot how to keep them right. Most got picked apart for swords, plows, all manner of useful things. Those that remained were unpredictable and dangerous.

"The crabs said you'd come." The ribbon man stood, turning to face them. One of his eyes was cold and dead, the glass black with ash, but the other flickered with strange brilliance—neither greenish-orange like a fire nor red like arclight, but a color Ama had never seen before.

He took a step towards them, quick and furtive as a sandpiper racing the tide. Up close, Ama could see his teeth were sharp bits of abalone set in gums of tarnished copper wire.

She swallowed. "They say you can fix anything."

"They're very, very wrong." Flecks of abalone fell as the ribbon man spoke, the writhing wire inside his mouth chipping at his teeth.

Ama lifted Kaito. "Can you fix my brother?"

"He isn't broken. The world is."

"But can you help him?"

"*That* I can do, for a price."

"I don't have much." She forced herself to meet his gaze. "But I can bring you new teeth, buttons and pretty shells for your skin, maybe even—"

"Oh, no, no, no." He loomed over them, moving with the metal-on-metal rasp of knives being sharpened. "I help him, you help me, perfect synchronicity."

"What do you want?"

"I want you to light the world." The ribbon man's breath smelled of scorched metal. A few knife-sharp strands flicked from his mouth to touch Ama's swollen cheek. There was no pain, but when she pressed a hand to the cut it came away bright with blood.

"Time grows short." He raised rusty skeletal hands to point at the clouds above. "But if we call, they will see."

"Who will see?"

"The gods." Kaito's response was barely a whisper.

"There are no gods," The ribbon man replied with a jagged smile.

"Of course there are." Kaito gave a weak cough. "They're just far away."

Ama grimaced, glancing from the ribbon man to Kaito. Her brother was barely breathing, every ragged exhalation echoing with his mad song. In that moment she saw him dead, salt crusting ragged eye sockets, his mouth an empty sea cave, slick strands of kelp wrapped like chains about his arms and legs.

"Whatever it is, I'll do it. Just help him." Ama turned to Kaito with a soft smile. "Better me than both of us."

"Yes, *both* of you." The ribbon man reached for them.

Kaito tried to pull away, but the ribbon man grasped his wrist, fingers tight as a manacle. Ama grit her teeth and took the other hand. Scabbed rust scratched across the flesh of her palm, but she held on, even when she felt the ribbons slide beneath her skin. Threads of gold and silver crawled up her arm, twining around muscle and bone to blossom in tangles of delicate filigree. Ama watched, wide-eyed, her sharp intake of breath expelled in a stuttering gasp as white-hot agony drove her to her knees. She heard Kaito scream and tried to turn, but the ribbon man had her fast, one eye blazing bright as the lighthouse.

"Don't worry." The ribbon man smiled as his face unspooled and light filled Ama's head.

"I'm not afraid anymore."

~

"You will be eaten by crabs," a small, chattering voice whispered in Ama's ear. She brushed the crab away before it could fulfill its prophecy.

Ama lay in the shadows of the seaward wall of the canal, a blade of crimson arclight halfway up the far side. She must have lain here most of the arc. Her first thought was that Haenyo would be furious she'd missed a day of scavenging. There would be a beating at best, at worst Haenyo would find another girl.

Kaito lay on the moss a short distance off, one arm across his face. Ama managed to get to her hands and knees before a wave of nausea made her wretch. Her head felt as if someone had packed it with mycelium, but when she looked down at her wrist, the filigree was gone.

Darkness had touched the water before Ama managed to crawl over to Kaito. His skin was warm to the touch, and with relief she noticed he was breathing. A few steps beyond, the ribbon man lay on his side in a scorched patch of lichen, little more than a twisted skeleton of smoking metal and abalone shards.

Kaito opened his eyes when she shook him. "It's so quiet."

Laughing, crying, she clutched him to her chest, after a moment he hugged her back. They lay there until the creeping shadow forced them to their feet.

Despite Kaito being able to walk unaided, the trip home took longer than the morning's journey. Ama felt ancient, her bones hanging heavy within her flesh, and soon it was she who leaned on Kaito for support.

He murmured wordless concern as they limped back to the hut, smoothing back the hair from her sweaty forehead. Ama grinned despite her exhaustion—with Kaito better they could leave the coast, get away from the lighthouse. There would be work on a farm, maybe enough to save up for a house of their own, maybe even a cabin with white shutters and a crooked chimney.

The bed of ferns was damp, but comfortable. Kaito moved through shadows of deepening scarlet, setting everything right. He sang as he used to back when they were scraping moss—old songs, familiar songs—the low thrum of his voice like the rumble of distant breakers. Ama tried to sit up, but the air seemed to press in all around her.

"Hush now, have some broth." He tipped a wooden bowl to her lips and she sipped. "You'll feel better after you rest."

"I love you," she whispered after he sat back.

"I love you, too."

Ama fought against sleep, needing to see he was truly free of the longing. Through heavy lids she saw only firelight in Kaito's eyes, the bloody glow of the lighthouse gone from inside him.

When the footsteps came, Kaito didn't even flinch, not even when the doomed called him by name. Ama must have moaned, because he leaned in to take her hand. The dead went to the sea, and her brother remained.

Smiling, Ama sunk back into the ferns.

"Don't worry," He murmured just as she slipped off to sleep. "I'm not afraid anymore."

When she woke, he was gone.

∽

The other girls stared as Ama walked toward the sea, indifferent to the shadows of the dead. She felt fine, at least in body, the terrible weight that had made a home in her bones was gone, leaving behind an emptiness that was somehow worse.

"Brave of you to come back." Haenyo stood on a small, flat-topped boulder, clear of the surf and shadows.

Ama's hands clenched and unclenched, legs aching to break into a sprint, but she kept her pace deliberate, fearing if she started running she might never stop.

"Got sea in your ears, girl? I'm talking to you." Haenyo stumbled as she hopped from the boulder, going down on one knee in the frigid, ankle-deep mud. The other girls made a point of looking away. When the overseer stood her smile had become something hard and familiar.

Yesterday, Ama would've cringed before that look, breath held, hands crossed across her stomach. Now, the overseer seemed small and furtive, the crosshatch of wrinkles on her windblown cheeks like cracks in an old limestone wall.

The old upswell of fear came and went, water poured into an abyss. Not knowing what to do in its absence, Ama smiled back.

"Something funny, girl?" Haenyo's fist flicked out, fast as an eel. There was a cold twinge, like a sharp blade lain across Ama's cheek, and the overseer flinched back, her bloody hand clutched to her chest. Ama saw a flash of silver, darting like fish in the shallows, gone as the ribbon coiled back around the bones of her face.

Haenyo glared at her, teeth bared, blood dripping onto the sand. "This is my beach."

The first stone hit Ama on the shoulder, knocking her back a pace. She turned in time to see another girl stoop to pick up a mud-covered rock. Others drew knives, still careful to step around the corpse shadows as they advanced, eyes wide, their faces shaded with fear and worry. Silt spattered Ama's forehead as she ducked another stone.

"Stop, it's me!" The gold filigree unraveling from Ama's arms gave lie to her plea. Streamers of shining ribbon hung loose and liquid in the air, their tips dotted with tiny beads of blood. Several of the girls darted forward to pull Haenyo back while others bounced stones from the tangle of wire.

Then, they ran.

Ama watched them go, surprise fading to sad comprehension. They had family as well, so many corpses on the beach. She would've done the same for Kaito.

A discordant whine slipped across the beach, distant as the roar of the sea in the conch shells Kaito used to keep back home. It grew to a tattered wail, the cry of a creature in pain, threading Ama's thoughts and setting the ribbon humming around her.

Slowly, she turned to face the tower.

As she stepped into the sea lengths of glittering ribbon coiled about her feet. Tight as bindings it wrapped around her legs, then her arms and chest to keep the bitter ocean chill from invading her flesh. A dozen steps and the sand dropped away. Panic seized Ama as icy water splashed across her face, but the cocoon of ribbon surrounded her, long flagella of glimmering wire pulling her through the depths. Ahead, the arc shone, crimson light shattered into a thousand sparkling motes of brilliance.

Ama was numb and quivering by the time she pulled herself onto the spit of rock at the base of the tower. The ribbon slipped from her like a shed skin, crackling under her feet as she stumbled on legs gone wooden. She hugged herself, thin clothes little protection against the cold.

Her brother lay face down on the rock. A crab tugged at Kaito's face, retreating with dire warnings as Ama approached. Tears ran hot on her skin as she knelt to cradle his head. The ribbon man had helped Kaito, just not made him better.

Cold and bloodless, his lips still moved, and Ama bent to listen.

"I can't do it alone." Then he sang, voice picking out the notes hidden within the tower's wordless shriek. Feeling as if someone had hollowed her out, Ama joined him.

The lighthouse howled the sound of storm wind whipping through rocks. Cold gusts whipped Ama's hair into wild tangles, cutting through her flesh like icy ribbons to chill the heart within. Ama could barely move, barely breath, and still she sang, her trembling tenor catching the high notes Kaito couldn't reach.

Like a body rising from murky depths, the song became clearer, each tone more distinct than the last. It rose above the shriek, then eclipsed it. The angry red of the arc faded, replaced by a clear brilliance that set Ama's eyes watering. It boiled away the clouds around the lighthouse to reveal a sky the color of the ribbon man's eye. Light radiated up the tower, bright filigree spreading up the sides to burst from the top in an arc of pure radiance.

Kaito's hand found hers. Warmth blossomed in Ama's chest, although she didn't know if it was the light or the sleepy calm before the end. Smiling, she realized the tower wasn't a lighthouse, but a beacon.

"Please come back," she whispered through stony lips.

Around her, the whole world hummed with light, so bright even the gods must surely see.

If they weren't too far away.

Deep Into That Darkness Peering
Anatoly Belilovsky

*O**ne could quite easily have ascribed my feelings of unease*
in Ascher's company to the rather startling selection of
art that hung in his home. It was decidedly *déclassé* even for a San
Francisco *nouveau riche*, with a copy of Goya's *Execution of the Rebels*
directly in front of me and no fewer than three different versions of
Saint Sebastian's martyrdom scattered about the other parlor walls,
as well as several *natures mortes* with dead hares and pheasants and
such visible in the dining room through the open French doors. Even
the prodigious quantity of excellent Cliquot I had consumed to the
accompaniment of Ascher's inane recitation of books he had read
recently did nothing to put me at ease. I nodded, whether I agreed
with him or not, as he opined that Twain's and Kipling's best days
were behind them, while Jack London's had hardly begun, failing even
to rise to the effrontery of his appraisal of Arthur Conan Doyle as a
"talentless hack."

But, truth be told, my first desire, upon spying Ascher as he
made his way toward me through the evening fog, had been to cross
the street to avoid meeting him. If I hesitated it was only because, for a
moment, my reluctance to tread the roadway mud surely ankle-deep in
springtime, outweighed my reticence to renew our acquaintance. For
only a moment—long enough to recall a small red-headed boy with
a perpetually running nose who followed me, doglike and worshipful,

down Sutter Street to the Lowell School—and then my childhood companion rushed toward me with a happy cry and seized me by the arm and from then on I found my retreat cut off and nothing for it but to follow him to his home and to accept his most insistent invitation to dinner.

He had never done me the least scintilla of harm, certainly none that I could ever remember, not as a studious youth full of admiration for my mental agility, not as the class salutatorian whose workmanlike oratory set the stage for my valedictory triumph, and certainly not in the subsequent years when we exchanged peremptory nods and tipped our hats each time we passed each other in the street; and yet each time I met him, a certain unease prevented me from pursuing companionship with him, and this unease now rose to apprehension no amount of spirits seemed able to soothe.

We ate a dinner of cold roast squab and venison with *rose d'Anjou* under the reproachful eyes of dead deer and pigeons in the ubiquitous still life paintings on the dining room walls. The servants had apparently been dismissed earlier for I saw none, and with the wine bottle nearly empty I recalled that poisoned *rose d'Anjou* had been the weapon with which D'Arthagnan and the Musketeers were nearly dispatched in Alexandre Dumas' eponymous book. But then Ascher emptied the dregs into his own glass and drank it in one draught; and I cursed myself for a fool and assayed a smile.

Ascher's answering smile looked as wholehearted as mine felt wan. He seized my hand in one of his and yet another bottle, that of Amontillado, in the other, and drew me into another room.

It was a windowless study, its gloom lit by a single candle just bright enough that I had no need to feel my way inside. Ascher let go of my hand once we were inside, put down the bottle on the table, and used the candle to light a pair of candelabra, and as the chamber suffused with warm flickering light, I felt a rising tide of chilling apprehension, for on the study walls there was the most extensive collection of tools of death that I had ever seen.

Ascher turned to me, his grin even wider. "If only you could see your face," he said, then sniffed and wiped at his nose with his fist.

The old familiar gesture failed to reassure me, yet I felt compelled to force a smile in return. "I hope your servants come back soon," I said. "We left a mountain of dishes in the dining room; the scraps will be quite high by morning—"

He waved me to silence. "Disposal of offal can wait; it isn't worth the interruption of our entertainment." He pointed to a curved pole-axe on the wall behind him. "We have spoken of literature—but if a picture is worth a thousand words, how much greater is the value of a touch?" He closed his hand about its handle. "This, for example," he continued, "is a *giserne*, which is the weapon with which Sir Gawain beheaded the Green Knight, in the chivalric romance named after them."

"How fascinating," I said.

"Indeed," he said, oblivious to any signs I may have given of my disquiet. "And this dueling pistol—" he released the axe to point at the wall behind me "—is of the same provenance as the one that killed the great Russian poet, Pushkin, at his ill-fated duel. You have read Pushkin, have you not?"

"Not in original, of course," I answered, clearing my throat.

"Oh, well," he said. "That's hardly reading it at all."

For what seemed an eternity Ascher held forth, apparently quite knowledgeably, about the provenance and literary mentions of the assorted revolvers, rifles, muskets, arquebuses, carbines, repeaters, shotguns, derringers and flint-locks arrayed behind me, and of the rapiers, halberks, bodkins, dirks, tomahawks and katanas displayed behind his back. His eyes glittered, he paced back and forth, he pointed at the weapons, he slapped the carved oak table, setting the candelabra to totter precariously as their flames flickered. With each sip of Amontillado his gestures grew ever more animated with unfeigned fascination for the subject of his speech.

I heard his clock strike, at long intervals one after another, the small hours of the morning. A bottle of excellent tawny Port followed the Amontillado onto the carved oak table and then into our glasses, and as the clock struck five—five in the morning!—one of the five candles guttered and went out, and Ascher froze on the spot.

All at once his face underwent a change. It was no mere darkening with the attenuation of light, nor growing ponderous with accumulated fatigue. No, from one second to the next he seemed to go from friend to fiend, his mouth from a slantwise smile to a bloodless gash, his eyes from twinkling to smoldering like twin matches poised over the touch holes of a brace of guns.

He stopped in mid-sentence—something about the dueling sword at the very top of the wall, some fifteen feet above us, of the kind that pierced Mercutio's breast in *Romeo and Juliet*; how strange to remember that fragment of a detail—stood up, drained his glass in one swallow and, with great violence, hurled it into the corner nearest me.

The deafening crash, and the resulting spray of fragments that missed me by the merest fraction, struck me immobile and dumb. On Ascher, they had the opposite effect. His mouth contorted in a mirthless grin, and he issued forth a bark of diabolical laughter.

"But what of Chekhov's Law?" he said, his voice now low and guttural.

"What—what of it?" I stammered. "I know of no bills sponsored by this Chekhov, nor have I ever heard of a Congressman by this name—"

"Fool!" Ascher snarled. "Yes, I chose wisely: you are indeed a philistine of no breeding; how you managed to best me— But I digress. Chekhov's Law is not a product of legislation but of Art." I heard the majuscule in his voice as clearly as I heard malice. "It states," he continued, "that a gun seen hanging on the wall in Act One of a play must always kill someone in Act Three."

He paused. I trembled where I stood.

"Act Three is now," he continued, more in a serpentine hiss than a whisper.

I stared at Ascher, then at the wall behind him. Edged steel weapons hung thick upon it, but all the firearms, it seemed, were out of his reach. I spun toward the wall behind me and snatched for the nearest weapon.

"The game's afoot," he said before I could touch the derringer toward which I had been reaching. "But I have not explained the rules. Bear with me, old friend." The word twisted with mockery, dripping off his tongue with scorn. "The gun which you are about to seize is unloaded. So is every other gun. Every gun but one."

He grinned again, and a rivulet of cold sweat ran down my spine. "Choose wisely," he said in a vicious sing-song. "Aim well. Sight on my heart. Squeeze, don't pull, the trigger." He opened his arms as if for an embrace, but then his right continued its arc, reaching back and back and impossibly back, until his hand closed on the hilt of a Turkish yataghan.

He swept it off the wall and spun it in an expert *moulinet.* Candlelight reflected off its mirror-bright blade both dazzled and mesmerized me.

"And if I live, I'll kill you." He brought the yataghan straight down on the longest candle yet lit; two halves flew to the sides. The flame, too, split in twain, an instant before the stroke extinguished it.

We stood in silence. I drew my hand back, slowly.

"Well, I refuse to play," I said, my tongue barely moving in my mouth. I took another sip of Port, then set it down quickly as a thought—*What if it's poisoned?*—raced through my mind. "Will you cut me down in cold blood?"

"I will do no such thing," said Ascher. "There is a second game, should the first end in a draw." He blew out another flickering flame, leaving two very short candles to light his visage from below. Not even Satan, at that moment, could have looked more demonic. "It's called 'Survival in the Dark.'"

He reached into his jacket pocket with his left hand, drew a box of matches and threw it on the table. It rattled as it rolled, coming to rest like a loaded die, predictably, on its broad side. "In the event you live," he said, sketching a fencer's salute in my direction, "it would be impolite to make you stumble about in search of an exit."

"But why?" I asked.

He reached for the half-full bottle of Amontillado, drank directly from it, then placed it carefully on the table. "Because I always wanted to," he said. "And it's my birthday, and my mother is dead, and no one gave me a present, so I must pamper myself." He blew out the penultimate candle. "Don't worry," he said. "I'll let the last one go out on its own. It has not long to burn."

I watched, by guttering light, the play of reflections across the walls, the mad glitter in the pupils of Ascher's eyes.

Which gun? He'd chosen a yataghan, an Oriental weapon—was that a Russian pattern on the stock of the double-barreled shotgun? Or would the yataghan's single-edged blade and angular hilt suggest a single-shot pistol?

My heart thundered, blood roaring in my ears. My hands and legs shook till I could stand no more. I reeled, clutching the table, but it seemed to move—the candle died, plunging all in darkness—I shook and tried to brace myself. I felt a great force strike me from the back. How could he have moved so fast behind me?

Another terrific jolt and a crash that seemed to go on forever, and through it I heard a shrill keening like that of a sinner burning in the fires of Hell. Something fell on me—my hand grasped it—it was a gun, a revolver, but I could not see to aim. I waved it about blindly, dropped it to grasp at something, anything, as I lost my balance again—

This time, the very floor seemed to rise up at my feet, a jagged fissure rent the ceiling, scant cold predawn light dazzled my eyes. And with a gasp I pushed away as I saw Ascher standing eye to eye before me.

Standing, yes, but hardly poised to strike, for from his collar protruded the Italian *spada*, the sword that topped Ascher's macabre collection. Its basket hilt perched on his shoulder like a second head while its tip affixed him to the oaken table. Blood ran down the weapon's blade protruding from his chest, and another rivulet trickled from his mouth: two scarlet blots swelling on the linen tablecloth.

A great wash of relief came over me then. Whether the ground quaked again, or my legs buckled of their own accord, I found myself kneeling, staring up at Ascher's pale, contorted face.

"I win," I said.

With the last vestige of life he turned his head and fixed his gaze on me. There was a cold light in it, a dying spark of unholy mirth.

"No," he croaked. "Chekhov...wins."

With that, the malevolent glow in his eyes went out. He slumped, the blade bending under his weight. The floor groaned once again and gave another lurch; the blade snapped with a soft, almost musical sound, and Ascher's body fell from sight.

I groped my way back from the now roofless study to what remained of the dining room, crawled between the broken timbers and exited through the gaping hole that once had been a window. All around me San Francisco lay in ruins, the first of the fires springing up as men and women and dogs ran about in mindless confusion.

As I stared aghast, with an awful crash the fissure widened; and as the walls fell in upon the house of Ascher, I breathed a great sigh of relief. A gust of wind parted the clouds of dust and smoke, and through them I glimpsed the bell-tower of Saint Mary's Church, still standing among the devastation.

I turned and walked toward this stalwart house of worship, past bleeding, crying, grieving people, past ruined homes and burning edifices, down streets strewn with fragments of lives destroyed. Saint Mary's was a Popish church, but I could think of nothing I desired more than to kneel within its hallowed precincts and thank Providence for sending me this most welcome, most merciful, most Divine deliverance.

Smoke and Sprites
Vonnie Winslow Crist

*A*s she approached the Northern Mars Waste Disposal
Facility, Cali adjusted the straps of her face mask. Even in
her truck, the edges of the apparatus needed to press tight against her
skin to seal out the acrid smell of the Waste Zone.

She was in no mood to deal with the stinging eyes and gut-
wrenching cough associated with exposure to fumes. Originally
scheduled for some down-time, she'd been called in to check the weather
phenomenon reported by the facility's workers after Silas cut himself.

"May you get toe rot, Silas Busbeel," she muttered into her
mask. Not that she really wished anyone ill, but trying to juggle knives
after drinking beer for hours seemed beyond stupid.

Before her, she saw a skyline of smoke stacks sprouting from
the NMWD Facility like giant redwood trees. But instead of branches
and leaves, the metal chimneys were crowned with clouds of smoke
and left-over gases.

As she sped closer, Cali briefly lifted her eyes from the road
ahead to study the billowy vapors. Sparks left over from the incineration
process glittered at the tops of the smoke stacks and tinted vermilion
the underbellies of the carbon monoxide and waste gas clouds. At least
she hoped still-burning bits were the cause of the bloody discoloration.

Just before she entered a fog of heavy gases which had sunk to
ground level, she saw a refuse train pulling under one of the off-loading

domes. There, the jumble of garbage would be sorted by machines. The reusable plastics, glasses, papers, and metals that hadn't been removed by scrappers would be taken from the heap. Then, the rest would be funneled to one of the enormous incinerators which not only disposed of garbage, but generated power.

Automatically, the fog lights on her truck flicked on. Thicker than usual ground vapors limited her visibility, so it took a few minutes before Cali could see the landscape again.

Like most Mars she'd seen, the red soil here supported stunted trees, straggly grasses, and prickly-looking shrubs. Of course, whatever plants and animals chose to make the Waste their home had to survive without human-made ponds, streams, and reservoirs. She suspected the drought-like conditions were partly responsible for the inhospitable terrain. But no matter what Mars Commercial and Planetary Management, Inc. reported, she knew the gaseous byproducts of the incineration process had to have some impact on the environment.

"Hey, California, you at the site yet?'

Just her luck, thought Cali. Silas was her base contact.

"Yeah. I just drove through the main facility domes and towers. I should be at the Southeast Spur in a few minutes."

"Wanted to let you know a storm's moving in your direction. You might have a chance to see whatever weather phenomenon is spooking the NMWD workers."

"Thanks for the heads up, Silas. California, out."

Cali had added the last phrase to stop any chitchat. She had little tolerance for Silas on a good day, and today she was sure she'd reel off a series of insults if pushed.

The Southeast Spur, like the main facility and the other NMWD Spurs, was a complex of domes, smoke stacks, power lines, and communication towers serviced by a web of train tracks. The facility ran night and day, employing combots and a skeleton crew of humans. Combots, half-robot half-computer machines, did all the labor under the watchful eyes of two human crew members per eight-hour shift. In addition, two facility managers oversaw the crew and arriving train engineers, and handled the planetary communications, operational reports, and any problems that cropped up.

It was one of those managers who'd contacted the Terra-forming and Climate Division of MC&PM, Inc. about weird lights in the sky during storms. Cali doubted it was more than lightning affected by the various gases released by the Spur's smoke stacks. Possibly there was some sort of electrical current from the power generating process charging the atmosphere. But if she had to place a bet, Cali would put her credits on lightning.

Workers at these remote sites tended to go a little buggy after a few years. Almost anyone would begin to imagine things if the only people they saw month after month were five co-workers, two managers, and engineers who just wanted to eat, sleep, and then, leave.

Careful to avoid the machines diligently performing their repetitive tasks, she pulled into the Spur's main dome and tapped her security code in on a virtual keyboard near the entrance.

A man's face appeared on the screen. "What can I do for you?"

"I'm the Terra-forming and Climate Division rep sent to evaluate your light anomalies. Am I speaking to Harold Bromski?" Even though it would have been easier for the facilities manager to see her without the mask, Cali refused lower it and breathe in the stench.

After leaning closer to the screen and squinting, the man responded, "Yeah, I'm Harold. I'll be down in a minute. Just have to let the crew know I'll be out of my office for a few hours."

Cali nodded, and then, turned her truck around so it pointed out of the dome. In truth, she didn't like being the only human in the company of hundreds of combots. Although their manufacturers guaranteed their safety, every now and again, a combot suddenly became non-compliant and sometimes violent.

She'd finished sending a message to Silas updating him on her status, and was checking her data-collection equipment when a loud rap on the passenger's side window of the truck nearly caused her to drop her camera. Cali hit the unlock button, and a gas-masked Harold climbed in.

"You might want to leave that on," she said when the facility manager started to remove his mask. "At least until we're away from the Spur's smoke stacks."

"I forgot the truck wouldn't be airtight," mumbled Harold as he adjusted his mask's straps. He continued, "There's an observation tower about a mile east of here where you should be able to see..." He paused, and seemed to be searching for the right word. "The lights. You should be able to see the lights."

Following Harold's directions, Cali wove through the Southeast Spur's buildings, finally arriving at a concrete block tower.

"Need some help?" asked Harold as she gathered various instruments to collect data, her camera, and a handful of spare batteries.

"Nope," she responded. She placed everything in a heavy-weight cloth knapsack, slung it over her shoulder, and followed the manager to the tower's door.

Harold fumbled with several passkeys, located the correct key, and swiped the lock-pad. The lock buzzed and the door swung inward. Lights must have been programmed to turn on when the door was opened, or perhaps when sensors detected humans, because the tower's interior was suddenly illuminated.

"Doesn't feel nearly as spooky, now," Harold said. He forced a nervous laugh. "Not that I'm afraid of a few lights in the sky."

"Never said you were," replied Cali as she brushed past him and began the climb to the observation room.

As soon as she reached the top level of the tower, it was clear Silas's weather forecast was dead on. Nimbus clouds lined up on the horizon like an army of charcoal gray soldiers. Lightning zigzagged from the thunderheads to the ground in an awesome display of electrical power. There must have been mica or some other reflective mineral in the soil, because the bolts appeared to not only strike the planet's surface, but to race across the ground.

"Are those the lights you reported?"

"No," answered Harold with eyes wide.

As Cali set up her Extra Low Frequency radio receivers, low-light camera, and various other instruments, she noted there were sweat beads on his forehead and upper lip.

The storm moved closer, and a pounding rain slammed into the tower's roof. Though it was hard to see through the heavy rainfall, the fierce lightning clearly split the sky, and the thunder seemed to rock the building. As quickly as it had started, the rain slowed to a mist, and what appeared to be flames shot upwards from the clouds.

"TLEs," gasped Cali.

"ETs!" Harold was clearly shocked.

"No, not Extra-Terrestrials." Certainly an incorrect nomenclature since they weren't on Earth, thought Cali. But alien species were still labeled ETs by most people. "TLEs, *Transient Luminous Events*. Sometimes people call them cloud-to-space lightning or upper atmosphere lightning. And I think what we have here is a variety called a sprite."

The manager stared at her as if waiting for more information.

The phenomenon occurred again. This time, she had the camera pointed in the correct direction and programmed to snap continuous pictures.

"Let's take a look," she said as she plugged the camera into her view-screen. Several finger strokes later, images of TLEs flashed one after the other on the screen.

First, there was a disc-shaped glow above the thunderstorm. Next, a column of red light shot up from the mesosphere and, Cali was sure, into the ionosphere. There appeared to be tendrils of purple and blue coming from the red cylindrical beam and dangling down to into the stratosphere, almost touching the clouds.

And then, the upper atmosphere lightning was gone. Within a split second, another red glow appeared, and the sequence began again. Though the sprites appeared to be the same phenomenon repeating itself, Cali knew the radio signature would be unique for each sprite.

Before she could continued her explanation of positive charges and atmospheric layers, Harold pointed at the view-screen and whispered, "What's that?"

She looked at the screen. There appeared to be a glowing disc-shaped vessel hovering at the base of a sprite. Before she could speak, it dropped groundward in a vivid display of lightning.

"Um, I'm not sure."

The final image was of a glowing disc resting on the planet's surface. She pressed her lips together as the pictures began to repeat.

Cali went to the window, held her binoculars up to her eyes and, using the night-vision setting, scanned the Martian terrain about where the disc should be. She observed the vessel less than two miles from the tower, skimming across the ground in their direction. It was definitely not human in design.

Perhaps the aliens were there to collect the carbon monoxide or other discharged gases from the Waste facility. Perhaps they were observing the sprites, too. Or studying the design of the power-producing incinerators. But there were also many nefarious reasons for ETs to visit a desolate, nearly deserted part of Mars.

As she lowered her binoculars, Cali saw the fear in Harold's eyes. He, too, knew there were rules, negotiations, and notifications if off-worlders wanted to land on Mars. But these ETs had chosen to arrive in secret. And she was certain no good would come of their visit.

Barely able to breathe, she activated her headset. She needed to report what she'd found while investigating the strange lights at the North Mars Waste Disposal Facility to her base contact. She hoped the communication towers still functioned. Hoped there was enough time left to get a warning out.

"Silas, this is California. Please, tell me you're there."

The Blind Queen's Daughter

G. Scott Huggins

*T*he heavy mauls swung inward, the only thunder in the soft morning rain. The priests watched, trembling. A small man from Arabia stared hungrily at the widening hole.

The bricks sealing the cell shivered, and Amren watched his father's jaw tremble under the blow—tremble as it never had in two desperate battles. Not even when the men of his auxilia fell about him in desperate retreat had Amren seen Sir Bedwyr's face show fear. Until now.

The brick fell inward under the final blow, and only gelid, tomb-like darkness crouched within. How long had she dwelt in this three-windowed cell, sealed up in brick, lest her anchoress's vows of solitude prove—like her wedding vows—too weak? *Since before my birth, nearly twenty years ago.*

From within the cell, a shape emerged, its dark cloak held fast about by two alabaster hands. Amren's breath caught.

Stiff with age she moved, her hands veined like marble. Reached up. Removed her cowl.

"Bedwyr," she said. "It has been long."

Amren sucked in his breath.

The rain caught in her raven-dark hair like glass beads; they glowed in the whiteness of her skin. Her eyes were the gold of a summer dusk. Rich, dark gold shot through her hair in strands. Gwynhwyfar. The White Enchantress.

"Not long enough, my lady," returned Sir Bedwyr.

"Is this your son?" she asked, and Amren felt his blood heat against his will with those eyes on him.

"Aye. His name is Amren. Sir Amren."

Amren shook himself, resolved not to show fear or shame, though the honor was scarce two hours old. He felt his unworthiness deeply, and the cryptic wrongness of it.

≈

The smell had choked him in the vast hall of Caerlon. His father had walked quickly past the empty round table, and Amren followed. When the sisters had opened the doors to the king's chamber, the bile rose in Amren's throat.

"Bedwyr," said the cassocked shape in the chair. Its white head lifted, bowed down under a long, carefully-tended beard, and the lightest of gold circlets. Beneath it, a black, spreading pool of liquid. "Bedwyr," repeated the voice, full of pain. "Have you come at last, to end it?"

"Aye, Sire," said his father, voice grim. "It ends soon. Grant me this last boon."

King Arthur coughed, grimaced, and spat. It was blood that he spat, and his own dark blood that dripped through the black cassock onto the ground. "Knighthood for your son? A fool's wish, and you know it. Sir Cei is dead. Sir Gwain, dead. This is your son, not a corpse."

"You swore, Sire," said Sir Bedwyr.

Wearily, Arthur nodded. "Help me." Arthur's right hand crept out, and clawed at a dark hilt. Sir Bedwyr helped the old king lift the great blade. The polished gems on its scabbard and pommel glowed in the room.

"Kneel," his father said. "Last knight of Arthur the High King, Dux Brittanorum of Rome."

"I dub thee," gasped Arthur. "Sir Amren, Knight of the Round Table." Then he broke off in a coughing fit, and the sisters rushed in to lift him from the chair to the bed. Amren had only a glimpse of Arthur's flesh as they laid

him on the bed, before his father hoisted him to his feet. His wound below the ribs bled reddish-black—and maggots spilled from the ragged flesh.

It was not until the door was shut that Amren noticed his father still held Arthur's great sword. Caledfwlch. Excalibur, the Romans called it. "He is worse now," said Sir Bedwyr. "Yet while this sword and scabbard remain, he cannot die. They hold him, past the dignity of the grave and his hope of heaven."

Amren found his voice. "Why has no one taken it from him until now?"

Sir Bedwyr frowned. "Do you not see it, boy? Only he has kept our folk and the Faith alive since Camlann."

Amren scowled. "I did not see him or that sword at Carmarthen when the Saechsen swelled about the tor like a sea of blades." He had lost friends there, before Sir Bedwyr's desperate charge had cut them a path home. They all had. And yet his father reddened and raised a hand as if to strike him. Then, he lowered it.

"The barbarians are worries for Rome. Arthur's fight is against… others. He is at the end of his strength now. As are we all. There are none left to return his blade. It is your duty, Sir Amren." And he held forth the sword.

More frightened than he had ever been, Amren took the blade.

❧

"Sir Amren," said Gwynhwyfar. Arthur's queen. "I greet you, in the name of the Father and the Son, and the Holy Spirit." She signed the cross, and Amren knelt, remembering that she was an anchoress and a holy lady. Caledfwlch caught awkwardly on the ground.

"How may I serve, my lady?" He blurted.

"Return the sword you bear."

He began to fumble with the belt.

"No!" She looked at her feet. "Speech is not so easy as once it was. Forgive me. Return it to the White Tower of Avalon, whence it came so that I, and my sisters, may take the king on one last journey."

Amren stammered. "I—gladly, lady. But I know not the way to Avalon."

Gwynhwyfar beckoned. "You shall be guided."

Another shape emerged. Cowled, like the lady, but lighter. The hands folded before the robe shone like the clouded moon. Someone gasped.

Sir Bedwyr found a voice. "Is it possible?" The priests crossed themselves.

"Yes," said Gwynhwyfar. "She is Mordred's—and mine. Her name is Gwynhwyfach. She will guide your son into Avalon. Together they must open the way for us—with one other."

The Arabian stepped to her elbow. "Your message was received. By the Holy Father. He sent for me." He spoke in Latin, with the oddest accent Amren had ever heard. "Show yourself, child."

Gwynhwyfach stepped forward. She threw back her cowl. Her face almost the mirror of her mother's, her hair black as night, her lips red as blood.

And her eyes were sewn shut with golden thread!

"Merciful Jesu!" cried an acolyte. One of the priests fainted, and a sister, too.

The Arabian merely nodded. "A most excellent guide, to Avalon." He stepped forward. "Even in my home, lady, I have heard of you. I am Abdullah al-Hazrat." These last words were run together, and sounded almost to Amren like *abdul-alhazred*.

"From Rome?" the lady asked, in the same tongue. "The Guide of the Mind?"

"From Arabia. And yes: to accompany the Guide of the Spirit." He turned to Amren. "We are your guides to Avalon. And now, I must speak with this great lady, for whose sake I travel."

They retreated into the church, followed by the eldest priest. Gwynhwyfar's daughter took her elbow and followed her mother, stumbling over the unfamiliar ground.

Amren turned to his father. "In Jesu's name, sire, what is all this?"

Sir Bedwyr looked down at his son. "You know that once, Caerlon was the very throne of honor under Arthur, Dux, the High King, and Gwynhwyfar the White, of Avalon. Their blessed union held the realm together, and we, their knights, kept the peace. This was before Arthur, enspelled by Morigena, betrayed her, and Gwynhwyfar, in silent rage, took Mordred's side and joined with him."

Amren shuddered. "And that's… Mordred's daughter?" She was at least two years his elder, and all that time, sealed up by brick and her mother's vows. Three windows to the world, and even that light denied her. "Why is she blinded?"

"I know not," said Bedwyr. "None of us knew of her, I swear by God. We would never… to a child…" His voice trailed off, and Amren saw his father's tears.

"But hear me: all was lost at Camlann. You see his hurt. Yet he endured, for his name alone kept the realm together. But now it must end, before his spirit breaks, and takes hers with him. They have both done more penance than ordinary men can bear. Yet, it is not enough.

"Arthur's knight must return his sword whence it came. And you are the last with the strength. He has made no more knights since Camlann, lest their souls be bound to his. I am sorry, son, but it falls to you to set this right."

Amren bowed. "Did you think to find me wanting, Father?"

"Never, son." Quietly, he pressed a strange, thin dagger into Amren's hands. "This is Carnwennan," he muttered. "'Twill serve Arthur better in thy hands than in his. Fight as thou hast ever fought, and it wilt make me proud."

Footsteps interrupted father and son. The Arab's eyes were alight with a strange look, and he clasped a thick tome to his breast. When he spoke, his voice was ragged. "We must ride now, or all is lost. We have no more than two sunsets before the way is forever shut."

～

The three of them rode into the sunrise. Gwynhwyfach rode behind Amren, her white hands clasped loosely about his waist. Her sealed eyes on the back of his neck made his hair stand on end. It was a relief when the Arab spoke.

"Gwynhwyfar and Excalibur came from Avalon," al-Hazrat said, when the horses left the road, and they had to slow, "to make an alliance of Spirit, to prepare the way for the world's salvation. Rome was falling, eaten from within and without by the machinations of the Elder Gods, who starved for lack of souls since Constantine darkened their temples. Did you think they would go quietly? Did you think it happenstance that the wastes of Leng disgorged the Hsiong-nu, driving the Alemanni and the Hun against Rome? Chance that sent plague to ravage the whole earth? Arthur and Gwynhwyfar were to unite, and bring a piece of the Blessed Realm again to Earth—for a time."

"What happened?"

"Like so many, they were unworthy. They betrayed one another: for lust, for power. The Round Table was broken. And the hundred million souls who would have been safe in Arthur's Empire lie in danger of damnation, prey of the Elder Ones. Only dying Caerlon remains."

Gwynhwyfach spoke from behind him. "Arthur's strength must not fail on this side of Avalon."

"But he cannot die," said Amren.

"Not die," said al-Hazrat, "yet his body and soul must go to Avalon with Gwynhwyfar—half passed to her when they were wed. If it does not, his soul will fall to the evil it has fought so long. The way to Avalon is closed by his own betrayal. On the other side of that gate is not Avalon, but the Otherworld."

Amren swallowed. "Ann..."

"*Do not speak that name!*" screamed the Arab. "You give it power. It is the Otherworld."

The Otherworld that hungered for the blood of the vanished, the Realm of King Arawn and his Wild Hunt. "It is a place? A true place?"

"Thither we go," said al-Hazrat, fixing Amren with a stare. "Beneath the Shadow of the Dark Tower—only there can Arthur's fall be stopped. There we must win through to Avalon, reopening it to Arthur, that he may find rest. I shall open the way. She will be our guide, and you, Sir Amren, must wield the sword and return it."

Gwynhwyfach's hand fell to its hilt. "Excalibur," she said, in Latin. She spoke no other tongue. "The sword that cuts steel." She took a deep breath. "The scent of rain, all around," she said. "Like living in a giant window. Now, turn thither." She pointed, without looking.

"How do you know?" Amren asked.

"I was born for this."

~

Again, Amren heard Gwynhwyfar's last words to her daughter as they approached. "…ever forgive the unforgiveable? Know only that you know all that you need."

Then, Gwynhwyfar had fixed him with her golden eyes.

"Trust my daughter. Guard her. She will tell you what you need to know. Ask nothing else!"

~

Gwynhwyfach had lived her life shut in a six-ell square room, with only her mother. She stumbled over every twig, and yet she guided them. How could she have been born for this?

"'Tis darkling," he finally said. "We must camp."

The Arab reluctantly nodded. "We must find the Causeway and the Gate. If we ride in darkness, we may *be* found."

~

Amren half-slept when she came to him. He started when she threw back her cowl. The gold thread through her eyelids caught the embers' glow and her raven-crowned face watched him.

"Do you fear me?" she asked.

"I fear your guidance," he said. "Have you ever seen aught?"

"My mother hemmed my eyes soon after birth. I have never seen."

"How can you guide us? If you mislead us in the Otherworld…"

"There," she said, sitting, "I shall have sight, and you shall see by it. Trust nothing there that you see yourself. It is the Realm of Shadows, and the Horned King's servants see you by those shadows."

"You speak in riddles," he said.

"All shall be plain," she said. "I shall lead you by the safest paths. But you must trust me with your life and soul."

"I shall trust you, lady."

She shook her head. "Your word is not enough. Not in this. You would not break it willfully, but… You must not hesitate, and nor must I. We must be one in all things. Even as Arthur and my mother once were one—before they fell."

"What are you saying, lady?" he asked. She moved closer.

"The King and Queen were joined to rule this realm—the blood of men, and that of Avalon. No other union can prevail against the Horned King on his own ground. We must go thence together or we die."

Amren's mouth worked. "There is no priest here."

"Nor was one in Eden," said Gwynhwyfach. "And yet Adam took Eve to wife. I know thee not," she said, "except that thou art prepared to fight this fearful foe from love of duty. I know thou art afraid, as I am, and yet you turn not back. I beg thee, be my husband, so we may have some chance of victory." Her face was nearly touching his, and Amren felt his blood race.

"Lady, if we wed, may I not look you in the eyes?"

"'Twould slay thee. Yet in the morning you shall open them."

He nodded. "Let it be as you say, lady."

She touched his face with one cool hand. "I, Gwynhwyfach, take thee, Amren, to my wedded husband, to have and to hold, from this day forward, with God and His creation witness."

Her face was warm to his touch. "I, Amren, take thee, Gwynhwyfach, to my wedded wife, to have and to hold, from this day forward, with God and His creation witness."

They kissed, surrounded by the dark they feared, opening to one another, trusting beyond reason where reason had failed, then slept one night beneath the stars of heaven.

She murmured to him, "In the Otherworld, you must loose my eyes. Carnwennan will open them, and I shall have my sight."

"How do you know?"

She kissed him. "My husband, my eyes and hands see more than you can imagine. Though I stumble, think me not a babe. I have trained in a school whose doors are as closed to you as sword craft is to me. Trust me as I trust you, and all will be well."

And Amren slept, without fear.

≈

At dawn they set off again, and though Amren's soul stayed still and calm, al-Hazrat's face grew more drawn, and he paged through his leprous, leather-bound journal more wildly each time Gwynhwyfach changed their course.

"What is it friend?" Amren said at last.

Al-Hazrat hunched over his saddle. "This land is strange to me," he muttered. "I see none of the signs. I know she must guide us, but I mislike her lack of learning. My life is built on study, boy. This book is my life's work. The Horned King, in his Tower, has another name. One even He must own. Today I put my studies to the test. But I swear, by Allah, I shall open the way, if she finds the Causeway."

The sun fell, and he sank further into a muttering fugue. Though Amren began to hear strange sounds, Gwynhwyfach never faltered. At last they descended, in the south, to the graying beach of Dyfed.

The beach stretched on, and seemed to have no end. The wood behind was veiled in fog that seemed more distance than mist. Ahead the stars rose above a sea that bulged and faded in directions that clawed at Amren's mind. And the hard and gibbous stars that rose were strange.

"*Allahu ar-Rahim!*" cried al-Hazrat. "He has shown me the way. And now, I shall defend His children." Turban askew, he clutched his book to him and stepped to the water's edge. From his robes he took a vial of clearest crystal, pouring out green-and-red fluid in a semicircle. He drank off the dregs, and opened the scrawled pages. "*Iä!*" he cried. "*Y'A'bdulal-Hazred. Yog-Sothoth H'ee – L'Geb! F'ai Throdog. Uaah!*"

Gwynhwyfach screamed and covered her ears. Amren retched at the sound of the unclean tongue. The Earth heaved, and an island loomed through the darkness as if it had always been there. Behind them, mist fell like a solid wall.

Like a man in a fever, the Arab stepped onto the causeway. Where he stepped, the black gelid mass of the water turned to solid rock.

Amren never knew if they walked a mile or only seven steps to reach the shore of the Otherworld, where strange stars shone like moons, and black crags reared to block the lower sky.

There was no way back.

In the darkness, Gwynhwyfach shone like a sword.

Amren raised his shield and drew Excalibur. Its pommel glowed like burning blood. Gwynhwyfach turned to him. "We arrived unseen," she said. Afterward, Amren remembered the way his heart lifted beneath her first smile. "I know the way. We—"

But a shriek rose and pierced the darkness. "Kadath! The Tower rises... Allah, it rises forever! And we..." He shot a glance behind. "We are too close! We are lost, and..." he gripped Amren by the sword arm. "I was wrong. The Dragon of the Thousand Young awakes...! The Horned King mounts—and he is but an aspect! The Utmost Gate is open! Yog-Sothoth has seen! It knows my name!" Al-Hazred turned to flee, but the glabrous, solid shadows with no color curled about him and pulled. Amren lunged after him, swinging at the grasping darkness, but clove only foul air.

"Amren!" cried Gwynhwyfach. "My eyes!"

Amren drew her to himself beneath his shield and slid Carnwennan from its sheath. He made two swift cuts with the glassy blade, parting the soft gold thread, leaving a single drop of blood on each closed lid. She kissed him. "Now I shall be thy light." She turned away.

He knew when her eyes opened, for the shadows parted beneath them as before a bonfire of stars. He saw the dead land, a high plateau whose walls were a city of ten thousand doors, that sprouted numberless towers, and one, a pillar like a hole in the sky, rising up to touch forever—the Dark Tower.

He saw the gibbering, ravening things that poured out from them. He saw tentacles sliding back into the ground, dragging shreds of turban and tattered pages. He saw the top of the tower—saw it unfold and scuttle through the air on wings of night.

The howling host charged. But the killing light of Gwynhwyfach's gaze stripped the shadows from them, dragging formless terrors screaming into visibility and space, freezing them to stone.

Perseus lied, he thought. *Medusa killed with beauty, not with fear.*

The dragon above stooped. The wind of its passage ripped them from their feet; its landing slammed the breath from them. A dozen cold eyes shone pallid hate from beneath curling goat-horns. Its cartilaginous plates twisted wetly; it scuttled on a hundred legs with the scream of damned souls. Staggering to his feet, Amren saw what they were: the lower parts of men, their upper halves fused and melted into the belly of the great wyrm, forever screaming with the pain of moving its purulent bulk forward.

Upon its neck, Amren saw the yellow-eyed horned god-king of the Otherworld. All hope left him. But he would not run. He raised his sword.

The Horned King laughed. The dragon's tail whipped around, shattering Amren's shield, felling him to the ground. Above him, the dragon reared to devour.

And then, Gwynhwyfach knelt over him, opening her eyes. Amren's ears bled, and the dragon screamed—its cartilage petrified and hardened. Cracked. *Shattered.* It cried in pain, its legs snapping beneath it. And yet it rose upon its belly, undying.

"Strike, Amren, now!"

He could not reach it with Excalibur. With his left hand he flung Carnwennan at the cracked and bleeding flesh. It spiraled through the air and struck.

The dragon screamed again, and fell; the shock flinging Amren away.

Vision blurred, he came up on his feet. A tall shape rose from the wreck, screaming in rage. It flung something that glowed. Gwynhwyfach screamed. It strode toward her, eyes blazing with vengeance, mouthless face writhing in fury. Amren raised Excalibur aloft.

"Arawn!" he cried

At the sound of its name, it turned from its victim, and fixed its yellow-eyed gaze upon him. Amren's skin boiled; he felt his flesh begin to melt, sliding from his bones, his soul sliding, too. A deathless prison opened its jaws to consume him forever.

Then, Gwynhwyfach looked upon Amren. Her eyes blazed; twin colorless suns. Elsewhere her gaze would have killed him. But here, beneath the putrescent glare of the Horned King, he felt his flesh firm, harden. The king's eyes widened, and he drew a sword black as the void between dying worlds. Excalibur leapt to meet it, pommel flaring as the blades met—then, Excalibur sliced through.

∼

The Horned King fell, mawless head rolling on a plain barren even of dust.

Amren knelt beside his wife. Her eyes were closed again. And from her side the white hilt of Carnwennan jutted, a font of crimson pouring on the ground.

∼

The Otherworld shook, but still he held her. He felt the ground split, receding, and did not care. She raised her face to his. "Please…" she said. "Take it out." It was the first time his wife had sounded like only a woman—a frightened woman, in pain. He eased the blade out, and her blood gushed forth. The wound was mortal.

"Look upon me," he whispered. Her gaze would turn his flesh to stone. And stone felt nothing.

"Not for the world," she whispered back.

He felt a wild hope. With fumbling fingers, he loosened the scabbard at his belt. He fastened it firmly upon her, as cleansing waves washed about their feet. They mixed with the blood, which did not slow. She smiled sadly at him.

"Yes, love. Now, I cannot die. But you saw Arthur's wound. I know you would not wish that for me. For a time, I hoped…but no. I knew how this would end."

The waves were waist high now, the Otherworld was sinking. In the distant dawn, a verdant isle rose in the East, the white tower shining in the twilight. He saw Gwynhwyfach turn from him and look thence. Toward home. "The way to Avalon is clear. And I will take the sword." She drew it, and held it aloft, over her head. "Let them behold our victory. And when we meet again, I will look you in the face, and never look away."

The land stood firm beneath his feet, while she slipped from him, into the waves. Amren cried great sobs into the sea, unashamed. She held the causeway to Caerlon's shore open behind him, but he could not look away from the white hand, holding the sword above the surface of the waves, until she faded from sight beneath the white tower.

About the Contributors

Daniel Beazley was born and raised in the South West of England. Growing up, he became captivated and drawn into the World of fantasy courtesy of the writings of Tolkien, Feist, Gemmell, Lewis, Livingstone and Dever. These together with films like *Conan, Red Sonja, The Dark Crystal, Willow* and *Krull*, truly inspired him to want to join the creative journey that is fantasy. He began writing in 1996 whilst spending some time in the sunny climes of Sicily. This continued periodically whilst working in the Army and then the Police; living in various parts of the country as well as overseas. Daniel now lives with his family in the rural countryside of Devon. You can keep up to date with the progress of his works at the following places: Facebook: www.facebook.com/writerdanielbeazley Twitter: www.twitter.com/Daniel_Beazley Website: www.danielbeazley.com

Anatoly Belilovsky is a Russian-American author and translator of speculative fiction. He was born in a city that went through six or seven owners in the last century, all of whom used it to do a lot more than drive to church on Sundays; he is old enough to remember tanks rolling through it on their way to Czechoslovakia in 1968. After being traded to the US for a shipload of grain and a defector to be named later (see Wikipedia, Jackson-Vanik amendment), he learned English from *Star Trek* reruns and went on to become a pediatrician in an area of New York where English is only the fourth most commonly used language. His original work appeared, or will appear, in the *Unidentified Funny Objects* anthology, *Ideomancer, Nature Futures, Stupefying Stories, Immersion Book of Steampunk, Daily SF, Mammoth Book of Dieselpunk*, and *Genius Loci* anthology, and has been podcast by *Cast of Wonders, Tales of Old*, and *Toasted Cake*; his translations from Russian have sold to *F&SF, Year's Best SF #32* (edited by Gardner Dozois,) *Grimdark*, and *Kasma*. He blogs about writing at www.loldoc.net.

Meg Belviso holds a BA in English from Smith College and an MFA from Columbia University. During the week, she chronicles angel encounters as an editor of a bi-monthly magazine on the subject, but her own tastes run more towards monsters and ghosts. As a freelancer, she has written for different properties from *Malcolm in the Middle* to *Dexter's Laboratory* to *Looney Tunes*. She's a contributor to the *Who Was...?* best-selling biography series for children, which she highly recommends. She's currently working on biographies of Lewis Carroll and The Three Stooges and has contributed stories to several anthologies. In her spare time she overanalyzes books, movies and TV series with alarming focus, struggles to learn to dance and converse in languages other than English. So far the results are mixed.

Richard Chizmar is the founder/publisher of *Cemetery Dance* magazine and the Cemetery Dance Publications book imprint. He has edited more than 20 anthologies and his fiction has appeared in dozens of publications, including *Ellery Queen's Mystery Magazine* and *The Year's 25 Finest Crime and Mystery Stories*. He has won two World Fantasy awards, four International Horror Guild awards, and the HWA's Board of Trustee's award. Chizmar and Johnathon Schaech have also written screenplays and teleplays for United Artists, Sony Screen Gems, Lions Gate, Showtime, NBC, and many other companies. Chizmar is also the creator/writer of *Stephen King Revisited*, and his next short story collection, *A Long December*, is due in 2016 (from Subterranean Press). Chizmar has appeared at numerous conferences as a writing instructor, guest speaker, panelist, and guest of honor. You can follow Richard Chizmar on both Facebook and Twitter.

Kelda Crich is a new born entity. She's been lurking in her creator's mind for a few years. Now she's out in the open. Find Kelda in London looking at strange things in London's medical museums or on her blog: http://keldacrichblog.blogspot.co.uk. Kelda's work has appeared in *The Lovecraft eZine, Journal of Unlikely Acceptances, Dreams from the Witch House* and in the Bram Stoker Award winning *After Death* anthology.

Evan Dicken studies old Japanese Maps and analyzes medical research at the Ohio State University by day. By night, he does neither of these things. His work has most recently appeared in: *Shock Totem, Analog,* and *The Lovecraft eZine,* and he has stories forthcoming from publishers such as: *Unlikely Story, Psuedopod,* and *The Overcast.* Feel free to visit him at: www.evandicken.com.

Kane Gordon is a UK based writer. He writes both fiction and poetry in various guises across all genres and age groups. His Facebook page can be found here: https://www.facebook.com/speculative.writer

Jeremy M. Gottwig is a librarian and programmer. Every morning at 4:30am, he stumbles out of bed to write science fiction. As a result, he's addicted to caffeine. His current project is a series of novellas collectively called *Employee of the Year.* He lives in Baltimore, MD with his wife and son. You can connect with Jeremy on Twitter: https://twitter.com/jgottwig, or at his website http://strangeshuttle.com.

Andrew Gudgel has always loved words and playing with words. He and his wife live in Maryland, in an apartment slowly being consumed by books.

Brad Hafford is a writer, traveler, teacher and archaeologist (not necessarily in that order). He teaches archaeology and critical writing at the University of Pennsylvania and writes speculative fiction in his spare time. He initially wrote *Freak Justice* at the Odyssey Writers Workshop where he was a student and later resident supervisor. The feedback he received there helped to make the story much stronger and his experiences at Odyssey have made him a stronger writer overall. Some of his other stories can be found on *Escape Pod* and in the anthology *Clockwork Universe: Steampunk vs. Aliens.* Follow him on Twitter: @BradHafford.

G. Scott Huggins grew up in the American Midwest and has lived there all his life, except for interludes in the European Midwest (Germany) and the Asian Midwest (Russia). He is currently responsible for securing America's future by teaching its past to high school students, many of whom learn things before going to college. His preferred method of teaching and examination is strategic warfare. He loves to read high fantasy, space opera, and parodies of the same. He has a column in the magazine <u>Sci Phi Journal.</u> He wants to be a hybrid of G.K. Chesterton and Terry Pratchett when he counteracts the effects of having grown up. When he is not teaching or writing, he devotes himself to his wife, their three children, and his cat. He loves good bourbon, bacon, and pie, and will gladly put his writing talents to use reviewing samples of any recipe featuring one or more of them. You can read his ramblings and rants (with bibliography) at https://scotthuggins.wordpress.com/, and you can follow him on Facebook.

Larry C. Kay is still mixing the concrete for his own tower, but he's fully paid up on his tithes to the forest sprites, so he expects no trouble with ents and such. When he's not dodging mosquitoes in Florida, or dutifully pencil-whipping, he indulges his appetites for Coppertail Brewing's Unholy Trippel, and raising three queens with only two pair. Find more of his grey matter at www.ScribbleNinja.com.

Ray Kolb is an assistant district attorney in Alabama. He spent nearly two years in Afghanistan working with Afghan judges, prosecutors, and police officers, training and mentoring each in Afghan criminal law. Ray has had more than a dozen stories published in *Pear Noir!*, *The Subterranean Quarterly*, *Morpheus Tales*, and elsewhere. Ray is represented by Paula Munier of Talcott Notch, who is currently shopping two of Ray's novels. Ray blogs way too infrequently at www. raykolb.com. You can find him on twitter @raykolb.

Edward McDermott, born in Toronto, has a professional day job but spends his spare time pursuing a writing career. Aside from taking writing courses and participating in writers' groups, Edward takes time for sailing, fencing, and working as a movie extra. http://edwardmcdermott.net.

Briana McGuckin lives with her family in an old house they call "The Wilde." She has cerebral palsy, and suspects that she took to writing as a child because her imagination leapt and bound in ways that her body could not. In her short time on this Earth, she has done many things; she has re-learned how to walk, she has spoken at the Library of Congress, and she has been pulled on-stage and sung to by Tim Curry. This is the first time her fiction has been professionally published, however, and she hopes this is the beginning of her grandest adventure yet. More about her may be found on her blog, Moon Missives: www.moonmissives.wordpress.com.

N.O.A. Rawle graduated MMU with a degree in writing and philosophy. She lives with her family in the middle of mythical Thessaly, teaching English by day and scribbling creepy weird tales by candle light into the wee hours of the morning. Works of her speculative fiction and dark poetry have appeared in numerous anthologies and magazines, won or been nominated for competitions, including being shortlisted for the AEON Award (2012). To explore the world inside her head, check out www.noarawle.blogspot.gr, tweet her on Twitter @NOARawle, and like her on Facebook N.O.A Rawle.

M. J. Ritchie grew up on a street in Philadelphia that no longer exists, listening to tales of banshees and ghosts from her Irish mother. A lover of words, and all things weird, she's been writing since the age of nine. As a volunteer tutor with various literacy programs, she's helped adults and children learn the joy of reading. She has degrees in business from Drexel University and Johns Hopkins University with experience in everything from accounting to sales. Her business writing focuses on management and employee development. As a faculty associate at The Johns Hopkins University Carey School of Business, she has helped graduate students learn the intricacies of business processes and organizational change. In her consulting practice, she works with organizations to improve performance. Her fiction writing indulges her desire to play god on a small scale. She hopes to make people aware of the importance of consequences whether they're implementing a system or selling their souls. She's married and lives in Maryland. Visit her at www.mjritchie.com.

Rie Sheridan Rose has been writing professionally since the turn of the century, having seen her first novel release in 2000. Her short stories appear in numerous anthologies, including *Nightmare Stalkers and Dream Walkers Vols. 1 and 2, Come to My Window, Shifters, The Grotesquerie* and *In the Bloodstream* as well as Yard Dog Press' *A Bubba In Time Saves None*. Mocha Memoirs has "Drink My Soul...Please," and "Bloody Rain" as e-downloads—and as part of the collection *RieTales*. Online, she has appeared in *Cease, Cows, Lorelei Signal*, and *Four Star Stories*. She is also the author of seven novels, five poetry chapbooks, and lyrics for songs on several of Marc Gunn's CDs. She edited the Steampunk Airship Pirates anthology *Avast, Ye Airships!* for Mocha Memoirs. You can find out more about her work on her website, www.riewriter.com or follow on Facebook. She tweets as @RieSheridanRose.

Peter Schranz's fiction has appeared on *Studio 360*, in *Mirror Dance* and *Breadcrumbs* magazines, and is forthcoming in *Weirdbook*. He is the webmaster of dailydoofus.com and the host of the podcast *Flight of the Fifty Fancies*. He lives in Philadelphia.

A.P. Sessler - A resident of North Carolina's Outer Banks, A.P searches for that unique element that twists the everyday commonplace into the weird. When he's not writing fiction, he composes music, dabbles in animation, and muses about theology and mind-hacking, all while watching way too many online movies. His short stories have appeared online at *Human Echoes Podcast* and *Acidic Fiction*, as well as print anthologies such as *Zippered Flesh 2, Dandelions of Mars, Star Quake 2* and *Cranial Leakage.* Find A.P at https://www.goodreads.com/author/show/6917738.A_P_Sessler, https://twitter.com/APSessler, and https://www.facebook.com/AP-Sessler-259899174205799/timeline.

Jonathan Shipley, a member of Science Fiction Writers of America, writes short stories and novels in the genres of fantasy, science fiction, and horror. Last year he was one of eight finalists for the Washington Science Fiction Association's Small Press Award with a whimsical story about Hell, and the *After Death* anthology where he was a contributing author won the 2014 Bram Stoker Award. His list of publications is pushing up to the half-century mark with a half-dozen additional stories sold and pending. With his short fiction on track, his on-going goal is to find a publishing home for his nine novels that range in a vast story arc from Nazi occultism to vampires to futuristic space opera. When not writing, he is immersed in the restoration of an old cattle baron's mansion in Fort Worth, Texas, which occasionally he also uses as a setting for stories—though not the overly grim ones. A hundred-year-old mansion has enough strange noises in the night without creating causes over and above the usual old house shifting and creaking. A listing of his short fiction can be found at www.shipleyscifi.com/publishedworks.

Laura Shovan is poetry editor for the literary journal *Little Patuxent Review.* Her chapbook, *Mountain, Log, Salt and Stone*, won the inaugural Harriss Poetry Prize. Laura edited the Maryland Writers' Association anthology *Life in Me Like Grass on Fire: Love Poems* and co-edited *Voices Fly: An Anthology of Exercises and Poems from the Maryland State Arts Council Artists-in-Residence Program*, for which she teaches. Laura is a Rita Dove Poetry Award finalist and won a *Gettysburg Review* Conference for Writers scholarship. *The Last Fifth Grade of Emerson Elementary*, her novel-in-verse for children, debuts in April, 2016 from Wendy Lamb Books/Random House. During the 2015-2016 school year, Laura is serving as the Howard County Poetry and Literature Society's Writer-in-Residence. She blogs about arts education at www.authoramok.com and tweets @LauraShovan.

Alex Shvartsman is a writer and translator from Brooklyn, NY. Over 80 of his short stories have appeared in *InterGalactic Medicine Show, Nature, Galaxy's Edge, Daily Science Fiction*, and many other magazines and anthologies. He won the 2014 WSFA Small Press Award for Short Fiction and is the 2015 Canopus Award for Excellence in Interstellar Fiction finalist.. He is the editor of the *Unidentified Funny Objects* annual anthology series of humorous SF/F. His collection, *Explaining Cthulhu to Grandma and Other Stories* and his steampunkthumor novella *H. G. Wells, Secret Agent* were both published in 2015. His website is www.alexshvartsman.com.

Steven R. Southard's short stories stack up in ten different anthologies including *Dead Bait, Quest for Atlantis*, and *Avast, Ye Airships!* He's the tall and looming author of the *What Man Hath Wrought* series, with thirteen stories at last count. An engineer and former submariner, Steve takes readers to new heights with engaging characters in distant places and varied historical periods. He towers over the genres of steampunk, clockpunk, science fiction, fantasy, and horror. Seek him in his lofty perches at www.stevenrsouthard.com, on Facebook at https://www.facebook.com/steven.southard.16, and on Twitter at https://twitter.com/StevenRSouthard.

Jeff Stehman and his wife live in the woods of northern Minnesota, where he divides the seasons into canoeing, cross-country skiing, and those few weeks in between when his writing output improves. His fiction has appeared in *Daily Science Fiction, Intergalactic Medicine Show, Jim Baen's Universe*, and the UFO Press anthology *Unidentified Funny Objects*.

Robert E. Waters has been writing science fiction and fantasy professionally since 2003 with his first publication in *Weird Tales*, "The Assassin's Retirement Party," his first Nalo Thoran story. Since then, he has gone on to publish many others, including the story contained in this anthology. Robert has also published 30 additional stories in various on-line and print magazines and anthologies, including Eric Flint's on-line *Grantville Gazette*, the magazine dedicated to publishing stories set in Baen Book's *1632/Ring of Fire* alternate history series. Robert lives in Baltimore, Maryland with his wife Beth, their son Jason, and their cat Buzz. Visit his website as www.roberternestwaters.com.

Jeremy Zimmerman is a teller of tales who dislikes cute euphemisms for writing like "teller of tales." He is the author of the young adult superhero book, *Kensei*, and its sequel is due out Winter 2015-2016. In his copious spare time he is the co-editor of *Mad Scientist Journal*. He lives in Seattle with five cats and his lovely wife (and fellow author) Dawn Vogel. You can find him at www.bolthy.com.

About the Editors

Kelly A. Harmon used to write truthful, honest stories about authors and thespians, senators and statesmen, movie stars and murderers. Now she writes lies, which is infinitely more satisfying, but lacks the convenience of doorstep delivery.

She is an award-winning journalist and author, and a member of the Science Fiction & Fantasy Writers of America. A Baltimore native, she writes the *Charm City Darkness* series, which includes the novels *Stoned in Charm City, A Favor for a Fiend,* and the soon to be published, *A Blue Collar Proposition.* Her science fiction and fantasy stories can be found in *Triangulation: Dark Glass, Hellebore and Rue, and Deep Cuts: Mayhem, Menace and Misery.*

Ms. Harmon is a former newspaper reporter and editor, and now edits for Pole to Pole Publishing, a small Baltimore publisher. She is co-editor of *Hides the Dark Tower* along with Vonnie Winslow Crist. For more information, visit her blog at http://kellyaharmn.com, or, find her on Facebook and Twitter: http://facebook.com/Kelly-A-Harmon1, https://twitter.com/kellyaharmon.

~

Vonnie Winslow Crist, MS Professional Writing, has had a life-long interest in reading, writing, art, fairytales, folklore, and legends. A cloverhand who has found so many four-leafed clovers that she keeps them in jars, she strives to celebrate the power of myth in her stories, poems, and illustrations.

A Pushcart nominee, she is a member of Science Fiction & Fantasy Writers of America, Society of Children's Book Writers & Illustrators, and Pen Women. Her award-winning books include *The Enchanted*

Skean, Owl Light, The Greener Forest, Leprechaun Cake & Other Tales, River of Stars and *Essential Fables.* Her speculative stories can be found in *Faerie Magazine, Chilling Ghost Short Stories, Dragon's Lure, Dia de los Muertos,* and elsewhere.

Ms. Crist is a staff writer for *Harford's Heart Magazine* and editor of *The Gunpowder Review.* She co-edited Pole to Pole Publishing's *Hides the Dark Tower* with Kelly A. Harmon. For more information, visit http://vonniewinsowcrist.com/home, http://vonniewinslowcrist.wordpress.com, http://facebook.com/WriterVonnieWinslowCrist, or http://twitter.com/VonnieWCrist.

www.ingramcontent.com/pod-product-compliance
Lightning Source LLC
Chambersburg PA
CBHW050357260626
47156CB00003B/771